An Unnecessary Deception

An Unnecessary Deception

Roy Bennett

AMHERST

ISBN 1 903637 27 9

Printed in Great Britain

First published in 2005 by

Amherst Publishing Limited
Longmore House, High Street, Otford, Sevenoaks, Kent TN14 5PQ

My grateful thanks to Don and Jenny
for their technical advice and support

Chapter One

The office was dimly lit from a shaft of sunlight, which streamed in through the small window behind the wide desk and shone, for a short distance across the floor. Unfortunately, this was the only window in the room, and due to the shadows cast by the other buildings within the vicinity; this sunny effect could not last for very long, possibly, any more than an hour or so each day. The ceiling light was on too, but the illumination from that appeared insufficient to make very much difference. It was in this gloom however; that one could make out two figures that appeared to be engrossed in conversation.

The room also had a slight musty smell about it, but that may have come from the old decaying plants in the terracotta pots on the window ledge, which were long since past their best, due to considerable lack of attention. On the floor was an old grey carpet that had seen better days, although still quite functional as a floor covering. Around the skirting board, numerous boxes and files of various sizes were piled high on top of each other. There were even more of the clients' files on the shelves that were screwed to the walls. These too were piled high and they bowed under their considerable weight.

Behind the large mahogany desk in front of the window, sat an elderly man, leaning forward in his black leather office chair. He was probably in his fifties, or possibly even older. It was hard to tell, in such a badly lit room. It was nevertheless a credit to the strength of his eyesight that he could still see well without the need for reading glasses, unlike most solicitors of his age whose eyes had deteriorated long ago from years of straining to read the small print in business contracts.

Slumped in the chair facing him on the other side of the desk, was a young man in his mid twenties. He was smartly dressed in a fashionable pair of jeans, which were fastened by a large buckled belt. He also wore a long-sleeved top, the hood of which hung down his back and was sandwiched between his shoulders and the back of his seat.

As he rested his head upon his arm, his nonchalant attitude gave the impression that he found the conversation that had been going on between the two of them for some time now, rather tedious. From his lack of respect, one could imagine a situation that had he been better acquainted with the elderly man, he would have probably rested his feet on the desk in front of him.

'Are you listening to me, Jon?'

'Of course I am, but I've heard it all before.'

'Yes, but this time it's more serious. You were lucky enough to escape a prison sentence on the last occasion but this time you may get sent down.'

'But it was only a car radio, for goodness sake. The way you're talking, you'd think I'd stolen something valuable.'

The solicitor shook his head. He was desperately trying to get through to the young man to get him to acknowledge the seriousness of the situation that he was in. Problem was, Jon seemed very flippant about the whole thing. Whether this was bravado or just plain lack of comprehension, he obviously wasn't making it very easy for his advisor to plan some kind of defence in Court to mitigate his actions.

'This isn't just a one off, Jon. You've been before the Court on a few occasions in the past. They won't take your youth into consideration this time. I can't see you getting just a fine or community service for a repeated offence.'

'So even you think I'm a nuisance to society as well, do you?'

'Well! I think that girlfriend of yours was right in what she told you. After all, she is very concerned as to the consequences of your misdemeanours.'

'Oh! Really!'

'Jon! You should appreciate the fact that she has always stood by you, when you've been in trouble in the past. You should listen to her more often.'

Jon rubbed his eyes and yawned, stretching his arms above his shoulders. He looked back at the solicitor with an air of indifference.

'You wanna live with her. It's just nag, nag, nag, all the time.'

'I'm sorry, Jon, but if you're not prepared to take good advice from anyone, I can see your spending the rest of your life in and out of prison. It may be car radios and shoplifting today, but you'll be progressing to something more serious in later life.'

Jon had already become bored with this lecture. First his girlfriend, and now the solicitor, had given him sound advice, but they failed to understand that he had a macho image to maintain. His peers would see any form of compromise as a weakness.

'Anyway. Where exactly do you see yourself, say, in ten years from now? Going straight? Wife, family, perhaps?'

'No! That all sounds rather boring.'

'Of course it isn't! It may even give you an aim in life.'

'What, and stay away from crime?'

'Well. A lot of young men start out in life falling foul of the law, but then they grow up.'

'But I don't want a wife and kids. They tie you down.'

'What you're really saying is, that you're not prepared to take on any responsibilities.'

'So!'

'Jon. I want the Court to hear that you're sorry for the things you've done wrong in the past. I want them to hear that you're now trying to get a proper job and go straight, and that you're looking to become a responsible member of society.'

'What?'

'Yes! Then, and only then, if your attitude comes across to the judge as one of contrition, we may just be able to persuade him not to give you a prison sentence.'

'Doing time, can't be all that bad.'

The solicitor threw up his hands in frustration.

'That's a ridiculous attitude. You've got to aim for something better than a life of crime.'

'Why? If I do something big-time, then perhaps I can retire on the proceeds. What d'you reckon?'

'Well. I put it to you this way, Jon. If you continue to maintain this childish arrogance when you appear in Court, you'll get at least six months.'

Jon shrugged his shoulders.

'Why don't you stay away from those friends of yours too? They're bad company and they'll only land you in more trouble. And there's that girlfriend of yours, who's been giving you such good advice? What about her? What's her name? Rebecca?'

'You mean Becky?'

'Yes. She sounds like a nice girl. I'm sure she'd like to see you do something useful with your life.'

'You mean, get a job?'

'Why not?'

''Cause then I wouldn't have the time to hang around with my mates.'

'But that just the point!'

'Yer, but they look up to me.'

'Why? Because you've committed more petty theft than they have? I'm really impressed.'

'You wouldn't understand. How can you? You're old and past it.'

The solicitor shook his head yet again. He now felt that

perhaps it was time to bring this meeting to an end. He would of course find counsel to represent Jon in Court, but after settlement of his bill, he hoped that he would never lay eyes on the belligerent young man again.

'Right. See you in a few weeks time, then Jon.'

Jon got up out of his seat, and looked across the room. The solicitor rose from his leather chair and came around the front of his desk to join him.

'OK, Mr Barrett. I expect if I ever get into the big league, you'll be able to afford a better office out of the higher fees you'll charge. That's assuming of course I get caught and need someone to represent me again.'

The solicitor wasn't smiling. He considered that it was a very stupid remark from a pathetic young man who had never matured. He firmly believed that this childish naivety that Jon had, would land him in some extremely serious trouble in the near future.

He led Jon across the room to the door of his office. As he opened it for him, he shook his client's hand firmly and then led him down the stairs to the reception area. At least, Jon had the courtesy to thank him for his concern, before making his way through the entrance to the building. The solicitor continued to watch as he swaggered down the path and back into the street. It was such a pity. He realised that the lad was going nowhere but was too foolish to see it.

Jon crossed the road and went straight over to the pub on the corner. It too was dimly lit. As he entered the premises, it seemed as though he was going back into the gloom that was reminiscent of the solicitor's office that he had just come from, after briefly being out in the bright early summer sunshine. Momentarily, he stood just inside the door and looked around the room, taking note of the customers, who were sitting at the tables, nursing their drinks. He recognised many of them as being out of work just as he was, although that didn't seem to stop them finding the money for a pint just as he was about to do. He headed across to the bar, where three of his friends were standing.

'Hi yer!'

'Hi, Jon! How did it go?'

'He reckons I'll get six months – and all for a car radio.'

'Yes, but it's not your first offence though. They'll take your rap sheet into consideration when they sentence you.'

'Bloody hell! You're beginning to sound like my solicitor now.'

Jon leaned on the bar and ordered a drink. The barman pulled him a half of lager and he searched in his pocket for a few coins to pay for it. After the barman had returned with his change, he leaned with his back against the bar and looked around the room once again.

'Where is everyone today? Where's Kyle?'

'Dunno!'

His friends glanced at each other and shrugged their shoulders. They hadn't seen him for a day or two, although normally wherever Jon was, Kyle was never very far behind. One of them offered up a suggestion.

'I expect he's gone down to the Job Centre in the town again.'

'He spends half his life down there, ever since Becky told him that he ought to make something of himself. I shall have to have a word with him about that. Don't know why he ever takes any notice of her. I never do.'

His friends laughed. Jon always considered himself in control of the relationship between himself and Rebecca, but she was in fact a very clever young woman who could run rings around him.

The four lads continued to pass the time of day. The subjects under discussion were always women and money, and usually they covered the same old ground every time they met. Somehow, they never seemed to get tired of the same repetitive conversation. However, the time had started to gather speed and the last hour had flown by, so Jon decided that he had better make for home to inform his girlfriend what had transpired at the solicitor's office.

He expected her to moan at him again and tell him what a

time waster he was, even though she occasionally benefited from his ill-gotten gains. In fact, he had even persuaded her to assist him in his latest scam, although he had yet to give her the details of her potential involvement. Nevertheless, in spite of all that, she would probably still suggest that he should join Kyle on his next visit to the Job Centre, to try and earn some money legitimately for a change.

'See you, then.'

'Here, Jon! Before you go. What's this we hear about a big job going down? One that Darren Baxter's set up?'

'Can't say anything about it at the moment, lads.'

'What's it drugs, stolen goods? What?'

'He hasn't told me yet. I only know it's pretty big stuff, and it's coming in from abroad. I've got to meet Darren soon, so he can fill me in on the details.'

'Lucky beggar! Bet it'll be worth a few bob to you?'

'Just the break I need actually. Still, catch up with you all later?'

'Yes, see you. Hope Becky doesn't nag you too much.'

'Yes. Try not to get caught again, Jon'.

Without turning to acknowledge their remarks, he gave them a hand gesture as he made for the entrance, leaving his three friends behind to continue their conversation and finish their drinks.

Once outside, Jon headed for home. He knew he would be back long before Rebecca returned from work, which meant that he would also have to wait for her to cook his evening meal when she came in. He was always too idle to prepare anything for himself and his girlfriend, so that it was on the table, ready for when she arrived home. A pity really, if he had been more considerate, it would have gone a long way to counteract the feeling of hostility that existed between the two of them, most of the time.

Anyway, he wasn't going to change now and besides, he considered that cooking was a woman's job. However, whilst he was waiting for her to arrive, he put on the television and helped himself to some biscuits and a can of beer from the fridge.

Chapter Two

It was in the early morning that Mike Stevens experienced a hard thump on his bed that caused him to open his eyes. Although it was already light, he was having great difficulty in focusing, after being in such a deep sleep. Initially, he tried to fix them on the light shade that hung down from the bedroom ceiling, but everything appeared as a blur. However, he persevered for a while by continuing to blink many times until eventually everything around him became much clearer, whereupon he was then in a position to investigate this unwarranted intrusion into his sleep.

He had gone to bed very late, the night before, and was therefore not too pleased at being disturbed in this manner. Besides, the sudden jolt had awakened him right in the middle of a beautiful dream and this interruption now meant that he would never know how it might have ended. Having now sufficiently focused his eyes, he looked across at the alarm clock on the dressing table and noticed that it had only just turned six.

'Oh no, not this early Suzanne! Can't you go and play in your own room and put the television on or something?'

The nine-year-old continued to bounce up and down upon the bed. Naturally, she was very wide-awake at this time in the morning, and wanted everyone else in the house to follow suite. Mike tolerated a further few minutes of this onslaught, before appealing to her once again.

'I said; could you go somewhere else and play? You are getting on my nerves.'

Again, the youngster took no notice of her father's request and continued to make a nuisance of herself. Mike decided that his best plan of action would be to ignore her completely, and so he turned his head sideways onto the pillow to pretend she wasn't there.

Having found that she was getting little reaction from him, she embarked upon a new bout of harassment. She slid right down to the bottom of the bed, and slipped under the covers to tickle his feet instead. This however was something that Mike just couldn't ignore.

'Please, Suzanne! Give me a break! It's Saturday, and one of the only days during the week that I ever get to lie in.'

The youngster ignored the remark and continued to run her little fingers under his instep. In doing his best not to encourage her, Mike tried to keep a straight face and not laugh. Considering the circumstances, this was quite difficult, as he was very sensitive on the soles of his feet. Nevertheless, he gritted his teeth and persevered.

As even this failed to provoke her father into some form of retaliation, Suzanne soon tired of the game. Unsure what to do next, she gradually worked her way up under the duvet until she popped her head out of the top. Momentarily, she rested her head on her father's pillow.

It was then that Mike's wife Julia began to stir beside him. She too had been in a deep sleep but the commotion had now woken her up. She turned her head to look at her husband and came face to face with the grinning youngster.

'Suzanne! Get back to your room this minute.'

Her mother's voice was very stern. There was no tone of compromise in it, unlike the pleas she had received from her father.

Suzanne protested.

'But I want us all to get up now. Granddad is coming to see us today and I'm really excited.'

'Don't make me repeat myself, Suzanne.'

The youngster's smile turned to a scowl.

'But he'll tell us lots of stories about all the places he's been to since we saw him last.'

'Out!'

'But...'

'No buts! Just do what you're told, or you won't be having your friends around to play next week after school.'

The reluctant youngster slowly dragged herself from under the covers and stomped back into her bedroom. Her mother had been very insistent and she knew it didn't pay to argue with her. She threw herself onto her bed and reached for the remote control handset. On went the television.

Once again, she heard her mother's voice calling to her from the next room.

'And you can turn the volume down too!'

At least this instruction had some effect, and the sound was promptly turned down.

'Thank goodness for that.' Julia added.

Mike and his wife rested their heads back onto their pillows and lay facing each other. Suzanne's early morning call was almost becoming a ritual every weekend, and Mike had even suggested to Julia, that they put a lock on their bedroom door to ensure that they had some peace, until a more respectable hour. He was joking of course. He loved his family dearly and wouldn't dream of creating any no-go areas for his daughter in the home. Besides, even if he did, Suzanne would probably bang on the door persistently until they were forced to get out of bed and let her in.

'Seriously though, Julia. Do we really have to listen to all of your dad's boring stories that we must have heard a thousand times before? I know every one of them off by heart.'

Unfortunately, Mike had picked the wrong time to make unsympathetic comments about her father. She was still feeling a bit frosty at having been woken up from a deep sleep at such an early hour and this, together with the subsequent confrontation with her daughter, would guarantee him a sharp retort.

'Look Mike. He doesn't visit us very often, does he? I'm sure on those few occasions that he does that we could at least put up with it for the short period that he's here. It isn't asking for much. You know that he lives on his own in that large empty house and doesn't have the chance to converse with anyone very often.'

'Yes, but why does he have to inflict them upon us?'

'Well, he's lonely, isn't he? When he does get the chance to relax with his family and to have a conversation with us, he's bound to go over old ground. Nothing too much happens in his life these days, that's particularly exciting to talk about. Look it at this way, Mike; we might be like that ourselves, one day.'

Mike frowned.

'I would hope that someone would put me out of my misery, long before I got to that stage.'

His wife began to smile.

'Even that can be arranged. Don't tempt me!'

Mike paused for a moment. He still wasn't completely wide-awake, and the last thing he wanted to have was an early morning confrontation with his wife, which inevitably he would lose.

'Ah well, I suppose you're right love, but it doesn't help matters with Suzanne always asking him to "tell us about the time you did this, granddad," or "tell us about that thing you made, granddad." After all, we have heard it all before, haven't we?'

'Yes, Mike. I know it can be irritating, but for Suzanne it's new and exciting. Didn't you like to listen to your grandfather's stories when you were a youngster?'

'I suppose so.'

'Well, it's nice for Suzanne too. I expect she'll get bored with them when she reaches her teens. Most of us do. Besides, I'm sure he'll spend most of the day out on his boat, so we shall probably only see him at meal times.'

'I still can't understand why he bought himself that boat. It's moored down here, so he can't get to use it more than a few times a year and then only when he comes to visit us. Then when he does take it out, he never goes more than a few miles along the coast and back. What's even worse, he can't swim.'

'I know, but it's something to keep him amused.'

'Yes. I suppose so. He spends hours and hours pottering around in it, even when it's moored at the marina.'

Julia smiled.

'Anyway, you always tell me that it suits us to have him stay with us, as he keeps Suzanne amused a lot of the time. I'm sure you won't object to him childminding so we can slip out and do some of the things we want to do, whilst he's here.'

With the back of his head on the pillow and gazing thoughtfully up at the ceiling, Mike nodded his approval.

'Umm! I expect we can manage two weeks of your old man. At least he leads an uneventful life so we're not likely to have any problems with him.'

'Well, don't sound so enthusiastic about his visit, Mike. After all, he is my dad, you know, and I do love him.'

Mike and his father-in-law very seldom saw eye to eye, since the day he married Julia. Generally speaking, they were polite together in company, but on many occasions in private, they could be heard, having a dig at each other. However, having thought about his earlier remarks, he felt that perhaps he was being a little ungracious to his father-in-law, so he decided to say something a little more congenial.

'I suppose he must get really lonely in that house on his own, since your mother died. I can't imagine what it must be like to have no one to talk to, most of the day. I can only assume that it must get really tedious, especially on those long, cold winter evenings. What he needs, is some regular company to break the monotony.'

'Am I to assume by that remark, that you are now suggesting you'd like my dad to come and live with us?'

'Heaven forbid, Julia! You're not seriously going to ask him to do that, are you?'

Julia laughed.

'No, but to be fair, he has done a lot for us. Look at that large sum of money he gave us to help buy this house, and we never did pay him back. Then there's the time he took Suzanne home in the school holidays, last summer, so we could enjoy that second honeymoon in Bali together.'

'All right, I get the point.'

'So you'll be nice to him whilst he's here, then?'

Mike didn't answer the question, but paused for thought again, before turning to face his wife.

'I'll tell you the best thing he ever did for me, Mrs Stevens, and that was to produce the most gorgeous, desirable woman I've ever met.'

Julia could anticipate what was coming next by the tone of his voice. Whenever her husband was losing an argument with her, he would always change the conversation, and that would lead to only one thing.

'I thought you were tired and wanted a rest,' Julia said, edging away from her husband.

'Well, I've suddenly changed my mind.'

'Now listen you - don't you start getting ideas.'

'That's not what you said last night, Julia. You couldn't keep your hands off me.'

'Yes; well, that was last night and I had too much to drink at the party.'

Mike slid across to his wife's side of the bed and Julia in turn moved further away. After a lot of constant shuffling, he was eventually lying next to her. She could go no further, as she had already reached the edge of the mattress. Mike whispered gently into her ear.

'And you were the most desirable woman at the party too.' He put his arms around her and began nibbling her ear lobe.

'Do you mind? Any minute now, Suzanne could come back again.'

'But her television is on very loud?'

'That's not the point, Mike. She could still come in on us.'

'So, you'd let a little problem like that come between us, would you?'

Mike tried to kiss her but Julia fought him off. After several further attempts, he decided to give up.

'Right then, Mike! I think this is the point, at which we should get up, don't you?'

She turned to push him away.

'In any case, I've got to get the house clean before Dad turns up - and remember, you did promise me that you would repair that gate this weekend.'

Mike groaned and turned his head back onto the pillow.

'I think I'll go back to sleep again.'

'No, you won't! You'll get up and help me to get the place ready.'

He watched as his wife got up and put on her dressing gown. She then proceeded to pull back the curtains and open all the windows much wider than they had been during the night, to allow the breeze to freshen the air in the bedroom. The bright sunlight shone into the room, ensuring that there was no possible way he was going to be able to doze off again.

'Are you going to get up then?'

Mike didn't reply.

Before heading for the bathroom, Julia turned and pulled the duvet completely off the bed, leaving Mike lying there and muttering to himself about his need for more sleep.

Chapter Three

'Where's that girl got to?'

The young man looked at his watch and then again along the harbour wall, expectantly. He had been waiting for some considerable time for her to show up and he was now becoming extremely annoyed. Patience was not one of his virtues. His friend, who sat beside him on the hard uneven concrete surface, was tucking into some sandwiches that he had brought with him. It was lunchtime, and many other workers had come out in the midday sun to sit around and eat.

'She said she would be here shortly, Jon. Don't get so wound up about it. She's a woman; she's entitled to be late.'

'Yes, but only at weddings, you Muppet.'

Jon had come into town to meet up with his girlfriend and his pal, Kyle, who, much to his disappointment, had recently started a new job. Being unemployed himself, Jon had all the time in the world, and was therefore exasperated at the fact that he had to comply with their lunchtime arrangements. Usually, most other things in his life revolved around him and he therefore found this get-together very frustrating.

Jon was a young man of twenty-four. He was very tall and strong, and prided himself on keeping very fit. His overall physique appealed to the woman of all ages, whom he seemed to attract with considerable ease. He excelled in all sports when he was at school and was captain of the football team.

Academically though, he hadn't done so well and his performance at some of the more basic subjects such as English and Maths, was a great disappointment both to his teachers and his parents. They considered he could have done much better if only he had put more effort into his studies, and that this dilatory attitude of his would adversely affect him when he left school. Now, as if to confirm their lack of confidence in him, he could not be bothered to hold down a job for any length of time, and even worse, had taken to petty crime as a source of income.

His friend, Kyle, on the other hand, was very different. He was of average build, average height, and average intelligence. He didn't posses that air of self-importance that exuded from Jon, but instead tended to live in his friend's shadow, seldom thinking for himself. Whatever Jon said or did, he was always happy to go along with.

His family had tried to get him to stay away from his friend's bad influence and to establish a life of his own. Had they succeeded in doing so, they had hoped that this would enable him to choose his own friends, and to be able to form relationships with the opposite sex. Any girl, who had so far taken a shine to this mild mannered lad, had come up against Jon, who quickly discouraged them. This emanated from the fact that he enjoyed having someone around him who was subservient and therefore he was very reluctant to relinquish the tight hold he had upon him.

Jon glanced down at his watch again. His girlfriend had been due to meet them half an hour ago and Kyle now had very little of his lunch hour left. It was fortunate that it was a warm sunny day too; otherwise he would have been really annoyed, especially if it had been raining. It was also possible that the uncertainty of the scam they were about to hatch was adding to his restlessness. Either way, he was becoming very impatient and that girl was going to get a piece of his mind, when and if she did eventually put in an appearance.

Jon looked up again. In the distance, he could see a young woman, ambling along as though she had all the time in the world. Seeing him look in her direction, she waved to him. She knew she was late and she also knew that her boyfriend would be going berserk, wondering what possibly could have delayed her.

She was the same age as Jon, very slim, and stunningly attractive. Then again, all of Jon's previous girlfriends were beautiful too. Jon liked attractive girls, as it boosted his ego whenever he saw the envy in the eyes of other men. For him, attracting women was effortless. He seemed to have that right chemistry; that unseen magnetism, which had them hanging onto every word he uttered.

Unfortunately for him, most of them could only put up with his good looks and his charm for a short period of time until his really cantankerous nature came to the surface. Having such a king-sized ego, it bothered him very little when they inevitably called it a day. As far as he was concerned, there would always be more women to take over where the last one left off. Besides, he considered that splitting up with him was their loss, not his.

His current girlfriend though had been very different. She wasn't put off by his awkward manner and gave him back as much stick as he dished out. She also had a wonderful way of deflating his ego, and therefore always seemed to have the upper hand in their relationship. That's not to say that Jon was a fool, but he was certainly no match for the quick thinking Rebecca.

As she drew nearer to them, Jon chose to ignore her completely. He sat with a sultry look on his face, staring out to sea. She crept up from behind and prised herself into the small gap between them. Once she had shuffled them from side to side and created sufficient room, she sat down on the wall.

She decided to acknowledge Jon's friend first.

'Hi, Kyle! How's the new job going?'

'Oh! Hi, Becky! I'm really enjoying it.'

'Got to be a week now, hasn't it?'

'Yes.'

From the corner of her eye, she could see that Jon was in a foul mood from the expression on his face. He didn't like to be kept waiting, especially by a woman.

'Where the bloody hell have you been? Kyle's got to be back at work in less than half an hour.'

'We've got as long as that, have we?'

Jon was in no mood for sarcasm.

'Don't try and be funny. There's not much time left for the three of us to talk now. We'll probably have to catch up with Kyle on some other occasion. He has to work overtime this evening.'

'All right! Don't go on about it.'

'Anyway, what kept you?'

'I got held up with a customer in the shop. Right!'

'That's no excuse.'

'Well! I'm afraid my job has to come first before any stupid idea you've dreamed up for us.'

'Only you, thinks it's stupid. Kyle reckons it's a good idea. Don't you, Kyle?'

'It seems a good idea to me, Jon, although Becky is entitled to her opinion.'

Kyle was hedging his bets, not wishing to fall out with either of his two friends. He was getting very good at being the peacemaker.

'Anyway! Why on earth we have to meet here at lunchtime beats me. Kyle could come over to our place in the evening.'

'But I've just told you, he's got to work overtime tonight. I wish you'd listen.'

'I didn't mean tonight, Jon. We could make it another night. What's wrong with that?'

'Because, you moron, I don't want all three of us to be seen together on our own patch. If you'd use your intelligence for once, you wouldn't need to ask.'

Kyle rushed to her defence. He didn't care for the hostile manner in which Jon always spoke to his girlfriend. Deep down inside, he had a soft spot for Rebecca. In fact, if the truth was known, he was probably in love with her. If only he could have been the one to attract her, he would have treated her with the respect she deserved.

'There's no need to be rude to her, Jon.'

'Oh, don't worry about me, Kyle, he's like this most of the time. It obviously wasn't his brain I was after when we first got together. In fact, I am now beginning to wonder why I bothered to hitch up with him in any case, as most of his other bodily parts are just as dormant.'

Jon took this hurtful comment as a personal affront to his manhood. He had always seen himself as irresistible to women, a bit of a stud, perhaps. Rebecca however knew just how to cut him down to size, with carefully chosen remarks. Kyle interjected.

'Look, I hate to break up this slanging match, but we do have very little time to talk.'

'Yes, shut up and listen, Rebecca!'

'Well, go on then. I'm listening.'

Rebecca looked across at Jon with a black expression on her face. It was times like this that she would dearly have loved to punch him in the face, but that could possibly inflame him further. During their hostile exchanges, he had never hit her, but she couldn't be sure how far she could go before he became violent towards her.

Kyle continued.

'Jon mentioned earlier, before you arrived, something about a boat with stolen gear on board?'

'Idiot! Keep your voice down, we don't want everyone to know what's going on.'

'Well, isn't that what we're here to talk about, then?'

'Well, of course it is.'

Jon had been very secretive about the entire scam, even to

Rebecca. So far, he had only given them the minimum amount of information, ever since he first suggested their involvement over a week ago. Truth of the matter was that he did not want them to know that he had not been privy to all the facts himself.

'Well. Who's masterminding this great heist?' Rebecca asked, sarcastically.

'Look, Becky! If you don't want to be involved, Kyle and I can always take it on, by ourselves.'

'Hold on, Jon! She does have a point. Who are we supposed to be working for?'

'Can't tell you at the moment. It's on a need-to-know basis.'

His remark at least intrigued Kyle, even though Rebecca shook her head.

'The gear is arriving on Wednesday evening by boat from Amsterdam. All we have to do is to collect it from them and take it in the car over to your house, Kyle. We'll store it in your dad's garage overnight.'

'Who's coming to pick it up, then?'

'Well, the next morning, someone will come over to you and take it off your hands. Later in the day, I shall meet my contact in town and he will hand over the money for doing our part in the job. I'll split it three ways with you two. It's all quite simple really.'

Kyle was very enthusiastic.

'Sounds quite an easy way of making money.'

'Sure, but there is one problem though.'

'Really, Jon. Just the one problem, is there?'

'Shut it, Becky!'

'Don't let me stop you. I just can't wait to hear what this one problem of yours is.'

This time, Jon chose not to respond to her sarcasm.

'They have refused to bring the boat into the harbour in case Customs become suspicious. Instead, they'll stay offshore and wait for us to come to them.'

Rebecca saw the problem immediately.

'Oh! Brilliant! Then we'll need a boat too. Where d'you propose we're going to get one?'

The two young men briefly sat in silence, pondering their dilemma. It was obvious that Jon had not clearly thought through this idea when it had been presented to him as a means of making a few easy bucks. He had been far too eager to become involved in the plan, without considering what was required of him. However, it was now left to Rebecca to offer up a sensible solution.

'If we need a boat, we've got to find one locally.'

'Why is that?' Jon asked.

'Well, for a start, taking it out and returning it won't then arouse suspicion.'

'You mean, one moored down at the marina?'

'Possibly.'

Jon scratched the side of his cheek and gave her suggestion some serious thought.

'Sounds OK in theory, but how do we get hold of a boat in the first place? We can't just go up to a boat owner and ask to borrow it.'

Rebecca came up with another idea.

'Just shut up a minute, Jon, and listen. I'm due to leave work early today. I could wander down to the marina and see what's available.'

'Oh, yes, and I suppose that when you see one that takes your fancy, you'll nick it?'

'I'm not that stupid, you moron.'

Jon was not being very helpful.

'You can just picture it, can't you, Kyle – "can I borrow your boat please on Wednesday evening, I just want to pick up some stolen goods?" That's not going to work, is it?'

'Of course it won't! It's not going to be like that.'

'Then what are you going to do? Flash your cleavage at the owner and hope that persuades him to hand it over to you?'

'Well! If you've got a better idea, then let's hear it. Otherwise, shut up!'

This time, there was a hostile silence between them. Rebecca hated Jon when he was in one of these moods. He was very good at criticising and belittling other people's suggestions, without offering up any solutions himself. Kyle was the first to speak.

'Let's give Becky's idea a try. If it doesn't work, then we're no worse off than we are now.'

'OK, then, Kyle, but perhaps I should go and sort it out.'

'No, you won't! Something would probably make you fly off the handle and then we'll all be in trouble.'

'All right! You do it then!'

'Don't worry, I will; and we'll stick to my plan. It'll work, you'll see.'

'It had better.'

Kyle looked at his watch. He had to be back at work within the next few minutes and that meant a swift dash across town if he was to make it in on time. The conversation had also come to an abrupt end and there was little more that could be said. In view of this, the three of them got up from the wall to go their separate ways.

'Hope it goes OK, Becky.'

'It will do, Kyle. I'll guarantee it. Catch up with you later.'

'Yes. See you.'

Jon nonchalantly grunted goodbye to his girlfriend and crossed the road with Kyle. They soon disappeared from view, down a side street. Meanwhile, Rebecca ambled back along the harbour wall, the way she came. Having been late leaving for lunch, she still had some time to spare. As she walked along, she muttered to herself as she began to form an outline of a plan in her mind.

'All we need is someone who has a suitable boat and is a bit naive and gullible. Now the point is, where can I find someone like that?'

Chapter Four

The new BMW zoomed along the A30 at speed. The traffic on the main road was surprisingly light for the time of year, so the driver was able to put his foot down hard. Anthony Lewis hoped to reach his daughter's home in time for lunch. He had made the journey dozens of times before and therefore knew how long it would take to travel from any one point on the route to any other. However, to be absolutely sure of getting there on time, he had left his home in South London very early that Saturday morning, in order to be well clear of the M25, before the holiday traffic built up.

On this particular occasion, he had accepted an invitation from his daughter to stay with her and her family for a couple of weeks. He was always ready to accept any offer she made, not only for the joy of seeing the family, but also because it was such a beautiful part of the country where he could go for long walks along the numerous scenic footpaths.

His wife had died some twenty years ago, leaving him to bring up his daughter on his own. Fortunately, Julia was fourteen at the time and therefore able to fend for herself most of the time. However, when she got married nine years later, he never quite got used to living entirely on his own, as the house always seemed so empty.

To add to this feeling of solitude, Anthony had recently

decided to retire from his job in the City, to have more time to himself and to leave all the frustration and stress of a high-pressure position to much younger men. At fifty, he didn't feel old, although he had to concede the fact that it took him a lot more time to perform the same basic tasks, that he had done in less time, when he was in his forties.

A few years ago, an opportunity had arisen for his son-in-law to join a solicitors' practice in the West Country, and so Mike and Julia sold their house in South London, and together with their young daughter Suzanne, moved west. Whilst Anthony was delighted for his daughter and family, it did have one drawback in that he could no longer occasionally pop round in the evenings to see them.

About the time that his family moved to the West Country, Anthony decided to buy a boat, in spite of the fact that his knowledge of such things was very rudimentary. Although it wasn't a large boat, the sports cruiser had a very powerful motor, and this gave Julia cause for concern, especially in view of the fact that her father couldn't swim. During the first few months after the purchase, he seldom took it out to sea, mainly due to the long drive to the coast in order to use it. To maximise its use, therefore, he decided to invest in moorings closer to where she lived.

The new sports car, a BMW Z4, was also calculated to enhance his feelings of being young at heart. He liked to think that it would impress the ladies, but so far, the vehicle had only received a few admiring glances from the kids as they got off the school bus.

There was one incident however on the way down, that almost had his pulse racing. He had stopped at a service station to fill up with petrol, and had just returned to his car, after paying for the fuel. As he got in to start the engine, he looked across at the adjacent pumps and noticed a young lady, sitting in the driver's seat of an open top Audi, and she was giving him the eye. He responded with suggestive gestures, which in turn was met with a rather seductive smile.

Unfortunately, what he had not seen, was the large burly boyfriend crouching down on the far side of the vehicle, checking the tyre pressures. When he became aware of the banter going on between the two of them, he was not amused. Anthony could see the conflict in his eyes, as the muscle-bound giant strode over towards his car, presumably to cause trouble.

Anthony turned on the ignition as the man quickened his pace. As he roared away towards the exit at speed, he looked into his mirror to see the man raising his fist towards him. One did not have to be a lip-reader, to interpret what the man was shouting at him.

Back on the road again, Anthony committed his thoughts of the past to the back of his mind. He had passed Exeter at ten-thirty, so he knew he could reach his destination in time for lunch. It was also quite hot now, and he could feel the rays of the sun, beating down upon him in the open-top car as he drove along.

Around lunchtime, Anthony arrived outside the family home. Getting out of the car, he strolled up the short drive and past Mike's new vehicle that they had recently purchased. It too was a BMW, but unlike his father-in-law's car, he had settled for a luxurious saloon. A mark of a successful solicitor indeed! As he turned to face the front door, he stood to admire the roses, which had been carefully trained around the porch. He scarcely had time to place his finger on the doorbell to ring it, when Suzanne opened the door.

His granddaughter was a cute little girl, very pretty and the image of her mother. She had a face that accentuated every expression. Gloom and sadness, happiness, joy, and love - they were all shown openly for all to see. When she gave you 'that look' though, it was always hard to get cross with her, even when your patience had run out long ago. It was also the same look that Julia had used on her father when she was younger, which guaranteed she could get away with just about anything.

She was just nine years old, although you'd be forgiven for

thinking that she was much older by her mannerism. “A proper little madam”, Mike had called her. He was right too. She would join in all the adult conversations and express views that would normally only come from someone considerably more mature. Often people found this annoying, even though some of the things she’d say would occasionally make the adults laugh. Although advanced for her age, she was still a little girl of nine, and Julia made sure that she was treated as such.

‘Hello, Granddad!’

‘Suzanne!’

Suzanne held up her arms towards him, for him to pick her up. He lifted her off the ground and she hugged him tightly around the neck and kissed him.

‘You’re getting a bit too heavy for me to pick you up nowadays. You’ve grown a lot since I saw you last.’

‘Well, that was last Christmas. I’ve had my ninth birthday since then.’

‘Yes, I received your little thank you note for the present. That was very kind of you.’

Suzanne struggled to get down again. She was very excited at seeing her granddad and there were lots of things she wanted to tell him.

‘Come on, follow me.’

Anthony lowered her to the floor and she led him by the hand down the hallway and through to the kitchen. The ground floor of the house comprised of a large lounge, a small kitchen, and a separate dining room.

‘Mum has spent all morning cleaning the house because Dad said it looked like a tip after their party last night. Dad said that Mum was drunk. Well he actually used another word but I’m not allowed to say that.’

Anthony smiled.

‘So you were at the party as well, were you?’

‘Oh, no. They wouldn’t let me stay.’

'Where did you go then?'

'Oh, they took me across the road to a neighbour's house. I came home very late.'

'I thought your mum told me that the lady next door usually looks after you?'

'Who? Mrs McBride?'

'If that's her name.'

'No. I couldn't stay there. She was at the party too. Mark was staying at his friend's house.'

'Mark?'

'Yes, that's Mrs McBride's little boy.'

'I see.'

'I think Dad likes Mrs McBride because I heard him talking about her to one of his friends on the phone this morning. He was telling him how attractive she was and what she was like at the party. He said he'd…'

'Yes, yes, thanks Suzanne. I don't think your Granddad's come all this way to hear about the party. Come on, go and play outside.'

An embarrassed Mike, had suddenly appeared on the scene and overhead the conversation. Rather red-faced and flustered, at what the eavesdropping Suzanne might have said he hastily ushered the youngster through to the garden. Having closed the back door, he quickly turned to greet his father-in-law.

'Lovely to see you again, Dad.'

'Thanks! How are you these days?'

'I'm fine. Business is good too.'

'I guessed it was by the new BMW on the drive.'

'Yes, it's a great motor. I'll have to take you out for a spin in it, whilst you're here.'

'Yes, that'll be great.'

'I think he gives more loving care to that car of his, than to me,' whispered a voice from behind him.

Anthony turned around.

'And how's my lovely daughter, then?'

'Pleased you got here safely, Dad. I watched you drive up. Don't you think you're a little too old for a sports car? Couldn't you grow old gracefully in a Vectra or a Mondeo?'

'But I want to feel young again.'

Julia went across and hugged him and then kissed him on the cheek. Pulling back, she looked into his face and smiled.

'But you seldom go anywhere, Dad; so who is there to impress?'

'I don't know. Maybe I will join some church social group and meet lots of old ladies with blue rinses. I can take them for a spin in my new car, whilst they tell me all about their latest operations or who had died recently or something.'

Julia smiled. Her dad had not formed a relationship with another woman since her mum died all those years ago. She had always wondered why that was, as many of her friends at school who had single mums, seemed to have strings of partners living with them. Perhaps, he felt that no one could replace her mum, who he had been completely devoted to for so many years. Who knows!

'Anyway, you're here with us now, Dad, and I want you to have a really good time.'

'Don't I always enjoy myself when I am here with the three of you? You never know, perhaps one of these days I'll come and live with you.'

Mike shuddered at the thought, even though he knew that his father-in-law was joking. The remark had been specifically aimed at him, as Anthony enjoyed winding him up.

The family wandered into the garden, where there was a wrought iron table and chairs, under a sun umbrella. It was quite a large garden, with a big spacious lawn, surrounded by flowerbeds. In one corner was a child's swing. Here and there were strewn a few toys that Suzanne had obviously been playing with earlier.

Julia set up another seat by the table, for her father to sit on. As they sat down, Mike brought them some cold drinks from the fridge, and then joined them. Suzanne sipped hers and then ran off to play on the swing.

Mike was the first to strike up a conversation.

'Julia tells me that you've just come back from a holiday in Spain. I take it you didn't drive there in the new car, then?'

'No, I went out on a scheduled flight and found my own accommodation in a small village away from the coast. It was my intention to take lots of photographs of the surrounding area.'

'I bet that made a nice change.'

'Yes. It did actually.'

Anthony guessed the remark was a dig at his favourite pastime, although he chose to ignore it. He had told himself on the way down that he would try to avoid the subject whilst he was at his daughter's house, knowing that Mike found the topic immensely boring. However, he did get a degree of wicked pleasure out of winding him up whenever he mentioned it.

'I went to a quiet part of Spain as I fancied a change from photography in Britain. I'm sure I've mentioned to you in the past that I've taken photographs of most of the scenic areas of our countryside and coastline. I shall have to tell you sometime about all the fun I've had doing it.'

Mike groaned. He imagined this was going to be the beginning of another of Anthony's repetitive stories. Anticipating what he was thinking, Julia gave her husband a stern look.

'So was it good staying in a small village, then?' Mike asked, trying desperately to look interested in order not to incur the wrath of his wife.

'It was all right, but to get served in the shops or the restaurant took ages. The pace of life out there is so slow. How on earth they managed to get an Armada together, I cannot imagine.'

Mike took a sip from his glass and placed it back onto the table. He was anxious to change the conversation, before his father-in-law had the opportunity to launch off into one of his long-winded yarns.

'I expect you'll be off to attend to your boat this afternoon, won't you?'

'Slow down a minute, Mike. Dad's only just arrived and I'm sure he has lots to tell us. Haven't you, Dad?'

'Well, maybe later I will. After lunch, I thought I would drive over to the marina just to make sure everything is in order, if that's OK with you?'

'Yes, that fine. Anyway, you go and bring your case up to the spare room, while I serve up the dinner.'

Anthony went out to the car and took his case from the boot. As he came back through the hallway and up the stairs, there was a lovely smell of cooking wafting through the house, which was beginning to make him feel hungry. His late wife had been a good cook, and as his daughter grew up, she too had acquired similar skills.

In the guestroom, he placed his case upon the bed. Before unpacking, he went over to the window and looked out across the bay. The view was truly magnificent. The sea glistened in the bright summer sunshine and there were no more than just a few traces of cloud in the sky.

'What a lovely view this house has,' he murmured to himself.

Before his wife died, they would bring Julia here to play on the beach on many a long weekend, just to get away from the noise of London. They would dig holes in the sand and build castles and tunnels together. Later, when there were just the two of them, they would still come to the district for a holiday, at least, until Julia started to take a keen interest in boys and preferred to stay at home. Strangely, he never imagined that one day his daughter and family would be living here.

'Ah,' he thought, 'One of these days, I shall live by the sea in a place like this.'

He unzipped his case and removed a few of his clothes to hang in the wardrobe. As he opened the doors, he chuckled at the sight of all the old wire coat hangers that they had placed along the rail. Even though Mike was tight and never believed in waste, Anthony considered that he should have at least purchased a few decent ones.

Having now taken all the clothes from the case, he placed the few presents that he had brought with him, onto the dressing table. He had purchased some perfume for his daughter, which he knew, was her favourite. She had tried the many new scents that had since come onto the market, but she still preferred the one she had first used, when she got married. There was also some after shave for Mike. He was always running out of it, as he tended to liberally splash it all over face. It was so potent that you could smell him coming, long before he appeared on the scene.

Finally, he had bought some sweets for Suzanne. Sadly, though, he had found them so mouth-watering, that he had already eaten most of them on the journey down. In contemplating whether his granddaughter would miss the last few, he decided to leave them in the car. After all, he could always take her up to the corner shop later to buy some more.

He was about to return to the window to admire the view again, when he heard his daughter shout to him from downstairs.

'Lunch is ready, Dad.'

He wandered down the stairs to the dining room with its large picture windows, overlooking the back garden. As the house was built much higher than the garden, one could sit in the dining room and see over the back fence to the bay below. A gate in the bottom fence, which incidentally was badly in need of repair, opened onto a path, which in turn led steeply down the cliff and onto the beach below. With such a wonderful outlook, Mike and Julia had been right not to miss the opportunity to relocate here.

During the meal, Mike discussed his influential clients with them, carefully avoiding any reference to their names, of course. You could never tell with Mike as to whether he actually knew these wealthy people personally, or whether it was all a product of gross exaggeration. Still, whatever the case may be, Mike's conversation was always guaranteed to be extremely dull.

Anthony knew how to taunt Mike too, by giving him immense praise for all the hard work he did. It was when you heaped such adulation upon him, that you could almost see his chest expanding with pride. To be fair though, he had done very well for himself and the family, but it would have been received with much greater recognition had he not felt the need to constantly remind everyone of this fact.

Mike's favourite topic of conversation was Mike and it was very unlikely he was ever going to change now. Amazingly, none of this lack of modesty seemed to upset Julia, who by and large, let it all go over her head.

Anticipating a pause in the conversation allowed Anthony to butt in.

'I too knew a lot of influential people when I was working in finance in the City. Did I ever tell you of the time that the hierarchy called me to their board offices in Mayfair?'

He knew full well that he had mentioned this incident to Mike on at least half a dozen previous occasions. As he began to relate the story, he could see Mike's eyes start to glaze over at the thought of a long boring tale that he had heard many times before.

'Well, I had to spend the entire night working in a hotel room around the corner from the head office. The chairman had loaned his secretary to me, to type all my figures onto acetates for the presentation the next day. It was five in the morning, when I completed the work, and I only had a brief time to wash, shave, and have some breakfast, before I was due to meet the main board again at seven am.'

Suzanne, who had been glaring at her granddad with her chin cupped in her hands, was hanging on to every word.

'Granddad.'

'Yes, love.'

'Last time I heard you tell that story to Dad, you said that you told the secretary that the chairman could stick his job up his bottom.'

'Suzanne!' screamed Julia. 'I won't have you saying things like that!'

'But that's what Granddad said.'

'I don't care! Leave the table and go and tidy your room this minute.'

'But I haven't had any pudding, yet.'

'Just do as you are told.'

The youngster got down from the table and reluctantly went to her bedroom.

'Honestly, Dad, you must be more careful not to say things like that in front of Suzanne. She picks up everything, especially if it's something that she shouldn't.'

'Yes. I'm sorry, Julia,' Anthony replied, rather sheepishly.

Julia then turned to face her husband.

'And what are you grinning at?'

'Well, I actually thought that was very funny.'

'Well, I didn't. Even you should have more sense than to encourage him. You can now wipe that grin off your face and start on the washing up.'

'But you haven't dished up the sweet, yet.'

'Tough! No one's getting any pudding now.'

Julia got up from the table and went upstairs. Mike knew better than to argue with his wife when he was in trouble. The two men set too and began to clear the dining room table, taking the dirty plates and bowls through to the kitchen. Mike then rolled up his shirtsleeves and started the washing up, whilst Anthony got a clean cloth out of the cupboard and began to dry the crockery as it was placed upon the draining board.

'How come a wealthy man like you never bought a dish washer?'

'Oh, don't get onto that subject with Julia, as I shall never hear the last of it. The truth is, that until I am able to extend the kitchen, there's no space for one.'

'I take it you row on occasions, then?'

'We have our ups and downs like most couples, but there have never been any serious problems.'

As Anthony had begun to touch upon a personal matter, Mike decided to change the subject.

'So you're off to look over your boat this afternoon, then?'

'Yes, it'll only take me twenty minutes or so to drive over there.'

'Julia and I checked it over about a month or so ago, to see that it had pulled through the winter period all right.'

'That's very kind of you, Mike. I'll give it the once over this afternoon so I can then be out of your hair until teatime.'

'Want a cup of tea before you go?'

'OK!'

The two men chatted whilst they finished washing and drying the crockery. Mike then put the kettle on to make a pot of tea.

'Look, Dad. We are always pleased to have you here. You know you can stay as long as you like. It doesn't have to be just two weeks.'

'That's very kind of you, son, but I do like to keep on the move. I know it isn't easy having Julia's old man around the place for too long, especially when he gets you into trouble.'

Mike laughed.

Chapter Five

Panting frantically, the young man paused by the rubbish bins, to get his breath back. He had been running across town for the last ten minutes, pursued by two very determined men. Thinking he had shaken them off after such a long chase, he had dashed down a wide alley between some old tall buildings, strewn with obstacles that could afford some cover. Safe at last, he slumped down between the smelly containers, which stood, piled high with rubbish, outside the back door of a restaurant. His heart had been racing, and resting for those few precious seconds, he was now beginning to calm down again.

As he looked up, his sense of temporary security diminished. Coming towards him from the street, was one of his two pursuers. His initial instinct was to start running again, but as he turned to dash off in the opposite direction, he encountered the other man, blocking his exit. It was possible that he could have got past him and on to safety, but the man was holding a knife in the palm of his hand. In the interest of self-preservation, he therefore decided to remain still and await his fate.

'What you gonna do now, Danny?'

The man, who was in his late thirties, spoke in a harsh gruff voice. As he drew nearer, he could see the fear in the young man's eyes.

'Look, Darren! Can't we discuss this sensibly?'

'D'you hear that, Nick? He's changed his mind. He wants to talk to us now.'

The other man was much younger, possibly in his late teens or early twenties. Still brandishing the knife, he stood a short distance away to ensure that their captive made no last minute dash for freedom. From his manner, one could tell that he too was out of breath.

'I'm knackered, Darren. I ought to cut him just for that.'

'You're out of condition. You're no good to me if you can't catch a wimp like our Danny.'

The older man stood, facing the trembling captive. His eyes showed no regard for the young man's feelings of fear. He paused for a moment, before he struck out at him, with his fist to the stomach. Danny doubled up in pain.

'That's for getting Nick out of breath.'

Although winded, Danny looked up at his assailant and tried to speak.

'What's it you want?'

'You owe me a monkey, and I want it now.'

'But it was only four hundred quid last week.'

'Well! That's inflation for you, Danny Boy.'

'I haven't got five hundred. You'll have to give me some time to get it together.'

The older man stood back and looked around him, as if appearing to consider the matter further. There was a certain wicked smile upon his face that revealed the satisfaction he was getting from making the young man squirm.

'What'd you think then, Nick?'

'Dunno, Darren.'

He placed his hand upon the young man's shoulder as if to reassure him.

'I'll tell you what, Danny. If you find me five hundred quid by this time next week, we're back in business again. If not, Nick here, is going to teach you a lesson. Remember, Nick can't think for himself, 'cause he's thick. He can only do what I tell him to. Got it?'

By this time, Danny had straightened up again, although he could still feel the effects of the blow to his stomach.

'OK! By next Saturday then, my friend.' Darren added.

The young man was still trembling with fear. He wasn't sure if he was going to get out of this situation without further injury.

'Yes. Anything you say. Don't worry. I'll get your money.'

Removing his hand from his shoulder, Darren started to walk away, closely followed by Nick. Neither turned to look back. Danny saw his chance to escape and immediately scurried off lest the two men changed their minds and returned to give him another pasting.

'You reckon he's gonna come up with the money, Darren?'

'He'd better.'

The two men strolled towards the end of the passageway and out into the street. It had been dark in the alley due to the shadows cast by the tall buildings, and now they were back again in the bright midday sunshine. As they ambled along, they discussed their next move.

'I'm going to meet up with Jon Dresner this evening. We're going to take a shot at a few car stereos. You know, just see what's about. Want to be in on it?'

'Yes. Count me in then, Darren.'

'Good. Between the three of us we should come up with something worth selling.'

They continued on in silence until they reached the first corner. As they were both about to go off in different directions, they stopped. Darren then turned to speak to Nick again.

'Got to have a word with Jon about another little scheme I've got going. I'm not sure if he's up to it, though.'

'Want me in on that too?'

'No! You're a bloody sight worse than he is, to give a job to. It's possible I might have to see to it myself. Tell you what, meet me in that wooded part by your housing estate, at around eleven tonight.'

'OK!'

Nick turned to go his separate way. He had not taken more than a few steps in the direction of his home, when his accomplice called after him.

'Oh, and Nick?'

'Yes, Darren.'

'Leave the knife behind, this time. We don't want you getting over enthusiastic.'

'Right!'

Nick gave Darren the thumbs up. Just as he was about to walk away for the second time, Darren called out to him again.

'Anyway! Where d'you get a blade like that?'

'Wot, this one?'

Nick took the knife from his jacket pocket and held it up, and in doing so, startled some of the passers-by. Darren shook his head in disbelief.

'Yes! That one, you moron!'

'Got it from a bloke up town. He sold it to me cheap.'

'Anyone we know?'

'He told me his name was Stanley.'

Darren drew breath. He couldn't believe his accomplice was so gullible.

'Stanley!'

'Yer.'

'He was having you on, mate.'

'Eh!'

Nick looked totally bewildered. He couldn't see the relevance.

'You know! Stanley the Knife!'

'Yes, that's right. So you know him too, then, Darren?'

Darren again shook his head in utter dismay and muttered under his breath.

'Give me strength! I'm working with a complete idiot.'

Chapter Six

Once Anthony had finished his cup of tea, he left Julia and Mike happily chatting together, and strolled down the drive to the car. The time had just whizzed by and it was already mid afternoon. Fortunately, the marina wasn't too far away, so it would only take a short while to get there. He decided that he should at the very least, check the boat over, even if there was insufficient time to take her out to sea. Having then reassured himself that the vessel had survived the winter moorings without any serious problems, he would be back at the family home again by teatime.

As he was about to pull away from the kerb, he noticed his daughter's neighbour further down the road. She was walking along towards the bus stop. No man could fail to notice Caroline McBride. She was a single mum in her early thirties, who always seemed to dress like a teenager off to a nightclub, when, in fact, she was often going no further than the shops. His daughter had commented on this fact over lunch, but had then added, that it was probably only her gorgeous figure that enabled her to get away with it.

Caroline had lived next door to Julia and Mike for about a year now. When she first moved in, Mr McBride was living at home too. He was a strange sort of chap and not very talkative. He seemed to work very long hours and it was often nine or ten at night, when his car would eventually return to the drive. He also had rather piercing eyes and Julia reckoned this made her feel very uneasy whenever she met him in the street. The couple never seemed to go out together either, and Mike said that they were always arguing, sometimes into the early hours of the morning. It therefore came as no surprise to anyone, even to Caroline, when he left home just before Christmas.

Caroline was a very popular lady, full of fun. She had a terrific personality and was always the life and soul of every party she went to. Julia and Mike were also surprised that she never had a regular boyfriend. She was lovely to look at and had men fawning all over her, everywhere she went. One or two had even taken her out for the odd evening and rumour had it, that when she invited them back for a cup of coffee, that was all they got too! Although she gave the impression of being “loose”, in reality, nothing was further from the truth.

Sadly, no man appeared to survive more than one or two nights out with her, although there didn’t seem to be a satisfactory explanation for it. On the whole she managed to keep herself to herself, and appeared to prefer her own company and that of her young son.

I suppose one can never really guess the real reason behind it all. Perhaps she had had such a bad experience when her husband left home with an eighteen-year-old girl from the factory where he worked, that she vowed never to trust a man again. Nevertheless, Julia reckoned she ought to find herself a husband, preferably one of her own, of course!

Feeling chivalrous, or at least, that’s what Anthony told himself that he was about to be; he drew alongside her to offer her a lift. As he lowered the car window to speak, he could see that she was lost in her thoughts. She hadn’t noticed him until he called out to her.

‘Can I offer you a lift anywhere, Mrs McBride?’

She turned and looked at his smart car and then back at him again. She was obviously impressed.

'Yes, you certainly can.'

She walked around the front of the vehicle to the passenger's side, opened the door and got in. Adjusting her short leather skirt that had ridden up her long shapely legs, she made herself comfortable in the seat beside him and put on the seat belt.

'Where to, then?'

'Well, I'm off to the school to collect my son, Mark, and then I'm taking him down to the hairdressers in town. He could go on his own, but I couldn't trust him to get there. He'd probably wander off somewhere along the way.'

'Fine! School, it is then!'

Anthony pulled away from the kerb and drove down to the bottom of the turning. The traffic on the main road seemed endless and it was difficult to find a gap in the line of cars, in order to pull out. Saturday afternoons were often busy in this area, especially during the tourist season.

Relaxing his concentration on the road again, Anthony continued the conversation. It had been the first real opportunity he had found to speak with Julia's neighbour, since the day she came to live next door.

'I hope you won't think I'm being impertinent but I understand your lad's twelve years old. Surely, by now, he should be responsible enough to go into town on his own to get a haircut?'

'You would think so, wouldn't you? It's not that he isn't old enough to go on his own, but he tends to bunk off to the amusements on the seafront and spend the money I've given him. He's a right little urchin.'

Not knowing quite what to say to each other there followed a period of silence. The car picked up speed and the breeze started to blow Caroline's long dark hair. Anthony began to think that perhaps the lift had not been such a good idea after all. If her hair became tangled, she may not like it.

'So you're staying with Julia and her husband for a while, are you?'

'Yes, I don't get the chance to pay them a visit very often. They've invited me to stay for a couple of weeks.'

'Well, you've certainly brought some nice weather with you.'

'I take it that it hasn't been too good lately?'

'The usual rain, my dear. Still, if you bring good weather with you, perhaps you should visit more often?'

'It would be nice to, but I don't like to get in their way. When you get to a certain age, nobody wants the old man around too often.'

Caroline looked across at Anthony and fluttered her long eyelashes.

'Oh I shouldn't think for one minute, Julia would agree with that'

'Really?'

'Yes. She often talks about you, and with great affection too. I think she's rather concerned about your spending so much time on your own though.'

'Well, I suppose she has got a point. I'm retired now, so I probably do have far too much free time on my hands.'

Leaving the stream of traffic on the main road, Anthony indicated left to go up the hill, in the direction of the local secondary school.

'I suppose it is this school he goes to.'

'Yep. Nearly all the kids go there.'

'I expect Julia's youngster will be here too, in a few years time.'

'I guess so; unless the wealthy solicitor decides to go private.'

Anthony smiled.

'I don't think that's really Mike. He'd be too concerned with what it would cost him.'

'Yes, he is a bit tight, isn't he?'

'Just a bit!'

'So you say, you're retired?'

'Yes. A man of leisure.'

'I wish I had more time to myself.'

Caroline pulled down the sun visor and looked into the vanity mirror. She then made a pathetic attempt to smooth down her hair. Fortunately, it wasn't tangled, just windswept.

'Sorry about your hair.'

'Oh, that's OK. I was going to wash it this evening in any case. Haven't anything else planned for later, at this precise moment.'

She pushed the sun visor back up again, and relaxed back into the comfort of the seat. She crossed her legs and the short leather skirt exposed her thighs once again. It was very distracting for Anthony whilst he was driving.

The car continued to wind its way up the hill and around the S bends, towards the school.

'Julia tells me that you work in the local supermarket.'

'Yes, I only do it part time, but it does help to pay the bills. My ex doesn't part with a penny for me or for my lad. With the bit of income support I get, I can just about make ends meet. I shall probably go full-time when he gets a bit older.'

'Your ex-husband should pay something towards your lad, even if he's not prepared to support you.'

'Yes, but you try telling him that. The CSA's been onto him on dozens of occasions to work out his child maintenance payments, but every time they catch up with him, he changes jobs and addresses. They're useless if you ask me. I've even given up on the idea of getting him to buy Mark the occasional shirt or a pair of shoes.'

'Does your lad see his dad very often?'

'No, but that doesn't seem to bother either of them. He wasn't much of a father to Mark when we were all living together, so there's no love lost between them.'

'I bet you find your lad a great comfort to you, though. I know Julia was to me, when there were just the two of us.'

'What my Mark! You've got to be joking! Most of my time is spent trying to find the little beggar when he goes missing. He usually wanders off after school. Then he doesn't turn up for tea, and I have to go out looking for him.'

'By the way, I hope you won't mind my asking, but what's he doing at school on a Saturday?'

'Oh, it's only football practice on the school playing field. When he said he wanted to join the team, I thought it would at least keep him out of mischief for one afternoon a week. He seems to enjoy it too.'

'Does his team play in a league?'

'In the wintertime, they play against other teams. It's then that he comes home covered in so much mud that I sometimes wonder if it's best to put kid and all, in the washing machine.'

Anthony laughed. Outside the school there were a number of parked cars, each with a parent sitting patiently inside, waiting for their child to appear. Anthony drove past the entrance, and almost to the top of the road, before he could find a parking space. It was then that Caroline spotted the bag of sweets.

'Wow, these are my favourites!' she exclaimed, whilst picking up the packet. 'Do you think I can be very naughty and help myself?'

'Feel free to be as naughty as you like.'

She guessed there was a hint of suggestion in his remark, but ignored it.

'I originally bought them for Suzanne, but they were so tasty that I've eaten most of them.'

Caroline took a sweet from the bag and popped it into her mouth.

'Well, my mother always told me not to take sweets from strangers otherwise it could get me into serious trouble.'

'So you've always behaved yourself and stayed out of trouble, like your mum said, have you?'

She chose not to answer the question, but just grinned.

'I don't know, men will always be boys whatever their age, won't they? Anyway, you can call me Caroline."

'Oh, thanks!'

She took off the seat belt and got out of the car. As she closed the door behind her, she leaned across the open top. She looked at him straight in the face and her big wide eyes lit up.

'And I will call you – "very naughty"', she added, in a rather seductive voice.

The remark had caught Anthony off-guard, leaving him rather embarrassed. He was too stunned to know how to reply to that. After all, he hardly knew her. By the time he had recollected his thoughts, she had gone. He looked into the rear mirror and noticed that she had already reached the school entrance.

'Wow! If only I was twenty years younger.' He murmured to himself.

Caroline soon disappeared from view, leaving Anthony to continue on his way.

Chapter Seven

Although it was only a few miles to the marina, the narrow roads were very congested. Once there, he was further delayed in trying to find a parking space. Fortunately, after he had made two circuits of the car park, he came across a vehicle pulling away and quickly parked in the vacated space. From there, it was just a brief stroll to the moorings.

Anthony's boat was a six-berth sports cruiser. She was almost nine metres long, with an open cockpit. Below deck, there were two cabins with all the modern conveniences, plus a full galley. The powerful 300-hp twin engines could propel the vessel through the water at considerable speed.

It was a ridiculously powerful boat for the style in which he used it. All he ever wanted to do was to be able to potter around in her and then take a trip along the coastline from one bay to another on a nice sunny day. The vessel was in extremely good condition too when purchased second-hand, and since he had transferred his pride and joy to the local area and it had been used more frequently, found that it needed very little attention. She had been a bargain at the price he offered, which the seller chose to accept without haggling.

The name was probably the first thing that had attracted him to the boat, when he was wandering around Brighton marina with his family. His daughter had been the first to point it out to them. She suggested that “My Julia” was a really good name for a boat. Now there’s a surprise! I expect the name “Julia” had some relevance to the previous owner’s family too.

That same day, they made some general enquiries and found that the craft was actually for sale. The family had a swift discussion on the spot and decided to buy it. Mike of course arranged all the legal side of the transaction, and Julia had her re-christened with a bottle of champagne on their first trip out, after bringing it to the area in which they lived.

Mike and Julia also used the boat from time to time. There was however only one downside to this, as far as Anthony was concerned. Unfortunately, Mike was not prepared to give the boat the loving care that he did. He seldom cleaned her, let alone maintained her, and always seemed to put everything back in a different place from where Anthony wanted it to be. It probably wasn’t such a big deal really, but the financial man’s tidy mind insisted on having a specific home for every item.

Upon reaching the boat, he tossed on board the large bag he was carrying, which contained the flares and navigational equipment. He always removed them whenever he was leaving the vessel for any length of time, as they were easy pickings for thieves. Besides, the kit could be plugged back in again and reset without difficulty.

His first job that afternoon was to check over the engine. No one had been out in the boat for a few months now, as the weather had been so bad during the spring. Fortunately, everything seemed to be in good working order, and when he came to start it up, he was pleased to find that it fired first time.

He then set to and cleaned below deck. As far as he was concerned, it was like a tip down there. He grumbled with mild frustration as he moved each item back to its proper place and put things away in the lockers. He was also put out by the fact that Mike had not had the decency to tidy up all of Suzanne’s sweet wrappers from the last time the family been out in her. As he was about to pick up the last of the mess, he heard a voice, calling to him.

'Hello! Is anyone down there?'

'Who on earth can that be?' he thought to himself.

It sounded like a girl's voice, although certainly no one he would recognise.

'Hello, is anyone on board?'

'Yes, just a minute and I'll be up.'

He placed the last of the litter in a black sack before going up on deck. Climbing the few steps of the short ladder, he came face to face with an attractive young woman.

'Is this your boat?'

'It certainly is. Why do you ask?'

She chose not to answer his question, but continued to look around her, smiling at him when she eventually caught his eye.

'Is there something wrong?'

'No, no. I was just admiring your very smart craft. Bet she's powerful?'

'So they tell me.'

The young woman was quite tall and slim, and very smartly dressed in modern casual clothes. Over her right shoulder, she carried a small matching bag. From her looks, he estimated her to be in her early twenties. He also noticed that her long, dark, straight hair was tied back into a ponytail and that her face bore little makeup.

Anthony wasn't aware of the fact that he was staring at her. Even though she had a beautiful figure that would naturally draw his attention, his eyes kept returning to that captivating smile. Sensing that perhaps he did not wish to be disturbed, she turned to leave the boat.

'I'm sorry, you're probably busy. Perhaps I should leave.'

'No! Please don't go. I'm sorry, you must think me very rude, staring at you like that. I was not expecting to have anyone come on board this afternoon. You've rather taken me by surprise.'

Anthony went across to the cockpit. As the seats were able to swivel, he turned them to face each other, before beckoning to her.

'Do come and sit down.'

She lowered herself onto the passenger seat and took the bag from her shoulder, placing it on the deck beside her. She then discreetly crossed her legs and leaned back. Anthony cleared away some of the mess, which was piled high on the opposite seat and then sat down to face her.

'What can I do for you then, young lady?'

'Well, I wanted to look over your boat.'

'Oh! Why?'

'Well! My dad owned a similar boat, when I was a teenager.'

'What, here? In this area?'

'Yes. We used to take her out at weekends. It was really great fun. I can still recall that exhilarating feeling of planing through the waves at speed, with the wind blowing my hair.'

'Did you go very far along the shoreline?'

'Yes. I do have very fond memories of our visiting a secluded sandy cove along the coast from here. It was there that we'd anchor and then swim ashore to sunbathe on the warm sands.'

Anthony observed the young girl's eyes that sparkled with excitement as she spoke.

'I take it your dad doesn't still own her, then?'

'Oh no; that was a long time ago. He sold the boat just after my sixteenth birthday. After that, I spent more time going out with my friends, whilst he fell in love with a tourist, who was staying at a guest house nearby.'

'Did he marry her, then?'

'Well, the woman was Australian. After their holiday romance, they continued seeing each other on a fairly regular basis, although it was very difficult to keep up a relationship across the world.'

'So! What happened?'

'Well! Naturally, they couldn't carry on travelling across the world to meet every few months, so Dad decided to go out there to live. From the photographs they sent me when he first arrived there, they appear to have a beautiful home. It's on the outskirts of Brisbane in Queensland. But that's a few years ago now.'

'You didn't want to go with him then?'

'No. I wanted to stay here where I was born and where all my friends live.'

'And Mum?'

'She died when I was only five.'

'Oh! I am sorry.'

'Yes. Dad brought me up on his own all those years. He and I became very close.'

She had been completely truthful in what she had just told him and was not to know that the story had struck a nerve. Unbeknown to her, he could relate exactly to what this young lady was saying.

'I too brought my daughter up after my wife died, so I know what it's like.'

'Were the two of you very close?'

'Yes. We still are, although she's happily married now.'

The young woman leaned her head to one side.

'I take it her name must be Julia?'

'How did you deduce that?'

Anthony paused to think for a moment.

'Oh, yes, of course - the name of the boat. You're a very astute young lady.'

She smiled and began to look around her again.

'Would you mind if I looked over your boat?'

'No! Feel free!'

She got up and wandered across the deck. She appeared to take a great interest in the way everything worked and what function it had. Anthony also took great delight in explaining things to her. Every now and then, she would pick up some piece of equipment to give it closer examination.

'Can I go below as well?'

'Yes. Sure.'

'It's amazing you know. Everything seems so familiar to me.'

She carefully took the few steps down into the living quarters. Anthony followed close behind her as she opened several lockers and peered inside them.

'I'm sorry it's such a mess down here. I've been trying to tidy things and put them away in their right places, ever since I got here. In fact, I had just finished clearing up the rubbish before you came on board.'

'Oh, don't worry. I think it's rather cosy.'

Her figure hugging white jeans accentuated her every curve as she wandered from one part of the boat to the other. Once again, he pondered on how old she was. Twenty, twenty-one, certainly no more than twenty-four. By now, Anthony was quite captivated by her. He had seen many a gorgeous looking girl walking along the High Street in town, and had only given them cursory glances, but this stunner was different. She was actually here on his boat!

After a brief look around, they came back up on deck again.

'Well, thanks for letting me look at your boat. It brings back a lot of wonderful memories.'

'Oh, that's fine. Anytime.'

She stood still for awhile, as if trying to work something out in her mind.

'Oh, well! I suppose I had better be getting home for tea.'

'Where's home, then?'

'Just on the other side of town. Actually, to be more precise, my home is just outside of town. My dad left the house to me when he went abroad to live.'

'He didn't need to sell it then?'

'No. Fortunately, this lady, who is now my stepmother, already had a home of her own. As Dad is fairly wealthy, he didn't need to sell the house in order to live out there.'

'That was fortunate.'

'Well, it certainly was for me. I couldn't afford to rent anything in this area, let alone buy something.'

As she started to leave, Anthony felt compelled to say something more to her. He had been really taken by this girl who had just paid him a fleeting visit. Now, having struck up a rapport with her, he wanted to talk to her again. He felt the need to say something quickly, otherwise she would be gone forever.

'Look. Once I'm all through with getting the boat ready, I'd be happy to take you out in her. Perhaps, tomorrow afternoon, if you're interested?'

She stared at him, pondering whether or not to accept his invitation. Suddenly, he realised the futility of what he had just said. All right, so she was interested in a bit of nostalgia, but come on, a really beautiful girl like that would rather be out with her friends, than on a boat-trip with a man over twice her age. Yes. It was a very stupid suggestion and now that he had made it, he felt rather foolish.

She stepped off the boat and back onto the pontoon. Pausing briefly, she smiled at him.

'Yes. I would like to come out with you on Sunday afternoon. Say, two o' clock?'

'What. Meet here?'

'If you like.'

'Yes, that's fine.' Anthony replied, in amazement.

'Well. Two p.m. it is then."

He watched as she strolled along the walkway in the direction of the road. Was he dreaming, or did he really just hear her take up his offer of a trip out? He was quite chuffed with the idea. After all, it wasn't a date, was it? He was merely satisfying the girl's curiosity, just a bit of nostalgia.

She hadn't gone very far when another thought struck him.

'Hey!' He called after her. 'I don't even know your name.'

Without looking around, she yelled back at him.

'It's Rebecca, Becky to my friends.'

Chapter Eight

After completing some maintenance work on the boat, Anthony decided to call it a day and return to his daughter's house. As much as he had tried, he just couldn't get the image of the lovely dark-haired girl out of his mind. It had all seemed so unreal, as though he had dreamed those events of an hour or so ago.

Ever since the moment she had left, his analytical mind had been working overtime, trying to establish a more convincing reason as to why she had come aboard in the first place. It was certainly most unusual. No matter how hard he tried though, he could not think of any ulterior motive she may have had. Finally, after much deliberation, he convinced himself, that as young women were very forward nowadays, he shouldn't be so surprised when one of them took him up on his offer, even one as beautiful as Rebecca.

As he was packing up, he noticed that it had already gone six. He had always prided himself on his punctuality and was therefore annoyed at the thought of keeping the family waiting for their tea. However, when he arrived back at the house, he was quite relieved to find that Mike's car was not on the drive. At least that meant they hadn't started yet.

He let himself in with the spare key his daughter had given him earlier. In the dining room, he found Suzanne busily setting the table for a sit down meal. She was neatly placing the knives and forks on either side of the place mats and he observed that the table was laid for five.

'Grandma's coming for tea this evening, Granddad. Dad has just gone to get her.'

Mike's mother Gina, was in her late sixties. She and her husband had lived all their lives in that area. Their son had even gone to the local school before moving on to university. After getting his degree, Mike returned to live with his parents in order to work in a local solicitor's office. Later, when he qualified, he needed to move away from the area in order to get a decent income and advancement in his career.

He first moved into digs in suburban London and joined a large practice in the West End. It was at a party there that he met Julia. She was new to the teaching profession and at that time she worked in a local primary school in London. For the two of them, it was love at first sight, and from then on they were inseparable.

After Mike's dad died of cancer, Gina remained living in the family home. She was fine for the first few months until it later became apparent that his death had had a more serious effect upon her than they imagined. She began to deteriorate both mentally and physically and became a constant worry to her son. She was always forgetful and often appeared distant whenever you spoke to her.

When the opportunity of a partnership position in a local firm of solicitors became available, Mike and Julia were happy to sell up and move to the area. As Mike had said on many occasions, it had not only been a good career move, but also had given them a chance to be near his mum, enabling them to keep an eye on her.

Anthony left Suzanne to lay the table and went into the kitchen to ask Julia if there was anything he could do to help out.

'No, everything's under control, Dad. You go and sit down and pour yourself a drink.'

'I'm sorry I was late, Julia. I didn't notice the time.'

'That's all right. Mike's gone to pick up his mum. We thought it would be nice to have both of you here for a meal at the same time.'

'Yes. How is Gina these days?'

'Well, I don't like to say anything to Mike, but I honestly think she's getting worse. Whenever you speak to her nowadays, she isn't really listening.'

'You mean, she's going deaf?'

'No, not that. She doesn't always seem to comprehend what you are saying. It often gets very frustrating.'

Julia had almost finished making the sandwiches and slapped her father's hand when he tried to help himself to the bowl of crisps.

'Look here! You can make yourself useful, Dad. Take these sandwiches and put them on the dining room table.'

Anthony did as he was asked. Suzanne had just finished laying the table, when the door to the room opened and Mike appeared.

'Hi, Dad. Had a good afternoon?'

Before Anthony had time to reply, Mike ushered his mother through the door in front of him.

'It's a long time since you last saw my mother, isn't it?'

'Yes, it is. How are you these days, Gina?'

Anthony walked across the room to her and gave her a hug.

'You're very familiar, young man,' she replied, trying to extricate herself from the grapple.

'I'm Julia's dad. Don't you remember me?'

She stood back and viewed him, looking rather puzzled.

'Oh yes. Tony, isn't it? Aren't you a bookkeeper or something?'

'It's Anthony actually, Gina, and I'm retired from finance work now.'

Gina had a habit of always shortening his name to Tony, which really annoyed him. As for the bookkeeper remark, she belittled everyone, except her son of course, who was nothing short of fantastic in her eyes. It was little wonder that Mike had turned out to be so full of himself.

Julia interrupted.

'Come and sit at the table, Mum. The food's all ready and I'm just about to pour out the tea.'

Mike sat his mother opposite Anthony, and Suzanne sat on the seat next to her granddad. That left Mike and Julia, sitting in the remaining two places, at opposite ends of the table. Julia brought in the remainder of the bowls and plates of food and placed them in the centre. She then returned to the kitchen for the pot of tea, before sitting down.

The sandwiches were handed round; some cheese, some beef, and some tuna. Julia always liked to make up a selection to ensure that she pleased everyone. She had also made up a separate bowl of mixed salad and put out other smaller bowls containing crisps and a selection of nibbles. As usual, Suzanne had her hand slapped on a couple of occasions for trying to reach across the table instead of asking for the food to be passed to her. On the whole, she had quite good table manners, but that seemed to deteriorate whenever there were guests present.

At the start of the meal, Mike spoke about a client who was giving him grief. Everyone around the table listened attentively to the story, whilst they continued to eat. The food was really good, and from the speed at which the sandwiches were disappearing, it would seem that they were all quite hungry. After he had finished his story, the conversation became just general chat.

'Did you come by car, then Tony?' Mike's mother asked.

'Yes, I've recently bought a new car. You may have seen it when you arrived as it's parked on the road outside. I had a really nice journey down and...."

'Oh, that's nice! Can you pass me the salt, son?'

Mike passed Gina the salt and Anthony continued his conversation.

'I left home early this morning...'

'Oh, really! My son's got a new car too. He works so hard, you know. He really deserves the best.'

'Yes, I'm sure he does.'

Anthony felt rather frustrated at not being allowed to end his sentences before she interrupted. However, he decided to be patient. It was then that Gina tried to reach across the table to the salad bowl but her arms were too short.

'Can I have some of that salad?'

Mike got up from his chair to assist his mother. He picked up the salad bowl and started to place some of the contents onto her plate. Anthony decided to change the conversation in the hope that he would have more of a chance with a different subject.

'Did you have a good journey over here, Gina?'

Mike's mother completely ignored him.

'You can take out those funny looking bits though, Mike. You know how they always get between my teeth.'

Mike dutifully took the bowl and attempted to segregate the bits of salad that his mother wanted from those bits she didn't. Frustrating really, as Julia would have done better to have had a separate bowl for each of the tomatoes, cucumber, lettuce, celery, and so on, if she had had prior knowledge that her mother-in-law would try to have them separated.

Anthony thought it best to keep quiet, as he was getting nowhere in trying to engage Gina in conversation.

'My boy's a solicitor, you know. He's very clever. Your daughter's very lucky to have married him. There were lots of other girls at his office, who were after him at the time.'

Mike positively beamed at his mother's adulation. It was then that Gina proceeded to remove her dentures. She had obviously got "one of those funny bits" stuck between her palate and the roof of her mouth. Julia looked on in horror.

'How come you can take your teeth out, Grandma, and I can't?' asked Suzanne.

'Do you know, my dears, I've had these teeth for twenty-seven years now.'

She pointed with one hand to the dentures that she held in the other. She had completely ignored Suzanne's question. Mike glanced across to Julia and noticed her revulsion. He decided that it was time to act before his mother's nauseating display got out of hand.

'I think we should put them away now, Mum.'

Gina proceeded to swish them around in the glass of water set beside her, before popping them back into her mouth again. Anthony's stomach began to churn as he watched all the little bits, floating around in the glass. He had a very sensitive stomach and this spectacle had been a little too much for him. Suddenly, he had gone off food and all he wanted now, was to scrape the remainder of his plate into the waste bin.

'Not going to eat those sandwiches then, Tony?'

'Well, I had such a large meal at lunch time, Gina, I'm not really hungry now.'

'I see! What was it you were telling me just now?'

'Well. I was talking about my trip down this morning. Then, I was about to tell you what I did after lunch.'

'Oh, yes!'

'Well! This afternoon, I went to look at my boat and...."

'Oh, that's nice! I do like your wallpaper, Mike. Did you put it up yourself? My son's so clever you know.'

The last part of her remark was directed towards Anthony. The lack of attention from Gina when answering his questions was now beginning to annoy him. To complete one full sentence was becoming a matter of principle. Not to be defeated in his attempt to get at least one point over to her, he continued regardless of the interruption.

'And whilst I was there, I washed the deck and tidied up the mess your lazy son left behind....'

'Oh, that's nice!'

'And then I took a machete and hacked the other boats to pieces....'

'Oh, really!'

'Yes, and then I took off all my clothes and ran through the marina, stark naked.'

'Oh, that's nice! Can you get me some clean water, son. This glass of mine seems to have bits floating in it?'

'And what's more, I was chatted up by a young girl and I'm taking her out on my boat tomorrow afternoon.'

Anthony hadn't realised that in his frustration, his voice had got louder and louder, to a point at which he was shouting. It was only during the deathly silence that followed that he noticed his daughter and son-in-law were not amused. Julia was the first to speak.

'That wasn't a very kind thing to say, Dad, was it? She can't help the way she is.'

Gina continued to eat the salad and her sandwich, totally oblivious to the bad atmosphere around the table that Anthony had created.

'Yes, I'm wrong and I apologise.'

He looked across at Gina, who was still stuffing food into her mouth.

'Gina, I apologise. Those remarks of mine were uncalled for.'

'Why? What on earth have you done then, Tony?'

Anthony threw his hands into the air and shook his head in utter disbelief.

'Anyway, the last part of the story wasn't made up. I did chat to a young girl today and I am taking her out on my boat on Sunday.'

Mike was still smarting from the onslaught on his mother.

'How old is she then? Ten, twelve, or what? This isn't "Swallows and Amazons", you know. Old men can't play with kids on boats these days.'

'No. She's a very attractive twenty something.'

'With a white stick, no doubt.'

'No. She's in complete command of all her faculties.'

'So what's she doing going out on a boat trip with you then?'

Julia had had enough.

'I want this conversation stopped right now. You're both acting like a couple of school children. What example does that set to Suzanne?'

Mike allowed her remark to go over his head. He didn't wish to leave it there, whilst he was scoring points against his father-in-law.

'OK. I'll come with you tomorrow, and see this girl for myself.'

Julia was now very angry with her husband.

'Mike! You are going nowhere tomorrow afternoon. You will be fixing that gate that I have asked you to do, time and time again. If you don't, another week will have gone by.'

The remainder of the meal was eaten in silence. Later, when tea was served in the lounge, the conversation continued and the two men remained fairly civil toward each other. By then, both had realised that they had been out of order at the meal table, and wanted to put the unnecessary quarrel behind them. Gina sat in the armchair and almost instantly nodded off, without drinking the cup of tea that had been set beside her. After a short while, Julia got Suzanne ready for bed.

'Are you going to take your mum back home tonight, Mike? It looks as though she's out for the count.'

'Trouble is, Dad, she always dozes off like this, whenever we invite her over lately. Julia often brings down some blankets and a pillow and we make her comfortable in the chair until morning.'

Mike looked sadly at the sleeping figure in the armchair. Anthony felt genuinely sorry for him. He realised that it must be awful to watch your mother deteriorate before your eyes, and Gina had really gone down hill fast.

'We can take her up to the guestroom, if you want to. I'm

quite happy to spend the night sleeping on the sofa.'

'No, that's OK, Dad. I'll just go and get some covers to put round her.'

His son-in-law went upstairs and returned with a blanket and a pillow for his mother. Anthony lifted her head whilst Mike slipped the pillow under it. Finally, they wrapped the blanket around her.

'It's possible she'll be too hot.'

'Well! You never know. It may turn cold in the night. Better to play safe.'

Having put Suzanne to bed, Julia returned to the kitchen to make another pot of tea. She contemplated whether to wash up the crockery straightaway or to leave it until the next morning. Feeling tired, she settled on the latter. Soon, she emerged with the tea and some after-dinner mints.

The three of them sat around in the easy chairs, chatting about amusing past experiences, and the earlier hostility was soon forgotten. Even their laughter failed to wake their sleeping guest. The lively conversation continued to just around midnight, whereupon they decided to turn in for the night.

Anthony retired to the guestroom. As he lay in bed, his thoughts returned to the events of the day, and in particular the girl he had met. He wondered if she would actually turn up the following afternoon, or have second thoughts concerning his offer. She was indeed a beautiful woman, and certainly not one who would normally take a shine to an older man. He couldn't imagine her actually fancying him, although she had given him the impression that she liked him. As he was evaluating the situation further, he fell asleep.

Chapter Nine

The clock on the local church tower had just struck eleven. In the shadows, alongside a wall on the edge of the estate, two figures were quietly conversing. Neither had been there more than ten minutes or so. Occasionally, they would retreat into the darkness as a vehicle passed them, which would then disappear down one of the many side streets. The loud banging of car doors, which resounded in the night air, would inevitably follow.

'Why are we here so early, Darren?'

'Cause we need to have a good look around first. We won't be so conspicuous, while there are people about.'

'So, we'll come back later to break into the cars?'

'Possibly!'

Darren Baxter and his accomplice, Nick Henderson, had been the first to arrive on the council estate that evening. It was an ideal place to meet. Where the wall ended a recreational area of trees and shrubland began. This afforded some cover. The plan was that once Jon had arrived, the three of them could move off into the estate. If they were seen talking together for too long, they may have drawn attention to themselves from the local neighbour watch.

'Do you think Jon's forgotten us?'

'Come off it, Nick! He wouldn't miss this for the entire world. He thinks he's Lex Luther, the greatest criminal mind.'

'Lex who, Darren?'

'Haven't you ever watched a Superman film?'

'No.'

'Well! You're about the only person who hasn't.'

Just then, there was a movement in the bushes up ahead. The two men withdrew into the shadows once again, whilst Darren strained his eyes to identify the black outline of a figure crawling around on his hands and knees.

'D'you think that's Jon, Darren?'

As Nick whispered the question, a shaft of light struck the figure as it came into the open.

'I don't believe it! What on earth's the idiot up to? He's creeping around like bleeding Quasimodo.'

'Ah! Now, that name does ring a bell, Darren.'

Darren drew breath. His accomplice never failed to amaze him.

'Oh, honest, Nick! Now you're a comedian.'

'Eh!'

'You know! The Hunchback ringing a bell.'

Nick's face bore a totally puzzled expression. He had no idea what his companion was on about.

'Don't get you! What have I said now then, Darren?'

'Just forget it, Nick. I really should give up on you.'

Having spotted the two men, the figure came out onto the street. He stood up straight and brushed down the front of his trousers.

'Hi yer! Can't be too sure nowadays, so I thought I'd stay out of sight.'

'But we've been here a quarter of an hour already, Jon.'

'Oh! I didn't see the two of you there, earlier.'

'Never mind about that. Let's get moving.'

Systematically, street by street, the three men scoured the estate for cars containing valuable equipment. As they went along, they made a mental note of possible break-ins. Jon was all for doing the jobs on the spot, but Darren sensibly suggested that it would be better to return in the early hours of the morning, when most potential victims were in bed asleep.

By midnight, they had marked out a number of targets. The majority of them had been older vehicles, which they knew they could break into with ease.

'Here, Darren! Why is it we can nick a car stereo in about thirty seconds, when a garage charges two hours labour to put a new one back in?'

No one could provide an answer to Nick's rhetorical observation. Besides, as most of his conversation was banal in any case, no one really took that much notice of anything he said. However, it was whilst passing by a brand new coupe that they had hit on, that a row broke out between them.

'I reckon we should go back and nick the entire car. We can always dump it later, after we've stripped it.'

'Jon. You can be such a pratt at times. The security on a modern car's too good. You've got to get past the immobiliser, let alone the alarm. That's why we pick older models. Mind you, I suppose we could always go in for car-jacking.'

'Yes. But older models have ropey stereos. Come and have a look at the gear in this one.'

'OK. But keep your voice down.'

At Jon's insistence, the three men returned to the coupe. It was indeed a smart looking vehicle. Looking through the windows, they observed that the owner had replaced the standard audio equipment with something far more upmarket.

'Can't be a local.'

'Why's that, Nick?'

'Cause a local who knows the district, wouldn't be so stupid as to leave all that gear in a car parked outside his house overnight.'

The other two were amazed. It had been one of the most intelligent observations that Nick had ever made.

'Nick's got a point, Darren. It's parked alongside a fence.

Probably a visitor to one of those houses across the road.'

'OK! We'll have a look at it again, when we come back later.'

Jon was impatient.

'I say, we do it now. After all, it probably won't be here later.'

His friends agreed, although Darren was still insistent that now was not the right time to steal the valuable equipment. Jon was rather annoyed with the attitude of his accomplice and began to protest. As they were getting nowhere in the argument that followed, Darren and Nick decided to ignore him and began to walk away. They had not noticed that Jon had taken the tyre lever from the inside of his jacket, until they heard the sound of breaking glass. Darren immediately swung around, to see Jon fiddling with the central locking of the car.

'You moron! The equipment's probably bolted in.'

It was too late. By this time, Jon had got the driver's door open, and the car alarm was screeching loudly. People, who had not yet gone to bed, came to their front doors to see what all the commotion was about.

'Leave it, Jon! For goodness sake, let's get out of here.'

'Hang on a minute! I think it's coming loose.'

The words hardly left Jon's lips, when a police vehicle came down the street at speed, no blue lights flashing or sirens.

'Where the bloody hell did that come from?'

'Something's not quite right here, Darren.'

'You're telling me! Come on! Go! Go! Go!'

Jon dropped the equipment that was still attached to the car's fascia, and began to run. Being so fit, he soon caught up his two accomplices, who already had a head start on him. They paused briefly on the corner of the street to assess the situation.

'You moron! What'd you go and do that for?'

Darren was angry.

'We had plenty of time to get that out of the car. Someone's stitched us up. The police normally take at least twenty minutes to arrive after someone's phoned them.'

Nick looked up. Two police officers had left their vehicle and were running in their direction.

'They're still after us, Darren.'

'Right! Let's split up!'

Jon headed for the recreation ground, whilst Darren and Nick went in the opposite direction.

'Don't follow me, you moron! Find your own way.'

'Oh! Sorry, Darren!'

Darren scaled the high wooden fence on the opposite side of the road. Before dropping down on the other side, he looked back to see that he was still being pursued by one of the officers. He presumed that the other had gone after Jon. Nick however, was nowhere to be seen.

Jon had made it across the estate and into the darkness of the recreation field. He found it difficult to run at speed and still know where he was heading. At one stage, he tripped and fell, giving the officer the advantage of shortening the distance between them. Fortunately, he wasn't hurt and was soon able to regain the lead over his pursuer.

As he reached the wooded area, he found it more difficult to keep pace. He paused for just a few seconds to give himself time to get his breath back but noticed that the officer was still on his tail. He considered it unwise to head across the open field and therefore decided to double-back on himself, using the trees for partial cover. At first, his plan worked well, and the policeman continued on in the direction of the woods. However, the rustling of the undergrowth as he ran, attracted too much attention.

Glancing over his shoulder, he could see the powerful flashlight of the pursuing officer, who was now gaining on him as he proceeded to run in the direction of the housing estate once again. He quickly assessed the situation and that meant that he needed somewhere to hide. He therefore jumped the low perimeter fence and into a garden. Crouching down behind a large shed, he could still observe the field.

When the police officer reached the fence, he didn't appear to want to go any further. This came as some relief to Jon, as his pursuer was only a very short distance away from him. Although he was panting heavily, he placed his hand over his mouth in order to muffle the noise of his breathing. He was also sweating and the drops of perspiration were rolling down his face.

The officer shone his torch into the garden, searching for any signs of movement. As the beam of light circled past the front of the shed, Jon sat back as far as he could against the neighbouring fence. For what seemed like an eternity to him, the police officer maintained his vigilance. He knew that even the slightest sound would give him away, especially in view of the very short distance between them.

Whilst Jon kept out of sight, he listened intensely as the officer relayed his position to his colleague. The police were aware that they had him cornered somewhere in the back garden and it would be only a matter of time before they caught him. He realised that he would now have to get away as quickly as possible before they brought in a police helicopter with a thermal imaging camera, or worse still, the police dogs.

Keeping the shed between himself and the police officer, he quietly climbed over the low fence and into the next garden. His fear of being caught receded, as he continued to do this for a few more gardens. Even so, he knew he had to be extremely careful not to make a sound, otherwise he would soon draw attention to himself once again.

Eventually, he reached the end of the row of houses, and could go no further, as the final fence was so high. Not to be thwarted by this obstacle, he followed it down to the back gate. He then paused to assess the situation and to calm down. His heart had been racing for the past twenty minutes, knowing that he had narrowly escaped capture.

On the other side of the gate, he noticed a low wall that ran the length of the house, separating the side entrance from that of the house next door. Beyond that path lay the street, and some familiar alleyways, which crossed the entire estate and ended back in town. His first problem however, was to get past the sensor on the security light.

Using the wall for cover, he crawled along on his front so as not to trip the sensor. As he was about to clear the obstacle, he felt someone climb onto his back and place a hand around his mouth. His assailant gripped him in a very tight hold, making it impossible for him to struggle free.

'I ought to kill you for this, you idiot! You almost got us caught.'

Jon recognised the voice instantly. Establishing that his accomplice had got over the initial shock, Darren gradually released his grip on Jon's mouth, to enable him to speak.

'Oh! I wondered where you got to.'

'Not so loud, you moron! People have got their windows open. Anyway, I'll deal with you later. Let's concentrate on getting out of this mess.'

The two men lay side by side, sheltering in the cover of darkness afforded by the wall. Some careful planning had to take place before the next move if they were to avoid arousing suspicion once they were out into the street again.

'It doesn't look as though the front gate has a lock on it.'

'You're right. I don't think they've got a dog either, or we would have heard it barking by now.'

Jon stretched his head around the wall to try and see beyond the gate.

'There doesn't appear to be anyone in the street either. I'll go first, and make it to the alley on the other side.'

'OK! I'll follow you, but if you mess this up, I'll get Nick to sort you out good and proper.'

Once clear of the security light, Jon was through the gate and across the road. Darren noted that there was nobody about and quickly followed. The alley was dark. The council had attempted to put a street light at the end of each section as it crossed the road, but these had been more or less vandalised. Each time they came to a well-lit area, they exercised caution, should a police vehicle be waiting for them in the next street. The law would have been well aware of this thoroughfare.

Upon reaching the centre of town, the two men could relax again. It had been an unnerving experience for both of them and they were relieved to have escaped their ordeal so easily without getting caught by the police. They stopped to talk for a while, before going their separate ways.

'What's this job I'm doing on Wednesday evening?'

'I'll say this, Jon. I've a good mind not to give it to you, after tonight's escapade. I still reckon we were set up. You haven't been grassing to anyone, have you?'

'Of course I haven't! You worry too much!'

'Well! I find that worrying keeps me out of prison.'

Darren was still extremely wary of Jon. He was far too flippant about everything, as far as he was concerned, and that spelt trouble. Nevertheless, Jon pursed his original line of questioning.

'This job. You say it's worth a grand to me?'

'Only if it all goes to plan. Did you get the boat?'

'Yep! I've taken care of that.'

Jon crossed his fingers behind his back. He was relying on Rebecca to get the boat. She had told him earlier that evening that she had sussed out a fast motor cruiser, and was now working on the old chap who owned it. However, he didn't feel the need to convey this information to Darren, as it would probably alarm him.

'You sure about that?'

'Yes! No problem! It's all in hand. Anyway, what am I picking up?'

'You don't need to know. It's just a very large package. Right?'

'Anything you say, Darren. You're the man forking out the money.'

Darren pondered for thought. He was still very unsure that Jon was the best person to entrust this job to.

'Know where you're taking it?'

'Yep! I'm leaving it in a mate's garage overnight.'

'Can we trust him?'

'Oh, yes! Kyle's OK.'

'Good!'

Darren began to relax again. He placed his hand on Jon's shoulder and his face broke into a false smile.

'Now! One last thing! I don't want to see your face again, this side of Thursday. Got it!'

'Yes! Sure!'

Jon left Darren to go his own way. He returned to his car, which he had parked down a street nearby, prior to walking across town to meet the other two. It was almost three in the morning, when he arrived back at Rebecca's place. She was of course sound asleep, having spent a boring evening in front of the television.

Chapter Ten

Next morning, Anthony's first recollection was of someone tugging at his arm. He first opened one eye and then the other, as he was having great difficulty in focusing them. The morning sun, streaming in through the windows, added to his discomfort and made him blink.

'Come on Granddad, wake up.'

The annoying youngster continued to shake him furiously.

'What time is it?'

'It's half past six.'

'Oh no, not this early! Isn't there someone else you can go and annoy for another two hours? Your mum and dad, perhaps?'

'But I want to come and annoy you.'

Suzanne was full of life and continued to bounce up and down upon the bed.

'I've made you a cup of tea. I made one for Mum and Dad too but they didn't want theirs. They said it was too early. They say that every time I make them tea on Sunday mornings.'

Anthony sat up and adjusted his pillow to lean back on.

'That's very kind of you, Suzanne.'

The youngster stretched across and handed him the cup. He took one sip and winced. It was barely warm.

'Do you like it, Granddad?'

'Yes, it's delicious.'

He lied of course. The tea was absolutely foul.

'I've made you some toast too.'

'Oh, boy! I can't wait to see what that is like!'

Although the toast was warm, well at least, warmer than the tea, it had been left rather too long in the toaster. After taking one mouthful, Anthony returned it to the plate, which he then placed upon the bedside cabinet.

'I'm sorry it got a bit black. You don't have to eat it if you don't want to.'

'Well, I'm sure it's very nice, but I'll leave it on the cabinet and eat it later.'

As he did not appear to want to drink the tea either, Suzanne took the cup from his hand and placed it carefully on a tray beside the bed.

'Granddad! This lady you're going to see this afternoon, is she very pretty?'

'Well, yes. She's very beautiful.'

'Do you think you'll marry her?'

Anthony smiled. What wonderful innocence, to think that every relationship between a man and a woman, however casual, should lead to marriage.

'I'm only going to take her for a ride on my boat.'

'What? Only the one ride?'

'Well, as far as I know; yes.'

The youngster paused for thought.

'Will I ever get to see her then?'

'I really don't know, Suzanne. I've only just met her.'

Suzanne put her head under her granddad's arm and snuggled up close to him.

'I don't ever want to have a boyfriend.'

'Why is that?'

'If you have a boyfriend and he likes you, then you'll have to marry him.'

'No, that's not true. Wherever did you get that idea from?

Anyway, there's nothing wrong in getting married one day, when the right boy comes along for you.'

'But I don't want to get married.'

'We all say that, but when we get older we change our minds.'

'I won't.'

Suzanne was very emphatic in her reply.

'Why not?'

'Dad deals with lots of people who are married and they all hate each other and do nasty things to each other. I've heard him telling Mum all about it.'

'It's not always like that, Suzanne. Your Grandma and I were very happy for years and years. Your Mum and Dad are happy too, aren't they?'

'But Mark's dad went off and left him and his mum.'

'Yes, I know, but it's only when things like that go wrong, that your dad gets involved and has to sort it all out. He only gets to see the unhappy marriages. There are thousands and thousands of people in the world who are really happy together.'

The little face looked up at him. He could see her trying to find an answer to what he was saying.

'Granddad!'

'Yes, love.'

'Why did God take Grandma away from us? I never did get to see her.'

Suddenly the sadness came flooding back to him and his eyes began to water.

'Your grandma was very ill and it was making her very unhappy. The doctors said that she wasn't going to get any better, so now she's gone to be with Jesus.'

'She feels much happier now, then?'

'Yes, I'm sure she does.'

Suzanne sat there in silence for a short while, meditating upon their brief conversation. Anthony decided to change the subject.

'Right! I think it's time for us to get up, don't you?'

The youngster nodded.

'You go back into your room, whilst I get dressed.'

'OK!'

Suzanne returned to her room and he heard her switch on the television. There couldn't have been anything interesting to watch at this time on a Sunday morning, but it got her out of his hair whilst he got ready. With his daughter and son-in-law still asleep in bed, Anthony headed for the bathroom. His plan was to get washed and dressed as quickly as possible and then go out for a stroll on his own.

Half an hour or so later, when he came downstairs, he noticed Mike's mother loudly snoring in the armchair, where they had left her the night before. He went across to her and tucked her in again, as one of her blankets had fallen onto the lounge carpet. Having then helped himself to a quick breakfast, Anthony left the house.

It was indeed a lovely day and without a cloud in the sky. As he walked along the coast path he met very few people. Of those who were about, some were exercising their dogs, whilst presumably on their way into town for the Sunday newspapers. Although it was still quite early, it was very warm. As he strolled along, he considered it would have been a pity to stay in bed on a beautiful morning such as this.

He left the path on the way into town, in order to walk across the beach. It was deserted, apart from a group of young men who were taking an early morning dip in the sea. The sandy patch left by the receding tide had started to dry in the sunshine, although it was quite heavy going under foot. Eventually, the beach came to an end, and he ambled up the slope and into the quiet narrow streets of the town.

Even here, there were very few people about, except those congregating around the newsagents. He stopped for a short while to look at some of the cards in the shop window, which offered all sorts of things for sale. It was amazing what people were willing to dispose of for a few pounds, including items that Anthony, to his shame, had tossed away in the rubbish bin over the years.

He then skirted around the harbour, where the moored fishing boats lay stranded in the mud, leaning to their sides upon their keels. The harbour always looked more picturesque when the tide was in. It was then that those same boats would be bobbing up and down on the glistening water in the sunshine, seemingly free once again. He sat for a while on the outer harbour wall, to look out to sea.

He was pleased that it was going to be another beautiful day, as it would add to the enjoyment of the impending boat trip that afternoon. Just as in one's childhood, one always remembered those days that were warm and sunny, he wanted this occasion to be just as memorable. His thoughts then turned to Rebecca. Would she turn up? She may have returned home the previous day and changed her mind. After all, it was a distinct possibility. Nevertheless, although he had a great feeling of anticipation and excitement welling up inside him, he didn't want to raise his hopes too high.

After being alone with his thoughts for some time, he looked around him and noticed that the holidaymakers were out in force. It was now mid morning. He rose from the harbour wall and started to walk back. It was then that he observed a young boy trying to walk across the mud.

From a distance, he thought he recognised the youngster. The boy had dark hair and was of slim build. He was dressed in a tee shirt and dark coloured trousers, the bottoms of which were caked in black slime. He looked about twelve or thirteen, certainly no older than that. The face looked familiar too but he couldn't quite recollect where he had seen the boy before.

As he attempted to cross to the other side, he seemed to be sinking more and more deeply with each step. Seeing the predicament that he found himself in, the boy then decided to take a short cut towards the harbour wall. As he got closer to him, Anthony could see that it was the young lad who lived next door to Mike and Julia. Unfortunately, when he reached the wall, he found he was too short to climb it. Bemused by the spectacle, Anthony felt it was time to lend a hand.

By the time he reached the lad, he was on his fifth attempt at trying to get a foothold on the rough concrete surface.

'Aren't you Caroline McBride's son?'

'What's it to you?'

'There's no need to be rude.'

'Yes, I'm Mark.'

The lad looked up to see Anthony towering above him.

'You're the old boy who's staying next door to us, aren't you?'

Anthony disregarded the lad's lack of respect.

'Yes, I'm Suzanne's granddad.'

He could now see that the boy's trainers and the bottoms of his trousers were covered in thick black mud. Where he had presumably fallen over, the knees were also filthy and so were his hands. The young lad was certainly living up to the awful reputation that his mother had revealed to him, the previous day.

'Your mum's going to kill you when she sees the state of your clothes. Why did you walk across the mud in the first place?'

'Look! Are you going to help me up or just prattle about all day?'

'You don't have to be so abusive, especially if you want my help. Here, I'll try and grab your hand.'

Anthony knelt on the edge of the wall and reached down to grasp the boy's hand. Once he had established a firm grip, Mark was able to drag himself up. The young lad showed visible signs of relief that his ordeal was now over. He then engaged in a pathetic attempt to brush the mess from his trousers, by using his hands, which were equally muddy.

'I think you'll only make matters worse by doing that.'

'What do you suggest then?'

Anthony noted an air of belligerence in the tone of his voice. There was no apparent reason for this unwarranted hostility towards him.

'Well, let's see what I can find. Stand still for a minute.'

He found an old discarded newspaper in one of the bins nearby. It wasn't the most ideal cleaning material but they used it to scrape off as much mud as they could. Hopefully, the remainder would dry in the heat, on the way home. Unfortunately, some of the mud had also transferred onto Anthony's best trousers and shirt in the lad's eagerness to grab onto anything to hand in order to hoist him up.

'Well, Mark. I suppose I had better walk home with you. I was heading that way in any case.'

'Can if you like.'

Anthony returned the bits of used newspaper to the bin. However, seeing Mark looking very dejected, he felt he should express some words of comfort to the lad.

'Never mind. Hopefully, some of the mud will have dried and fallen off by the time your mum gets to see you. Perhaps it won't look so bad by then.'

Mark grunted in agreement.

The two of them set off around the harbour. It was now crowded with tourists, looking in the numerous gift shops which skirted the quay. Occasionally, passers-by would give them strange looks as they tried to ascertain how the lad managed to get his clothes and his trainers into such a state. It was very embarrassing for both of them. What was more annoying to Anthony though, was the fact that Mark had now decided to drag his feet.

After crossing the beach, they climbed the narrow footpath to top of the cliffs. It was a long and frustrating hike for Anthony. Frequently, he had to wait for Mark to catch up. Then, within a few minutes of setting off, the infuriating youngster was dawdling again. He also tried to engage the boy in meaningful conversation, but every sentence was met with a grunt that must have indicated either, “yes”, “no”, or “mind your own business”. It was difficult to tell which alternative was correct, as he showed a complete lack of interest in anything that was said.

Almost halfway home, the gap between the two of them had extended considerably, as Anthony had become tired of constantly stopping and waiting for him. Mark was now lagging some distance behind.

‘Why don’t you try to keep up? Anthony shouted. ‘It’ll take us all day to get back at this rate.’

‘What’s it to you?’

Anthony was annoyed. Mark’s offhanded attitude was totally uncalled-for. Admittedly, boys of this age were often aggressive without good cause but how Caroline managed to put up with this behaviour day after day, he couldn’t imagine. Most children were nowhere near as disrespectful as this lad was.

Suddenly, he felt something hit the back of his head. It took him completely by surprise. Anthony turned to face the nuisance, who he guessed must have lobbed the missile.

‘What was that?’

The youngster grinned mischievously.

‘It was only dog pooh.’

‘It had better not have been.’

At this stage, he realised that if he had any common sense, he should now walk off and leave the boy to face his mother on his own. After all, it wasn’t his fault that he got into such a mess. If his mother got mad at him, then it was no more than he deserved, especially in view of his current display of disgraceful behaviour. The only problem about that idea was the fact that he now felt responsible for him and therefore felt it inappropriate to walk off and leave him. Besides, he wanted to ensure that the boy at least went straight home.

The lad continued to drag his feet, and Anthony slowed the pace to a mere crawl to ensure that the gap between them got no longer. He had given up on trying to talk to Mark and so they plodded on in silence.

Suddenly Mark yelled out to him.

'I bet you fancy my mum, don't you?'

Anthony stopped and turned to face him. Mark stopped too, not wishing for the gap between them to be closed. The remark had been calculated to goad him into some sort of hostile response, and he therefore considered that he might need a head start if the "old chap" came running after him. He stood his ground with a smug look upon his face, which Anthony would have dearly liked to remove at the first opportunity he had; that is of course, assuming he could get hold of him first.

'Your mum is a very nice lady. It can't be easy for her having to go to work, run a home, and bring up an obnoxious youngster, like you, all on her own. You should be very pleased she is so patient with you.'

'So you don't fancy my mum, then?'

Anthony realised that the boy was just trying to be provocative, so he decided that the best idea was to ignore him. There was no point in trying to reason with him as he obviously thought it was all a "bit of a giggle". Leaving him some distance behind, he continued to walk on up the hill.

'What are you, queer or something?' said the lad, trying to sound as controversial as he could.

Anthony ignored the remark and walked on ahead. He considered that the boy was now being so stupid, that his questions didn't even warrant a reply.

'Pervert, pervert!' The boy shouted.

Anthony stopped and turned around yet again. His comments were now getting beyond a joke.

'Mark! Must you persist with this childish behaviour? Why don't you grow up? You couldn't even spell pervert, let alone know what it means.'

'Yes, I can. P.u.r.v….'

'Wrong.

'P.u.r.r…'

'Wrong again.'

'All right then! Queer, poofter, pansy, faggot…'

Anthony switched off, whilst Mark continued to work his way through his entire vocabulary of extremely rude words. As he reached the next bend in the path, a young girl about Mark's age came walking down the hill. As she drew level with Anthony, she stopped to speak to him.

'Isn't that Mark McBride down there?'

'Yes, it certainly is.'

'He's in my class at school.'

'Lucky, you!'

'Do you know; all the girls at school really fancy him?'

'Oh! Do they?'

'We think he's really lovely.'

'Yes, he certainly is that; and so articulate too.' Anthony added, sarcastically.

'What's articulate mean?'

'I'll tell you what! Why don't you go and ask your "lovely" friend. He's got a way with words and such a wonderful command of the English language that he's bound to know the answer. In fact, you'll find that he's working his way through his entire vocabulary as we speak.'

'Oh, OK! Thanks!'

Anthony's further attempt at sarcasm had completely gone over the young girl's head. He turned and watched her stroll down the footpath and then stop for a chat with her vulgar school pal. As they soon became engrossed in a dull conversation, he decided to walk on.

A short while later, the discussion came to an end and they parted company. The girl continued down the hill, and Mark thought he should now get a move on. Some of the mud on his trousers had already dried and he was able to brush it off. It still left dirty marks though, but at least he didn't look quite as bad as he did down by the harbour. Looking ahead, Anthony was nowhere to be seen.

As he turned the bend in the path, he spoke aloud to himself.

'I wonder where that old boy's gone to? I bet he's back in doors by now, stupid old git! Can anybody hear me?'

Suddenly a hand came out and grabbed him. Before he could ascertain what was happening to him, Mark was pinned firmly up against the wall. He had been so taken by surprise that it had knocked all the wind out of his sails.

'Listen, you obnoxious little brat. I've just about had it up to here with you.'

Anthony was gripping the front of the boy's shirt.

'Don't hit me! Don't hit me!'

'Who said anything about hitting you?'

Mark was now panicking.

'I'll tell my mum if you hit me. You're not suppose to hit little kids, like me.'

'Don't flatter yourself. I wouldn't waste my energy on you.'

Anthony released his grip upon the boy's shirt.

'How old are you?'

'Twelve.'

'Well, if you want to see thirteen, you had better start behaving more sensibly.'

Anthony didn't smile. This time he was being serious. He felt that someone should drum some sense into the kid, and it might just as well be him.

'Now let's get one thing straight, shall we?'

'What's that then?'

'I want to see some respect from you, and so does your mother. You can't go through life being rude to everyone you meet.'

Mark was stunned into silence.

'In fact, you can make a start by helping your mother and going straight home from school each day, so she doesn't have to spend her valuable time searching for you. Got it?'

'Yes! OK! Anything you say.'

'Good.'

Anthony softened the tone of his voice.

'Now we understand each other, we can take that brisk walk back home, together. All right by you?'

'Yes! All right!'

Anthony and Mark set off on the last part of the walk home. After the shock to his system, the boy seemed rather more subdued and a little more sociable.

'Will you come and explain this mess to my mum? She might take more notice of you.'

Anthony agreed. The boy still seemed dazed by the unexpected nature of his ordeal. He now seemed quite content to trot alongside the older man, all the way home. Anthony, in turn, made no big thing of the incident and chatted to him about football and other hobbies that interested him. He was sad to hear that Mark had few friends outside of school though. Apparently, their parents wouldn't allow them to invite him back home. It wasn't really surprising, when considering Mark's discourteous attitude. Parents don't like their children to mix with bad company, and Anthony supposed he was considered to be just that.

What the boy really needed was a father figure who would take him in hand and teach him how to respect people. It would need to be an adult who, besides his mother, would take a genuine interest in him; essentially, someone he could look up to. He had never found that quality in his father and, as his mother had rejected all men who were interested in her, there was no surrogate replacement either.

As they reached home, Anthony kept to his word and walked down the path to the McBride house. As he rang the doorbell, Mark hid behind him. They waited for what appeared to be ages for someone to answer. As no one came to the door, Anthony decided to ring again.

Eventually, Caroline opened the door. It was obvious that she had been sunbathing in the back garden, as she was wearing a brief bikini that was clearly visible under the flimsy coat she wore over the top of it. It also explained her delay in answering the front door. She looked at Anthony and then at her son, skulking furtively behind him. Upon seeing the state of his clothes, the expression on her face turned to one of anger.

'What have you been up to?'

The boy didn't answer. He could see his mother was furious.

'Just look at the state of you!'

Anthony spoke in an attempt to defuse the situation.

'Can I say something here?'

Caroline's eyes moved across to Anthony.

'He accidentally got stuck in the mud down by the harbour.'

'Accidentally! Did you say accidentally? Mark doesn't do anything by accident! He only does things on purpose to annoy me.'

She then turned to look at her son again.

'You! Get inside this minute and get those filthy clothes off.'

Mark dashed through the gap between his mother and the door opening and managed to dodge the swipe she took at him as he went past.

'You're really asking for a damn good spanking,' she added.

With the same fixed hostile expression, she turned to face Anthony.

'Yes?' she asked, abruptly, almost anticipating a question.

'Well. I was down at the harbour too. As you can see, I also got muddy.'

'So!'

'Does that mean I'm up for one as well?'

Realising the implications of this saucy remark, Caroline's expression changed to a broad smile. She tutted; shook her head; and then gently closed the door in front of him.

Anthony stood for a moment, and chuckled to himself.

'I guess I'll take that as "No".'

Chapter Eleven

Rebecca sipped her drink as she sat on the bench outside the pub, in the beautiful bright sunshine. Her boyfriend had gone inside to order them a meal, and had yet to return. It was too good to stay at home for lunch on a day like this, so they had decided to eat out. It was very relaxing for Rebecca and got her away from the chore of having to cook, with the added bonus of not having any washing up to do either.

When she first met Jon, he would often bring her here for a drink in the evenings. In those days, he was very attentive and she enjoyed his company. Now, when she came home from work, all he wanted to do was to lounge in front of the television, and only go out when Kyle called for him. She liked Kyle a lot, but found it tedious always having to have him along with them, everywhere they went. Today, however, was one of those rare exceptions when he was not around.

The pub was crowded with people and it had been difficult to find a parking space in the car park. Like most of the other customers, they had found it far too hot to remain inside, and had therefore ventured into the garden to sit on the benches under the parasols, which provided some welcome shade. Fortunately, when they arrived, a family had just got up from one of the tables, which enabled them to have the unoccupied seats straight away. Others had not been so fortunate, and had therefore resorted to sitting in groups and eating their meals outside the bar, on the recently mown grass.

'Who would want to be in their kitchen, cooking a meal in this weather?' she mused.

The two couples on the adjacent seats, all of whom were in their late thirties or early forties, were engaged in a long discussion about politics. What had started as an almost inaudible conversation on some current topics, progressed as they began to raise their voices, each one becoming more impassioned about getting over their own points to the others. The argument between the two men was noticeably very heated. It was obvious that they had two diametrically opposite political views on most subjects. It never ceased to amaze Rebecca, how people could get so worked up over political issues that she would consider as relatively unimportant.

She contrasted this, with the young boy and his girlfriend on the opposite side of her, who were making it very apparent how deeply in love they were with each other. Every so often he would tenderly hold her hand and she would gaze lovingly into his eyes. They said very little, and for that matter, ate very little of the food on the plates in front of them. She observed, as the young man prodded his fork into a chip from his meal and offered it up to her. The girl, in turn, brushed it aside and gently kissed him on the lips. Jon had never been like that.

'I couldn't get chicken breast as they've run out, so you'll have to make do with nuggets. OK?'

Rebecca looked back to see Jon sitting on the opposite side of the bench.

'Oh well! Back to reality.'

Jon caught the remark, but didn't understand what she meant by it.

'What d'you mean by that?'

'Ah! Nothing! Nothing at all!'

What would he understand about romance? The truth was

that there had never been any romance between them from the beginning of their relationship.

Jon made himself comfortable at the bench and handed Rebecca her cutlery and a table napkin.

'I saw you staring at that couple over there. Not getting any romantic ideas, are you?'

'As if I would.'

Rebecca lifted her glass to her lips to take another drink.

'Why can't you be like that, once in a while?'

'What? Like him over there?'

'Well! What's wrong with that?'

'Oh, come on, Becky! Just look at him! It's almost sickening to watch.'

'But it's nice to have a man show you lots of attention.'

'Yes, but not like that.'

'But they're in love with each other.'

'Well, they've certainly been up to something. It looks as though he's got a love bite on his neck.'

'So what if he has?'

'You know, I had one once, and it hurt.'

'I guess it must have been self inflicted then, seeing how you love yourself so much.'

Jon made a rude gesture with his fingers.

'I hope they won't take too long serving the meal. I'm starving.'

'Actually, Jon, I've never known a time when you're not.'

Jon started to raise his glass to his mouth.

'Well, the queue at the bar for meals was awful. It's going to take ages before our number comes up.'

'Then, why don't you just relax like me? I'm happy just to sit here in the sun.'

'Well! I'm not.'

'Oh! Who's the grumpy one today?'

Jon refused to answer. He was annoyed at having to wait in

the queue to order the meal and now frustrated at having to wait for it to be served. Patience was certainly not one of Jon's strongest points. He then picked up his drink and downed it with one long swallow.

'I was really thirsty.'

'I can see you were. It can't do you any good, drinking like that. After all, we're not in a hurry.'

'I'll drink anyway I want to.'

Rebecca could see no point in continuing with this banal dialogue. Jon was in such a bad mood again that he probably wouldn't snap out of it until his food came. She offered up a suggestion.

'Shall I go and find out for you how long it'll be?'

'No. Don't bother.'

'Do you want me to get you another drink?'

'No. I'll save your offer till later.'

Jon nursed his empty glass, whilst Rebecca looked back at the young couple again. They were now so busily kissing that their food must have gone cold, even in this heat. That was something Jon would never allow. Filling his stomach had always taken priority over anything else.

'I'm not keen on your seeing this old guy, this afternoon.'

'Yes, I know. You've already told me that a hundred times, before we arrived here.'

'Perhaps I should go and look him over.'

'Honestly, Jon! What on earth do you think we're going to do when we get out on this boat then?'

'I bet he fancies you.'

'I expect he does.'

'If he tries any funny stuff, I'll sort him out.'

'Oh, grow up! He seems a very nice man. I feel bad enough about going this afternoon in any case, since it's only his boat we're after.'

'Don't you start going sweet on him.'

Fortunately, the waitress arrived with the food and therefore a possible full-scale squabble was avoided. At least, whilst they were eating, they weren't arguing. Jon always lacked the co-ordination to be able to have more than one bodily function working at any one time.

He soon scoffed his meal and then sat watching Rebecca picking hers over. She eventually ate most of it, although she wasn't that hungry. She also wasn't looking forward to the afternoon boat trip, as the whole thing seemed so deceitful.

With the meal finished, Jon was back on the same topic again.

'Make sure you get the boat from him for Wednesday evening.'

'Yes, Jon.'

'Don't whatever you do, let him suspect what's going on.'

'Yes, Jon.'

He paused to think of another question.

'You won't let him try anything on with you, will you?'

'No, Jon.'

'Are you going to eat those last two chicken nuggets?'

She gave out a sigh.

'No, Jon.'

John leaned across the table and picked up the nuggets with his fingers, putting them straight into his mouth. Anyone would have thought he hadn't had a decent meal for a month at the speed at which he ate them.

'I could go that all again.'

'Yes, I bet you could, you pig.'

His eating habits always disgusted her.

Rebecca had become tired of hearing him drone on about the boat trip and this so called "scam" of his. He had started on her first thing that morning when they got up, and he hadn't let up since then. Now, his persistence was really beginning to grate on her nerves.

He had gone along with her idea when she first suggested it as means of "persuading" someone to lend them their boat. He hadn't realised at the time, that being devious might require some association with the boat owner. Initially, if that meant merely accepting a trip out in it, then he had very little to complain about. However, Jon's problem was, that he was so jealous of other men even so much as looking at her, that he couldn't contemplate the thought of her having an afternoon in another man's company.

'Look, Jon. It's one 'o' clock and I had better get going. Let's have the keys to the car so I can go home and change. Kyle will pick you up later.'

'Make sure you don't wear anything that's too revealing.'

Rebecca drew breath.

'Jon! Just give me the damn keys!'

Jon handed over the keys to the car and she left. As she drove home, her attitude to the trip changed. She was now looking forward to the afternoon out but was not exactly sure why. Maybe it was the thought of getting a break from Jon for a few hours or the thrill of flirting with this mild and seemingly embarrassed man she had met the day before. She was not entirely certain which of the two thoughts excited her more.

At home, she had a shower and washed her hair. Unfortunately, she had left it rather late to get ready and didn't have too much time to look for the hair drier, which Jon had used earlier. He must have put it somewhere other than in its usual place. As she couldn't find it after a brief search, she decided to leave her hair wet. She thought about putting it into a ponytail again, but instead she combed it straight, to enable it to dry quickly.

She decided to put a bikini on under her clothes, on the off chance that she might get the opportunity to sunbathe, while they were out at sea. It seemed a good idea, providing she didn't get it wet. Just to be sure, though, she thought it best to take a few items to change into that would fit conveniently into her small shoulder bag.

Searching through her wardrobe, she picked out various tops and tried them on. She couldn't afford to be too selective as it was already ten to two. She finally settled for a linen shirt, which she tied in a knot under her cleavage, leaving her slim waist and navel exposed.

'That'll get his pacemaker running at full speed,' she muttered to herself, mischievously.

Turning then to look at skirts and trousers, she tossed several of them onto the bed. Which was it to be? She put on different skirts but none of them seemed to compliment the shirt. Eventually, she settled on a pair of tight trousers of a light material that would keep her cool.

'Make up? I haven't really got time for make up.'

She continued to mutter to herself, as she quickly gave her face the once over with the lipstick.

'Well! That'll just have to do. I can't afford to miss out on this trip. There's too much at stake.'

Chapter Twelve

On the other side of town, Anthony was sitting patiently on his boat. He had arrived there at half past one, in plenty of time to get everything ready for the trip, and it was now gone two. He was beginning to wonder whether she was going to turn up and was trying to work out how long to give her, before he should pack up and return to his daughter's house again.

Julia had arranged for an early Sunday lunch so he could get away and over to his boat on time. She had also silenced her husband, who was anxious to make comments about his father-in-law's stupidity over this young woman he was meeting. For him, the whole idea made no sense.

One of the most annoying things for Anthony, was the fact that he had only packed one pair of good trousers for the stay at his daughter's house. Following the escapade that morning with Mark, these were covered in muddy stains. He knew that there was no way he was going to get them washed, dried, and ironed in time for the trip, so he just had to settle for a pair of dark coloured jeans. It was not the ideal dress for taking a lady out, but then again, he had not come prepared for that.

By twenty past two, he had convinced himself that she was not going to come. He was very disappointed and mulled over the problem, as to how he was going to break the news to the family. Julia and Suzanne would probably be sympathetic, but

Mike would have a field day. Anthony had always been very trusting and took people at face value. He always kept to his word and therefore expected others to abide by the same principle. Still, it wasn't the first occasion that he had been made to look a fool and, unbeknown to him at the time, not the last either.

He continued to potter around, finishing the jobs he was unable to complete the day before, due to lack of time. Suddenly, he heard a familiar voice.

'Am I still welcome aboard? I know I'm very late?'

He had been so engrossed in his thoughts that he hadn't noticed Rebecca arrive. She looked beautiful, in fact, absolutely stunning. Yes. She was very late, but with such a lovely smile, how could any man be annoyed with her.

'Yes, Becky. Of course. I'm really pleased you made it.'

'I expect you thought I wasn't coming, didn't you?'

'Well, it did cross my mind but I'm really pleased you're here now.'

She clambered onto the deck and came over to him.

'You're not annoyed with me then?'

'No, of course not.'

'Are you sure?'

'I don't mind being kept waiting by a lady.'

'A lady, eh! No one has ever called me that before.'

'Well, I think you are.'

Anthony blushed.

'Well! That's very kind of you.'

She leaned over and kissed him endearingly on the cheek, which only added to his embarrassment.

'You know, it's been a long time since I've been kissed by anyone.'

'Except your daughter, Julia, of course.'

'Yes, except Julia, and of course, Suzanne.'

Rebecca smiled.

'Suzanne! How many more women are there in your life?'

'Suzanne is my granddaughter. She's only nine, so it doesn't really count.'

Anthony started up the engine and manoeuvred the boat around the other moorings and steered it out past the end of the mole. In the open sea, there was a light swell, which caused the boat to rock gently from side to side. They had all afternoon to spare, so he drove quite calmly. The engine purred as the boat cut effortlessly though the waves.

Just off the coast, there was a lovely cool breeze, which was welcome on this sweltering hot day. There were few clouds in the sky too. In fact, everything was just about perfect, even more so, due to having this beautiful woman on board.

'I'm sorry, Becky, but I forgot to tell you my name, yesterday. It's Anthony.'

'Well, I was wondering whether you would want me to call you captain something or other.'

'No! I wouldn't advise you to do that with my hopeless sailing skills.'

'Tell you what! Anthony sounds rather formal. What if, I call you Tony instead?'

'Yes! If you like.'

After all the fuss he had made in the past about people shortening his name, he was now prepared to accept it from a complete stranger and without protest too. He considered that his acquiescence had nothing to do with the fact that she was a gorgeous looking young woman though. Perish the thought!

Rebecca made herself comfortable, sitting up on the foredeck, with her back against the screen. She removed her shirt, to reveal the top half of her bikini, and then, putting on her sunglasses, settled back to sunbathe.

Anthony kept the boat close inshore, where there was plenty of deep water and no danger, except for the occasional rock, for which he kept a watchful eye out. On the cliffs above, people were sitting and admiring the view or ambling along the coast path to the next inlet. Every so often, the seabirds would sweep over them and then back up again to their hideaways in the cliff face.

After about twenty minutes or so of lying peacefully in the sun, Rebecca turned on her side and rested her hand on the screen to steady herself. She then removed her sunglasses and spoke to him.

'So, Tony! Does the family know you're taking a "lady" out on your boat?'

'Yes. I did mention it to them yesterday. They didn't seem to mind my disappearing for the afternoon though.'

'What will they be doing now then?'

'Oh, their Sunday afternoons are usually spent pottering around the house, or a taking a short walk down to the beach.'

'Not as adventurous as Dad then?'

'I wouldn't say I was adventurous.'

'Didn't they want to know who this "bird" was, that you were taking out?'

'Suzanne was curious as to what you looked like.'

'And what did you tell her about me?'

'I told her that you were very attractive.'

Anthony almost blushed again with embarrassment. Rebecca noticed his shyness and grinned.

'That's the second compliment you've given me this afternoon.'

The boat rounded the headland and another bay opened up. Here, there were a number of white-walled buildings on either side of a valley, which cut through the cliffs. There was a tiny harbour with just a few small craft sheltering in it, and then a beach where they could clearly see children playing on the sand. A jetfoil passed them, nearer to the shore, leaving a trail of white water in its wake.

Rebecca got up and joined him at the wheel. Anthony felt it was now his turn to ask questions.

'Anyway, what exciting things have you been up to so far this weekend?'

'Well, I had to work most of yesterday.'

'Where? Locally?'

'Yes. I'm the assistant manager of a shop in the High Street.'

'Do you like working there?'

'It's OK. I have made a few friends amongst the other staff and, of course, it does pay the bills.'

'So, how did you happen to be at the marina, yesterday?'

Rebecca had anticipated this question turning up at some point in their conversation, so she had planned a plausible reply.

'I finished work a couple of hours earlier than usual, as we didn't have a lot of customers. It was such a beautiful afternoon, that I didn't want to go home straightaway, so I thought I'd go for stroll along by the marina. It was then that I saw your boat and decided I'd take a closer look. The rest you know.'

'And then?'

'What? After I left you?'

'Yes.'

'I went home for something to eat. Then, later in the evening, I met some of my friends from work and we went out for a drink. Nothing wildly exciting, I'm afraid.'

Being anxious to divert the conversation away from her own private life, she proceeded to ask him questions about himself.

'What do you do for a living then, Tony?'

'I used to work up in London, but I'm retired now.'

'You don't look old enough to be retired.'

'What do you mean? Sixty-five? No, I retired early, at fifty.'

'And now you occupy your time with your family and this boat?'

'Something like that.'

Suddenly, a small sandy beach caught Rebecca's eye. It was very secluded and surrounded by tall cliffs. It was also completely deserted, probably due to the fact that there was no obvious way to get down to it from the path above.

'Can we anchor the boat over there?'

'Yes, if you like.'

Anthony headed for the cove. As he drew near, he throttled right back and eased the boat gently towards the shore, checking the decreasing depth on his echo sounder. When he had brought the boat to a virtual standstill, he dropped the anchor and chain, and gently reversed to ensure that it dug firmly into the seabed. When he switched off the engine, all around was peaceful and calm. The only sounds to be heard were the gentle lapping of the waves upon the shore and those of seagulls, squawking, as they flew up onto the high cliffs above.

Rebecca made her way to the stern of the boat.

'I'm going to swim to that beach. Coming?'

'But I can't swim.'

'Oh, you're an enterprising man. You'll find a way there.'

Rebecca placed her sunglasses into her shoulder bag, which she then tossed into the cockpit. She took off her trousers to reveal the full extent of her bikini. Anthony was rather taken back by the suddenness of it all. Before he could utter another word on the matter, she slipped over the side and her lithe figure disappeared into the sea. He went over to the side of the boat, from which he could see her swimming towards the shore. She was indeed a very fast swimmer, and had already covered half the distance between the boat and the beach.

'Well, I can't just stand here,' he muttered to himself.

Fortunately, on the stern of his boat was a little inflatable dinghy. He had never used it himself before, as it looked rather small and unseaworthy. He stood staring at it for short while, assessing whether or not to use it, convinced that it was too unstable. Eventually he came to the conclusion that there were no other alternatives if he was to join Rebecca on the shore.

He slid the small craft into the water and gingerly lowered himself into it. As he attempted to sit down, it tilted precariously from side to side a few times until he managed to stabilise it.

Once he felt confident that it was not about to capsize, he reached out to unhook it, and then, picking up the paddle, he headed for the beach.

I've got to be mad,' he muttered to himself, 'if a wave washes me over the side, I'll probably drown. The family will never believe I'm doing this.'

At first, he found himself almost paddling in circles until he managed to get the hang of it. Once in control, he headed in a straight line towards the coast. Upon reaching the shore, he got out of the dinghy and pulled it up the beach a short distance. He looked up and noticed that Rebecca was already lying back on the sand. She had her head resting in her hands and had been observing him for some time.

'What took you so long, then?' she asked, with a beaming smile across her face. 'That was pathetic!'

'I did tell you I couldn't swim.'

He dropped down on the soft sand beside her.

'Anyway, I don't know how I let you get me into this. I might have drowned out there if that stupid inflatable had capsized.'

'No, you wouldn't. I would have rescued you.'

'Well, that's very sweet of you, Becky, but I'm not too good in the water.'

'Yes. I have noticed.'

Rebecca giggled.

'I don't know. It's worse than being out with a schoolgirl.'

'Make a habit of that too, do you?'

Anthony smiled. Rebecca was indeed the master of the witty retort. She was so bubbly and full of fun. He leaned back on the sand and propped himself up with his arms behind him for support. Rebecca turned and rested her head on his thigh, and looked up at him.

'I used to come here with Dad.'

'I had guessed, only I expect he could at least swim to the shore.'

'Yes. My dad was a very strong swimmer.'

'I get the impression that you miss him very much.'

'Umm! I really do. He was always there for me whenever things went wrong. Always looking out for me.'

'And now you have to fight your own battles, eh?'

'Yes. That's right.'

Rebecca placed her arm around him and then relaxed and closed her eyes. Anthony began to wonder what was going through her mind.

'Penny for your thoughts, then?'

'Oh. I was just thinking what a nice man you are. I bet you were always there for your Julia?'

'Yes. That's true. The times we had together made up some of the best years of my life. I'd do it all again if I had to.'

Anthony now moved into a more relaxing position and lay back with his hands at his side. Rebecca moved around to lie beside him, with her head tucked into his shoulder. It seemed so natural to put his arm around her as she snuggled up closely to him. He turned to her and gently kissed the top of her head. Again, she looked up at him.

'I like being here with you, Tony. I feel so relaxed.'

'I can assure you the feeling is mutual.'

She paused for a moment.

'Do you know, you are the first male who hasn't made a pass at me?'

'Well, I've always been told that I'm slow on the uptake.'

She smiled.

'By now, I would have been told at least a dozen times how beautiful I was. Well, at least, the nicer guys would have. The not-so-nice ones are usually crude.'

'That's a rotten thing to have to put up with.'

'Yes, I know. But then again, both types are only after one thing.'

'You can always tell them to get lost.'

'Most of the time I do, but you don't always know what a guy is going to be like until you've been out with him for a while. By then, it's too late.'

'You mean, by then, you've fallen in love with him.'

'Something like that.'

She now moved her body even closer to him, this time, resting her head upon his chest. He tenderly ran his fingers through her wet hair, which had now started to dry in the hot sunshine.

He watched as the waves broke upon the shoreline, making damp patterns in the soft dry sand, before returning to gather momentum once again. Beyond that, the sun glistened as it struck the boat, casting dancing reflections of the sea on its paintwork, as it bobbed gently from side to side on the calm waters of the inlet. It was an idyllic setting for the two of them, as they lay in complete tranquillity together, at peace with the world.

'I wonder what attracts a man and a woman to each other?'

'It's called chemistry, Becky. There's a real joy in living with a woman who knows all about you, how you think, and how you feel.'

'And that's chemistry?'

'Yes, if you like. You have that certain empathy between you. I'm no psychologist so I'm probably not explaining myself very well. I expect it all sounds too much like a romantic ideal in this day and age, when attraction has become more basic'

Rebecca was silent for a short while, considering his words before answering.

'I think I know what you mean. I like the idea of true romance, although I can't say that it's ever happened to me.'

'I think that's rather sad.'

'Umm! I expect you're right. How was it with you and your wife? Was she romantic?'

'Yes, she was. We were very much in love with each other. Whenever things went wrong at work, I didn't have to tell her. She could see there was a problem as I walked in through the door. She would never actually ask me about it straightaway but gave me space until I'd settled down and felt more relaxed.'

'I take it she'd find out eventually?'

'Oh, yes. Later that evening, I'd tell her what was really troubling me and she'd be very supportive.'

'You must miss her?'

'Yes. I did after she died but then again I couldn't dwell on it for too long as I had Julia to look after. She had lost her mother too of course so I had to devoted all my time, love and energy to her.'

'And now that she's married and off your hands, it's only your boat that gets all your loving care?'

'Yes, but it isn't quite the same though, is it?'

'No. I'm sure it isn't.'

In the period of silence that followed, Anthony looked down and noticed that she had closed her eyes again and fallen asleep. He continued to gently caress her hair and then run the back of his hand over the soft silky cheeks of her face. He began to wonder what he was doing here on this deserted beach with this attractive young lady. It was like a beautiful dream, one that was pure and clean and innocent.

An hour or so passed during which time he also fell asleep. He could vaguely remember having a wonderful dream of being on a desert island with a gorgeous woman. There was the blue sea with its waves lapping on the shore and the palm trees, swaying in the breeze. Sadly, as the sun beat down upon them, all he could think about, was where they were going to get something to eat before they starved to death. Whilst he was desperately struggling to overcome this dilemma, he was gently awakened by the soft touch of someone's lips against his lips. He opened his eyes to stare straight into Rebecca's beautiful smiling face.

'I hope you didn't mind, Tony? I just wanted to wake you with a kiss.'

'No, of course not. Although I think it's supposed to be the other way round, isn't it? At least, it is in fairy stories.'

'Well! I'm afraid it's time we returned to reality, as it must be getting late. Come on. Let's go back to the boat.'

Rebecca was soon on her feet again and running towards the water's edge. He watched as she began to swim towards the boat. On this occasion though, she swam some way out and then waited for him to launch the dinghy and catch her up. It became very apparent that she wanted to ensure that he was safe in the water and for them to arrive at the boat together.

Back on board, Rebecca stood by as he secured the inflatable. The drips of water were rolling off her hair and down her cheeks, and the cold seawater had started to make her shiver.

'I expect I shall soon dry out in the warm sunshine.'

'No! Hold on a minute! I think I've got a couple of bath towels down below somewhere. I noticed them when I was tidying up the other day.'

Anthony went below and returned with a large white bath sheet. He threw it across to Rebecca, who then picked up her shirt, trousers and shoulder bag, and clambered down the steps to the cabins to change.

Whilst she was getting ready, he started the engine. He edged the boat forwards until the anchor chain was up and down, before he winched it in. Setting a course for home, he opened up the engines to full speed.

Soon Rebecca appeared again on deck, this time fully dressed. She had even made some attempt to dry her hair too. Anthony, who was standing behind the wheel, had not yet noticed her return. Holding on to the nearest thing to hand in order to steady her, she made her way over to the cockpit. The boat was now travelling at some considerable speed, in fact, much faster than he was accustomed to. It was quite exhilarating. She looked across at the shoreline and saw that they were already half of the way back to the marina.

'Can I steer the boat?'

Anthony turned and beckoned to her.

'Come over here and take hold of the wheel.'

Rebecca ducked under his arms and popped up on the other side, facing the wheel. She put her hands just below his, and he let go. The boat planned the tops of the waves at speed and every so often they would be showered with water that would come over the side and into the boat. Rebecca drove with an air of confidence that conveyed to Anthony that she was very experienced in seamanship.

What incited Anthony to do what he did next defied explanation? Perhaps it was the tenderness that they experienced between them or the need to feel her close to him. Who knows?

Anthony rested his hands gently on Rebecca's hips. He then leaned forward and tenderly kissed her on the cheek. Without a word being spoken, she let go of the wheel and turned to face him. She slid her arms around his neck and kissed him passionately on the lips. He put his arms around her and pulled her to him. Both of them closed their eyes and were lost in the excitement of the moment.

The kiss seemed to last forever. When Anthony did open his eyes, he found himself looking fondly into hers. Suddenly, he detected a moment of fear in her expression and she pulled back from him.

'Oh! Tony! This was not supposed to happen.'

'I know! I wasn't expecting this, either.'

He could not possibly be aware of the true implications of what she was saying.

'But you don't understand! It should not have happened!'

'But, Becky! I'm sorry! Have I done something wrong?'

'No, of course not!'

She stretched out her arms and held him close to her again, kissing him with such force; he had to hold her back to breathe.

'Tony! What am I going to do?' she asked, wistfully.

'Do what? I don't understand.'

'This should not have happened.'

'You've really got me confused now, Becky.'

'You're confused! You want to see things from my side of the fence.'

Anthony was now baffled. He couldn't understand her at all.

'Look. Perhaps I shouldn't have taken advantage of you. You probably think I'm much too old for you in any case?'

'Oh do stop it, please!'

'I just enjoy being with you.'

'And I enjoy being with you too.'

Anthony took her hands in his. They were very soft and gentle. He looked into her beautiful wide eyes.

'Does that mean you'd like me to take you out again?'

'Of course it does. Do I have to spell it out for you?'

Suddenly, he realised that the boat was heading towards the rocks. No one had been steering for the past few minutes and it had been going at some considerable speed. Instinctively, he leaned forward, and in grasping the wheel, he flattened Rebecca up against it.

'My goodness, you're masterful all of a sudden,' she giggled.

Anthony eased back the throttle, and slowed the boat right down. She kissed him again.

'Hold on a minute, you sexy madam. I'm trying to get us back on course.'

'Now tell me, Tony,' she asked, in a low husky voice, 'would that be "madam or Madame"?'

Grinning, he shook his head and moved her to one side. Concentrating on what he was doing, he changed course and took the boat back up to speed again. Rebecca on the other hand sat back in the comfort of the passenger's seat.

'How does dinner tomorrow night grab you then, Becky?'

'And perhaps a nightclub afterwards?'

'Yes, sounds great.'

On the last part of the journey, Rebecca stood up and put her arm around Anthony's waist and hugged him as he manoeuvred the boat back to the marina. Upon reaching the moorings, she gave him directions to her home, so he could pick her up the following evening. She also gave him her mobile phone number lest anything should crop up in the meantime. He then watched as she crossed the quay and went up the hill to where she had left her car.

Rebecca's mind was in turmoil. All of this was supposed to be so simple. Her original intention had been to go out with him on a couple of trips and then ask to borrow his boat. Falling in love with him had certainly not been part of the plan. The speed at which the events had happened sent her feelings into total confusion and her cleverly conceived idea had now been completely shot to pieces.

She drove back home at speed. As she opened the front door, she was relieved to find that Jon had not yet returned. He would have gone ballistic if he had seen her come home in that state, with damp hair and a wet bikini rolled up in her hand. Even so, she knew that it was a certainty that she would get the third degree from him when he did eventually show up. It was a daunting thought for her that she had all of that unpleasant experience to come.

She threw her shoulder bag onto the bed and headed for the bathroom, where she quickly showered and washed her hair, this time blow drying it. She changed her clothes and put those she took off back into the wardrobe. She knew Jon wasn't sufficiently astute to work out what she had worn that afternoon, even if he did cross-examine her. Besides, she knew just how to fob him off with any reasonable explanation.

She sat down on the bed to concoct a plausible story to tell him about the events of the afternoon. However, that was the easy part, as she needed to say very little other than how pleasant the trip had been. The difficult part would be asking for his co-operation in staying out of sight, when Anthony came to pick her up the next evening. It was, after all, part of the plan, so he shouldn't really object. However, the matter that affected her most was lying to Anthony. This lovely naive man wouldn't suspect anything.

'No, he wouldn't, would he?'

She quietly spoke out her thoughts.

'He's a kind, trusting man and he doesn't deserve this. It's going to hurt him badly if he ever finds out that it was all part of a con. Worst still, he'll never believe that my feelings for him are real. He's going to think that was all part of the deception too. What am I going to do?'

As she thought more about it, she felt physically sick. No one had ever treated her with such respect before. If only she had met Anthony when Jon wasn't around, then there would have been no problem.

'If only my dad was here now, he'd know what to do,' she murmured.

A tear rolled down her cheek.

'Oh, Dad! Why can't you be here with me now? I do need you. You would know what I should do.' she cried aloud.

She took a tissue from the box in the dressing table drawer. She couldn't stop the flood of tears that followed. At last, she had found the romance that had eluded her for so long but it was based upon dishonestly. She was now in a quandary.

It was then that she heard a key turn in the lock on the front door. Jon was back. She quickly wiped her eyes and put the tissue into the bin. She looked into the mirror and saw that her eyes were very red. It was too late to do anything about it now. She heard him climb the stairs and when he reached the landing, his head appeared around the bedroom door. Jon could tell instantly that something was wrong.

'Hey, what's up? Have you been crying or something?'

'No. I just banged my head on the edge of the dressing table.'

'Are you sure that's all it is?'

'Yes, it made my eyes water.'

It was a very poor lie but she couldn't think of anything more credible on the spur of the moment. There wasn't even a bruise to back it up. Although Jon wasn't too bright, he wasn't that stupid either.

'That old guy hasn't tried anything on, has he?'

'No. I've had a really good time.'

Rebecca was now becoming more composed.

'Well, something must have upset you.'

'I'm OK. Right?'

'If he's been forcing himself on you, I'll...'

'Jon, please! Just leave it, will you?'

Chapter Thirteen

Nick Henderson was up early on Monday morning. His weekend had been a disaster. He had been picked up by the police on Saturday evening, and had undergone a lot of questioning. He had told them nothing, of course. Nick could survive even the most gruelling inquisition. It wasn't that he was clever and could therefore avoid giving away vital information, it was just that he was so thick, that even the most persistent questioner would be left as hopelessly confused as he was about the incident.

Since that evening, he did at least have the common sense to avoid any contact with Darren Baxter, suspecting that the police would keep a close eye on his whereabouts, and whom he came in contact with. That meant that he was forced to spend a rather dull Sunday in the company of his parents and younger sister.

Spending a lot of time with his family gave them the opportunity to get at him. His father suggested that he should start looking for a job first thing Monday, and not waste time hanging around with dubious friends. He was not known for taking too much notice of his parents' advice but nevertheless decided to show willing.

As he strolled through the streets, heading for the Job Centre, he got the distinct feeling that he was being followed. He couldn't quite understand where this suspicion lies, as each time he looked around him, the person that he considered was trailing him was nowhere to be seen.

Crossing the road, he decided to duck down the first alleyway he came to, and then wait for his pursuer to catch up. He did not have to wait too long before a familiar figure arrived on the scene.

'Hi, Nick! How's it going?'

'Oh! It's you, Darren! I thought someone was following me.'

'Yes. You've been quite elusive, lately. I'm glad I caught up with you at last.'

Darren pulled Nick into a doorway, to be sure that they could not be seen talking together, from either end of the alley.

'So! What have you got to tell me, then?'

It was obvious that he was aware of Nick's arrest.

'I didn't say anything, Darren. Honest!

Darren placed his hand upon the shoulder of his partner in crime, in a reassuring way. He forced an unconvincing smile.

'Of course you wouldn't, Nick. I always knew I could count on you in a crisis. So, what did they want?'

'They said they were looking for some "Mr Big". You know. Like that Lex bloke you were talking about. They knew Jon was there.'

'Did they?'

'I said I had no idea who he was.'

Nick continued to babble on. However, Darren was more concerned about any reference to him.

'And me? What did you tell them about me?'

'I told them that the two of you were just a couple of guys I'd met in a pub earlier. I said we were just walking home together.'

Darren put his hands into his pockets and leaned back against the door.

'Where does Jon fit in all this, then?'

'The police seemed to think that he was out to meet someone important.'

'Who?'

'You! I suppose.'

'Me!'

'Yes. They had no idea who you were, but they were certain that something big was going down, and that you were part of it'

'So! Jon must have told them that we were all meeting up together. That explains the police car being on the scene so quickly. Did they actually mention my name?'

'No! Honest, Darren! They didn't know who this "Mr Big" was.'

'You're confusing me now, Nick. Let's get this straight. Jon tells the police that he's meeting us on the estate to talk about a big job we're into, yet, he doesn't tell them who I am.'

'Yes. Something like that, Darren.'

' I wonder what he's up to.'

One could always guarantee that Nick would add further misunderstanding to an already confusing set of facts.

'It must be something to do with that job on Wednesday that you mentioned. That's the only thing we've got planned.'

'I think, my dense friend, that you are right for once. Umm! You did well, Nick.'

'What do we do now then, Darren?'

'Well! I'll tell you what you're not going to do, and that's breathe a word of this to Jon. We mustn't let him know our suspicions. I reckon he must have grassed on us.'

'But that don't make sense. Why would he want to do that, Darren?'

'Don't know, but I've got to be careful what I tell Jon, in future, until we establish which side he's on. I think I'll have to arrange a nasty surprise for that cocky little swine.'

'What d'you intend to do, Darren?'

'Don't worry about it, Nick. I've got it all in hand.'

'You don't want me to cut him, do you?'

'No. I've a better idea than that. We'll get even with him. He was always getting in my way in any case.'

After a few more brief exchanges, the two men parted company. Nick had already forgotten why he had come into town that morning and went back home again.

Darren was sure that Jon was the root cause of his recent problem. The more he thought about it, the more he was convinced that he must have turned police informer. That incident on the estate on Saturday night, which almost got him caught, was no fortuitous accident for the police. The only thing he could not explain was why he would want to shop his accomplices.

He decided that he would now give Jon a wide berth until after the planned pick up on Wednesday, assuming he would still want him to go ahead with it after all that had transpired. He would have to give that very careful consideration to see what was in his own best interest. Jon of course was oblivious to all of this, and was in for a rude awakening.

Chapter Fourteen

Monday morning, Anthony got up late. He hadn't slept too well the night before, thinking about Rebecca and all the things that she had said to him that afternoon. He couldn't remember the last time he had enjoyed himself so much with someone and he wanted to be out with her again. But still, he knew he had to be patient until the evening, when he would pick her up from home and take her out for a meal - and, of course, the nightclub.

It was on this last matter that he had a problem. He had never been inside a nightclub before. He had seen them from a distance, and noticed the numerous young people congregating around outside, so he had always assumed that it was for a much younger age group. Those who frequented these places had also told him that the music played inside could be deafening. Therefore, he found the prospect of going there, quite daunting. When he and his wife were much younger, they never ventured further than the local disco, so he wasn't sure what to expect.

"Oh, well. I shall play it by ear," he thought.

He waited until he heard Mike's car drive off before he left the bedroom to come downstairs. Each day, on his way into work, his son-in-law would drop Julia and Suzanne off at the local primary school. Julia had been working there ever since they moved into the district and was very popular with the other teachers and the children. Suzanne wasn't in her mother's class, but she liked her teacher very much and received some very good reports from her on her schoolwork.

When he reached the kitchen, he made himself some breakfast. Reflecting upon the previous evening, he was pleased that he had successfully avoided responding to too many questions about his boat trip with Rebecca, preferring to give one-word answers, whenever it was mentioned. Mike mistakenly deduced that the whole thing must have been something of a non-event, and soon turned to a different topic to talk about, that of himself.

Yes. Mike was heavily into narcissism, so Anthony escaped having to give them detailed information. Julia, on the other hand, was not taken in by her father's apparent lack of interest in the subject and although she didn't quiz him on the matter, she would still give him 'knowing looks' every time their eyes met. My goodness, she was so much like her mother. So astute!

It looked as if the weather was going to be nice again, so he thought he would make the most of it and drive to the beach. As the children had not finished term yet, the local beaches were never crowded and there were always spaces in the seaside car parks, even on a sunny day. Having eaten his breakfast, he washed up the bowl and placed it upon the draining board, beside all the other crockery that had been left to drain.

It didn't take him too long to drive to one of the more secluded beaches, which stretched out along the coastline of this beautiful part of the West Country. Upon arrival, he noticed that it was surprisingly quiet even for a Monday. From where he parked the car, he could see two people hand gliding off the hills above; their brightly coloured gliders set against the clear blue sky.

As he strolled along the sand, he observed an elderly couple, attempting to dodge the waves as they rolled onto the shore. To Anthony's practical mind, it seemed such a pointless exercise for two retired people to engage in. At one stage, the old chap wasn't quick enough, and the sea saturated his shoes. It didn't seem to bother them though as they were both laughing at what had happened.

After walking the length of the shoreline and back, he decided to sit on the sand for a while. He was still tired after having a disturbed sleep, so he thought he'd lie back and doze. Every so often he would nod off, and then the noise of someone passing by would wake him up again. After an hour or so, he became restless and returned to the car.

As he crossed the near empty car park, he noticed a young woman who appeared rather distressed. She was having trouble starting her vehicle. Each time she turned the key in the ignition, the engine chugged a couple of times and then died away. Anthony could see that she was becoming more frustrated with each abortive attempt.

'Excuse me. Would you like me to lend a hand?'

The young woman looked up to see who was speaking to her.

'Yes. I'd be delighted if you can make this damn thing start.'

Anthony reached inside for the bonnet release and then went around the front of the vehicle to raise it.

'Know anything about cars?'

'A bit. At least I do know that you've now flooded the engine. You can smell the fuel.'

'I'm sorry I bought this rubbish car. It does nothing but go wrong.'

'I expect it'll go better with a new battery.'

'No. Stupid me left the sidelights on when I parked it. I must have caught the switch as I got out. This old banger doesn't take kindly to something like that.'

Anthony looked around the engine compartment to ensure that no leads had come loose.

'Tell you what. I'll move my car over to yours and we'll see if we can jump start it.'

'OK! My name's Natalie, by the way.'

'Oh! Without the 't' in it, no doubt.'

Anthony suddenly realised, that what he had said in humour, was probably rather rude. However, the implications of his remark went over her head.

'Eh!'

'Sorry, Natalie. My name's Anthony. I just hope I can help.'

'Oh! Right!'

He collected the BMW and drove it around to the front of her car. He opened his boot and took out the jump leads.

'Tell me. What's a guy with a brand new upmarket car like this, doing with a set of jump leads in his boot.'

'Ah! Thereby hangs a tale. My last car wasn't known for its reliability, so I often had to use them. Still they've come in handy again now.'

Anthony clipped the leads onto the two batteries and started the engine in Natalie's car. After a lot of whirring, it burst into life.

'Keep your foot on the accelerator, you don't want it to die on you before the battery has had a chance to recharge.'

'Thanks mate. You're a star. I must get back into town now. I'm already late.'

'Look. I'll drive behind you some of the way, just in case it stops again.'

'Great! Thanks.'

Anthony followed Natalie's car along the road, until they reached the outskirts of town. At a road junction, he sounded his horn to indicate to her that he was turning off in the direction of his daughter's house. Natalie gestured with her hand to say "goodbye and thanks", as she continued onwards.

On arrival, he found Julia and Suzanne at home. He was rather puzzled at this, as it was only just on two-thirty.

'Yes, I know I'm home early. I got a call at school to say that Mike's mum is seriously ill and they've taken her into hospital.'

'Does Mike know, yet?'

'Well, his secretary says he's been in Court all morning and his mobile is only taking messages. She wasn't sure when he could get away.'

Just as she finished speaking, Mike drove onto the drive. Julia went out to meet him and then returned with a proposition.

'Dad! Do you think you could do me a favour and look after Suzanne for me till we get back from the hospital?'

'Yes, of course I will.'

'I can't say how long we'll be though.'

'That's all right. You go now.'

'Oh, by the way, Dad, I washed and ironed those new trousers of yours. They're hanging upstairs in the wardrobe.'

'Thanks, Julia. I hope you don't find it's anything too serious when you get there.'

Anthony's heart sank. He was due to pick up Rebecca at seven-thirty. What if they weren't back in time? Anthony mulled the problem over in his mind, whilst Julia went upstairs to collect her handbag. He knew it was ungracious to think like that. Poor old Gina was ill in hospital and Mike and Julia were understandably very worried - and all he could think about was taking Rebecca out for the evening.

'We're off now, Dad. Thanks again.'

Julia kissed him and ran to the open door of the car. It was just Anthony's bad luck that something unexpected like this had to turn up on this particular evening. Even his best trousers were now poised on their 'wire hanger' in the wardrobe, waiting to be used. Nevertheless, he pushed such selfish thoughts to the back of his mind as he gazed through the window to see his daughter and son-in-law, drive off at speed.

'It's just you and me then, Granddad!'

Suzanne stood beside him, watching them go, with her head resting on her hands.

'Yes. It looks that way.'

'Why don't we play a game?'

'All right! You go and fetch one.'

To pass the time, Suzanne returned with one of her favourite board games for the two of them to play. After she had won for the fourth time in succession, Anthony decided it was time to pack it away. Besides, it was teatime.

'So what's it to be, Suzanne?'

'Fish fingers and chips.'

'I'll have a look in the freezer to see if there are any.'

Anthony went into the kitchen, followed by his granddaughter.

'Mum won't let us have chips very often. She says she never wants to see another chip ever again, after being brought up by you.'

'Oh! Charming! And what's wrong with my cooking?'

'She said it was always the same. Sausages and chips, eggs and chips, fish fingers and chips, burgers and chips..."

'Yes, all right! I get the picture! I'll cut up some potatoes and fry them, but you'll have to promise not to tell on me.'

'Oh! Good!'

'You won't tell on me?'

Suzanne made a sign as if to zip up her mouth.

Anthony checked the freezer and was relieved to discover a small packet of fish fingers. He sorted out some large potatoes and cut them up into chips, and popped them into a pan of hot oil. After Suzanne's remarks, he guessed that his daughter would not possess a chip fryer. In a very short while, the meal was prepared.

'There we are, Suzanne. Get your laughing-gear around that.'

Anthony took the food into the dining room. Suzanne had already poured them cold drinks, so they were now ready to sit and eat. It was very true what she had said though. He had enjoyed much better meals once Julia had become of an age to take over the responsibility of cooking them.

The two of them tucked into the food, whilst Suzanne told Anthony all about her day at school. Her teacher had been so pleased with her standard of reading that she had been asked to read out aloud to the whole class. She had told her mum all about it on the way home, and Julia was very proud of her. When she had finished eating, she dutifully placed her knife and fork together on the plate.

'Granddad. When are you going to see Becky, again?'

'Well, I was going out with her this evening but I can't now.'

'Oh! That's a shame.'

The tone of her reply sounded very grown-up.

'I think the fact that your mum and dad have gone to see your granny, is far more important.'

'Will you have to tell Becky that you can't come?'

'I expect so.'

'If you go over there to tell her, can I come with you?'

Anthony could tell that Suzanne was anxious to satisfy her curiosity, surrounding his newly found friend.

'She did leave me her mobile phone number though, should anything crop up. I only have to ring her'

Suzanne's face broke into a frown.

'I know what! Why don't you ask Mrs McBride to look after me at her house? You can then go out with Becky after all?'

'Oh! That wouldn't be fair on you.'

'I don't mind. Becky will miss you if you don't go.'

'But I've promised to look after you.'

'I don't mind, Granddad. Really, I don't.'

'I'll have to think about it.'

Suzanne seemed a little too eager to be accommodating, which signified that there was probably an ulterior motive.

'So, why are you so keen to get to next door then?'

Suzanne's frown changed to a smile.

'Mrs McBride lets me bake little cakes.'

'Really!'

'Yes, and she lets me watch what I like on television and stay up very late.'

'I knew there was a catch. You're not your father's daughter for nothing, are you?'

'What d'you mean by that, Granddad?'

'Oh, nothing! I'll go and see Mrs McBride after tea.'

'Oh! Yes!'

Suzanne jumped up with both her thumbs pointing upwards.

'Don't get too excited. I can't promise anything, as she might be too busy and say "no" to the idea.'

'But Mrs McBride never says "no".'

'Well, at least, not to childminding.'

Suzanne heard him mutter the remark under his breath.

'What do you mean by that, Granddad?'

'Nothing!'

After the meal, Anthony walked across the drives, with Suzanne close on his heels. He rang the doorbell. It was Mark who opened the door.

'Mum! The old boy next door wants you.'

Mark disappeared down the hallway, presumably to fetch his mother. They stood on the doorstep and waited.

'Is Mark rude to everyone he meets, Suzanne?'

'Usually he is. He always calls me motorgob, because he says I never stop talking.'

It probably wasn't a bad description of her, if a little discourteous. Soon Caroline appeared at the door. She saw the two of them and smiled.

'You'll have to excuse my ignorant son. Politeness is not one of his finer points. Anyway, what have you been up to this time?'

Anthony laughed. Caroline was obviously reflecting upon the last conversation that they had had on her doorstep.

'I was wondering if you could do me a favour?'

'Oh, yes!'

'Mike and Julia have had to rush to the hospital to see his mother. She was taken ill earlier today. I've been asked to look after Suzanne until they get back, but that could be much later this evening.'

Before he could finish his explanation, Caroline butted in.

'And you have plans to go out this evening with this young woman that Julia has told me about?'

'Oh! So you know all about her then? Is nothing sacred?'

'I don't know. You men are all the same. The excitement of

going out with a younger woman and your brain goes to mush.'

'I'd be ever so grateful. Really, Caroline!'

'Where are the two of you off to then?'

'It's only for a evening meal'

'Yes. OK!'

'You really don't mind.'

'No, of course not. She can come in now, if she wants to.'

Suzanne needed no further invitation.

'Wow! Thanks Mrs McBride.'

She stepped up to the door and, after giving Caroline a big hug, went inside.

'She's a good kid.'

'Well, she's told me that she likes coming over to your house.'

'Yes. I know she does.'

'Incidentally, I see Mark has not gone wandering off this evening.'

'No. He's doing his homework.'

'His homework!'

'I know. I can't believe it myself. You must have said something that got through to him at last when you brought him home yesterday. Mind you, I did say that if he didn't get up to date with his schoolwork, he wouldn't be going on this school trip tomorrow.'

'Where are they going?'

'Somewhere in Wales. Only for a few days though.'

'That'll give you a few days peace.'

'I expect so. Ah! That reminds me. You may be able to do me a favour. Mark is going in on the school bus in the morning. You wouldn't mind giving me a lift in with his case a little later, would you?'

'No, of course not.'

'That's very kind of you.'

'It's a pleasure!'

'Right then! If I hear Julia turn up before you're back, I'll take Suzanne home.'

'Thanks, Caroline, you're a real pal. If you jot down your telephone number, I'll give you a ring on my mobile later, to make sure everything is all right.'

Caroline took a pencil and pad from her hall table and wrote down the number. She tore off the sheet and handed it to Anthony, who put it into his pocket.

'OK! Have a good time.'

'Yes. I'm sure I will.'

Anthony returned to the house to change into something more suitable to go out in. Upon closer examination of his best trousers, he discovered that Julia had made a good job of getting the stains out of them. He then hunted through the clothes he had brought with him for a suitable casual shirt to go with them. He was also pleased to find some decent shoes as well, although he hadn't anticipated going anywhere special, when he packed them.

As he had plenty of time, he sat for a short while to watch television. In spite of the late lunch, he was looking forward to the evening meal, as he was still feeling rather hungry. He didn't find the television programmes very inspiring and was glad when the time came to switch off.

At seven, he left and took a slow drive over to Rebecca's place. It wasn't too difficult for him to find the location, as her directions were very precise. He pulled up outside her house and was about to get out of the car, when he saw her come to the front door. She waved to him and then turned to close it behind her.

He sat and waited for her as she came swiftly down the path and got in. He noticed that she was wearing a rather attractive top and skirt, although he could well imagine her looking smart in any outfit she chose to wear.

'You're early.'

'Yes. I found my way here more quickly than I expected.'

As she was putting on her seat belt, he leaned across and kissed her. Looking over her shoulder, he noticed her curtains move.

'You haven't got company, have you?'

'Why?'

Rebecca suddenly felt rather nervous as he may have spotted something suspicious that she had overlooked.

'I could have sworn I've just seen your curtains move?'

'Oh, no. That's only my cat. He's probably sitting on the windowsill.'

Rebecca's quick thinking had provided an instant intelligent reply. Nevertheless, she was relieved that Anthony made no more of the incident. Damn that jealous boyfriend of hers, trying to spy on them!

They drove into town and parked. It was just a short walk from there to the restaurant that he had chosen for them. That evening, tourists were everywhere, in the bars and cafes, looking in shop windows, or strolling around in the last of the day's sunshine. Anthony held her hand as they walked along the narrow streets.

He had not anticipated that the restaurant would be so busy and was beginning to wish he had telephoned earlier to book a table. Once inside, he was relieved when the waiter ushered them to a corner of the room where there was a spare setting for two. They sat down and were each handed a menu. Rebecca studied hers for ages, having great difficulty in making up her mind what to have from the long list of choices.

'Having problems?'

'Isn't it difficult to choose something when you like everything?'

'That's a relief. I thought perhaps there was nothing you liked.'

Anthony peered at her over the top of his menu card.

'I suppose I could ask them to put a bit of everything on the plate for you.'

'Fine. But I don't think meat and fish together would go down very well, though.'

She continued to look up and down the card and then became more positive.

'I think I'll go for the steak. Yes, that'll make a change. It's not something that I have very often.'

'Right. Two steaks it is then.'

The waiter brought them bread rolls to go with their starters and Anthony ordered a bottle of wine.

'I suppose you're like me and don't bother to cook very much at home. It always seems such a waste of time just preparing a big meal for one.'

Rebecca realised that she had to keep her wits about her in order to reply to such embarrassing questions. Although she had been looking forward to going out for the evening with Anthony, she was conscious of the possibility that she might say something that didn't quite add up.

'I often treat myself to a lunchtime meal in town, so I don't have to cook for myself when I get home in the evenings.'

'Someone from work go with you?'

'Yes. One of the other shop assistants who I'm friendly with.'

'Well, that's better than eating alone.'

At least she could derive some comfort from her remark, as she had not actually lied. She did occasionally have lunchtime meals with her friend, at a pub, near to where they worked. However, she conveniently omitted to say anything about cooking for her hungry boyfriend, when she returned home.

As the meal progressed, Rebecca carefully answered all the awkward questions he put to her. Even though Anthony suspected nothing, she still felt bad at having to deceive him. She now had feelings for him and it hurt her deeply to know that she was concocting the whole story about her domestic life and with whom she mixed socially. She wanted so desperately to tell him the truth. Sadly, one set of lies led on to another, and she felt ashamed of the fact that she was becoming rather good at it. If only she had met him in different circumstances, and Jon and his scam never existed, she could openly enjoy their new relationship.

The meal was enjoyable and she felt quite light-headed after several glasses of wine. As the plates were cleared away, she stretched her arm across the table and squeezed his hand. In turn, he placed his hand upon hers, in a reassuring way. Her eyes sparkled in the light of the candle that flickered on the table in front of them.

'Anthony. Thanks for everything.'

He took both of her hands and held them in his. They felt very soft and delicate. He then took one and gently kissed the back of it. He could have been mistaken, but he thought he'd caught a glimpse of a tear in her eye.

'It's I who should be thanking you.'

'In that case, I'll let you take me to a nightclub. Shall we go?'

Anthony called for the bill. He paid it at the desk and they left. Outside, it was dark, except for the lights from the shops and the street lighting. Even those establishments that usually stayed open late had long since closed and there were now just a few holidaymakers still wandering around and looking at items in the windows. Rebecca turned to him and kissed him hungrily.

'Goodness, Becky. Didn't you have enough to eat in there?'

Rebecca grinned.

'Food - yes, but I've only just started on you.'

She took hold of his hand and raced him back to the car. Maybe it was the wine or perhaps the freedom from Jon, but she had not felt like this for as long as she could remember. For the time being, the reason that had brought them together was committed to the back of her mind. Tonight, she was on cloud nine and was going to enjoy every minute of it.

Back in the car, she kissed him again, and he reciprocated. However, he became mildly embarrassed when he noticed an elderly couple across the street, giving them looks of disapproval.

'I think we'd better get going, Becky, before they come over and tell me that I should be ashamed of myself, to be seen kissing a woman, young enough to be my daughter.'

Chapter Fifteen

Rebecca gave Anthony directions to the club. It soon became apparent to him that they were going somewhere that she had been to on many previous occasions. Before leaving, he had intended to put the top up on the car, but at her insistence, he left it open. It was however still quite warm and the wind gently blew her long dark hair as they sped along the open road out of town. Eventually, they reached an entertainment complex with cinemas, restaurants and bowling.

Upon entry to the club, the doorman greeted her like an old friend. He did seem rather puzzled though, when she introduced her companion to him. He had been used to seeing Jon with her and could not figure out where the older man fitted into the relationship.

'I don't think he approves of me, Becky.'

'Oh, take no notice of him. He doesn't often meet the more-mature clubber.'

Once inside, they went up to the bar and Anthony bought the drinks. He nearly threw a fit at the prices they charged, but felt it wholly inappropriate to make any comment to her about it. They stood at the bar for a while, trying to make polite conversation by passing the occasional remark about the decor and lighting, and peering through the gloom to see if they could recognise anyone. Anthony found the music to be both repetitive and deafening.

As time went on, several people who knew Rebecca came up to her and engaged her in brief conversation. Each time, she introduced Anthony as her friend. Although they appeared to accept him without comment, he did feel awkward due to their difference in age.

Rebecca took the drink from his hand and placed it on the table nearby. She then took him by the arm and dragged him towards the seething mass of bodies on the dance floor. It was so crowded, that there was barely enough room to shuffle, let alone dance. It didn't seem to matter though as nobody took too much notice of anyone else's dancing abilities. Every so often, Rebecca's arm would snake around Anthony's neck and she would kiss him upon the lips.

As the night wore on, Anthony found it exhausting trying to shout to her over the loud music. He could well imagine that his voice would be hoarse later and that the heavy beat would still be ringing in his ears when he arrived home. Leaving the dance floor, they made their way over to a corner of the room.

Anthony leaned across to speak directly into Rebecca's ear.

'I promised I would ring Caroline to see if Suzanne is all right.'

'You'll have to go outside to do it.'

'I know. I don't really have a choice. It's absolutely deafening in here and I don't suppose I'd get a signal on my mobile anyway.'

'OK! I'll come with you.'

Outside the club, he rang Caroline. She answered the phone almost immediately. She told him that Suzanne had dropped off to sleep on the carpet in front of the television, and that Mike and Julia had returned home from the hospital several hours earlier. He had not realised that he had phoned Caroline so late until she mentioned that she was already in bed and talking to him on the bedside phone. He felt very embarrassed about this and apologised. Fortunately, she always read for a while and had not as yet settled down to sleep. He thanked her for her help and ended the call.

He returned the mobile phone to his pocket and looked around for Rebecca. She was standing a short distance away, and was engaged in conversation with two young men. Both appeared to be about the same age as her.

She seemed to be rather cross with one of them. He was quite tall and smartly dressed in dark casual designer clothes. Each time he spoke, he would point in Anthony's direction with a sneering look upon his face, and answer her abruptly. Anthony tried to listen in but couldn't quite hear what they were saying to each other.

'So this is the old guy you're going out with, is it?'

Rebecca found it difficult to hide her frustration.

'Isn't there somewhere else you should be, Jon?'

Rebecca was hoping that Jon would leave before his reaction to seeing them together, got out of hand. It was obvious that he had drunk far too much. His words were slurred and his actions were slightly uncoordinated. His companion, on the other hand, appeared sober.

'Hey Kyle, the old git looks even older than your dad.'

'Will you shut up, Jon, or he'll hear you!'

'I don't care. Anyway, what's it to you?'

Anthony decided that it was time to join them. He could see that Rebecca was holding her own, but he was curious to see what all the hostility was about. As he approached the three of them, they turned to face him.

'Are these friends of yours, Becky?'

'Yes! This is Jon and that's Kyle.'

'Pleased to meet you both. Have you known Becky long?'

Jon ignored the remark. His face was like thunder and did not appear to be pleased with Anthony's interruption. He looked at him with contempt.

'So what's an old boy like you doing with a woman half your age?'

Anthony immediately sensed the hostility in his voice.

'I don't think that's any of your business.'

'Oh! But it is my business.'

Anthony remained calm.

'Do you know what he's talking about, Becky?'

Rebecca threw Jon a hostile look. She realised that she had to think quickly before Jon said something that would give the game away.

'Just ignore him, Tony. He's far too drunk to know what he's saying. Why don't we go back inside?'

Rebecca attempted to divert the conversation away from the subject of their relationship, but Jon was having none of it. He continued to butt in.

'I bet I know what you're after, you disgusting old man?'

Anthony had heard enough. He wasn't prepared to take this sort of abuse from anyone, even a drunk. However, as they were Rebecca's friends, he decided to keep his reply relatively pleasant.

'Look! I think you've had too much to drink. It isn't very nice to hear that sort of talk in front of a lady.'

'A lady? Who? Becky? Hear that, Kyle?'

'OK! Maybe you don't think so, but I do.'

'Listen, you old fool. You don't know her as well as I do. Becky is a just tart. Got it? A tart!'

As Jon was now becoming very personal in his abuse, Kyle stepped in.

'Come on, Jon. The man's right. You've had too much to drink.'

Kyle grabbed Jon by the arm and tried to pull him away, but he stood his ground. Jon was unfortunately sparring for a fight. Rebecca stood there in fear, wondering what else Jon was going to come out with. She wasn't a tart, but this didn't put her in a good light with someone who had only just started to get to know her. Nevertheless, Anthony sprung to her defence.

'I know Rebecca well enough to know you're talking rubbish. She's a very beautiful, sensitive, young woman, who probably wouldn't look twice at bloke like you.'

'You reckon?'

'Yes, I do! Becky could have any man she wanted. She's much too good for most men so I'm sure she'd be too good for you.'

'What d'you mean? You don't know her at all. She's only going out with you because....''

Rebecca hurriedly interjected before Jon could end his sentence and blow the whole deception apart.

'Look! Let's end this conversation right now. Why don't you get your pal, Kyle to take you home?'

'Trying to get rid of us now, are you? I expect he's taking you back inside to get you drunk, eh? Then, what are you going to get up to?'

'What!'

'Don't listen to him, Becky. He's just trying to be controversial.'

Although Anthony could tell that the young man was deliberately being contentious, he was nevertheless offended by the suggestion.

'As a friend of Becky, I'm surprised you feel it necessary to make such disgusting remarks about her.'

Jon registered the older man's apparent lack of insight into his relationship with Rebecca. He wanted to make him wise to the fact that she was his girlfriend. Although it would have serious repercussions in respect of his scam, he still felt compelled to tell him the truth.

'You don't know who am I, do you?'

'Now let's see. Small cranium, low forehead, knuckles scraping the ground – Neanderthal Man?'

It was now Jon's turn to be on the receiving end of abuse. Unlike Anthony though, he was not prepared to take it. He lashed out at him with his fist, but was too wasted to aim accurately. The blow missed by a mile. Whilst Jon recoiled from the abortive punch, Rebecca took hold of Anthony's hand and dragged him away from the boys and back into the club. Fortunately, they did not immediately follow the couple inside.

She was immensely flattered by Anthony's show of chivalry but was deeply concerned at Jon's incredible display of jealousy. Had they stayed and continued the conversation outside the club, she knew that his remarks would become even more abusive and inevitably lead to violence. It was also possible that Anthony might then hear the truth.

Back on the dance floor again, they put their arms around each other, and Rebecca expressed regret for the incident. Anthony was prepared to put the matter behind them and insisted that Rebecca should forget it. He also felt that there was absolutely no need for her to apologise for the disgraceful behaviour of her friend. She tried to reassure him that Jon was quite amiable and good-natured when he was sober. For her, it was just another lie to add to the seemingly endless deceit. She was beginning to feel like the children's character, Pinocchio, apart from the obvious physical attribute.

Rebecca was furious with Jon. She had specifically asked him not to come to the nightclub. Yet, seething with jealousy, he had ignored her request and deliberately searched them out to see what they were up to. However, the shameful exhibition he had now made of himself in front of Anthony, only made her more determined to see it through. There was no way that he was going to ruin everything. She loved Anthony and nothing was going to spoil the feelings that she had for him. If Jon wanted to make a scene, then that was his problem.

As Rebecca was a frequent visitor to the club, she knew many of the young people there. Every so often, she would stop dancing and exchange pleasantries with friends and acquaintances. On each occasion, she would introduce them to her partner.

As the night drew on, she stopped to chat to a colleague from the shop. Lynn was a very short, round, outgoing girl who had quite a lot to say, and for awhile Anthony listened whilst she told him her life history. He found it very interesting, and was amazed at what she had got up to in such a brief span of existence.

Eventually, the conversation turned to the subject of her current boyfriend, who had apparently been two-timing her. This topic however, he found rather dull, although Rebecca seemed very intrigued.

Leaving them to continue with their "girls talk", Anthony fought his way back across to the bar to order another round of drinks. As he stood, waiting to be served, Jon once again homed in on him, accompanied by his friend, Kyle.

'Enjoy your grope on the dance floor, then?'

'You're drunk, Jon. Just go away. Please!'

'You obviously didn't hear what I said. I suppose that's because you haven't got your hearing aid switched on?'

Anthony was getting sick and tired of this constant barracking and wanted to ignore him. Jon nevertheless repeated the question.

'Well! Did you enjoy groping her?'

'Yes, you're right, Jon. I can't hear very well over this loud music. My hearing has not been so good since I turned fifty. What was it you're trying to tell me?'

Anthony anticipated the next move. Jon leaned forward to shout his remark into the older man's ear. As he did so, he brought his knee up and struck Jon in the groin. Instantly, he fell to his knees, groaning in pain.

Apart from Kyle, no one else witnessed the assault. He bent down to try to help his friend to his feet. Jon however was in too much distress to move and pushed Kyle away from him. Just then Rebecca appeared.

'I thought I'd come over to see what was taking you so long.'

She looked down at Jon, who was rolling about on the floor in agony.

'What's wrong with him?'

'I think he's too drunk to stand up,' Kyle replied, trying to diffuse a potentially embarrassing situation.

Rebecca knelt beside the writhing figure to ascertain how inebriated he was. She spoke to him fondly but he did not reply.

As it appeared to her that Jon wasn't in the mood to talk, she now felt that this might be the right time to get away.

'Do you want to stay any longer, Tony, or would you rather go now?'

'I honestly think I've had enough excitement for one night. Let's go home.'

'OK, then! Just let me tell my friend, Lynn, that we're leaving'

She returned to where her pal was sitting, amongst a group of young lads and girls.

'We have to go now. See you later, Lynn.'

'Yes! See you at work, Becky.'

The couple headed for the exit. Upon reaching the door, they came across Kyle, supporting an intoxicated Jon down the steps. He was still groaning but seemed to have lost his appetite for confrontation. Although she was still very annoyed with him, she was also concerned.

'Do you think Jon will be all right, Kyle?'

'Don't worry about him, Becky. I'll see that he gets home safely. You two go.'

Outside, in the cool morning air, Anthony and Rebecca walked back to the car. The car park had started to empty, although there were still quite a number of night revellers inside the club. Upon reaching the vehicle, Anthony wanted to raise the soft-top but Rebecca had other ideas.

'Leave the top down, Tony. I'm OK, if you are?'

'I think you'll find it a bit cold when we get going.'

'Don't worry, you can always put the heater on. I want to drive somewhere quiet, so I can gaze at the sea.'

Anthony laughed.

'What! In the dark.'

'Why not?'

'Is this the romantic occasion that you've always wanted?'

'Yes. I know it's silly, but don't spoil it for me.'

Anthony held the passenger door open for her to get in.

'Thank you. No one has ever done that for me before.'

'All part of the service, madam - or is it "Madame"?'

Rebecca chuckled.

Closing the door behind her, he then went around to the driver's side and got in. It was a beautiful night and certainly not as cold as he imagined. They drove out of the car park and onto the main road and then across town. The well-lit streets were empty, apart from the infrequent car that passed them. The houses too were in total darkness; their occupants presumably snuggled up in bed asleep.

On the outskirts, they veered off down a long narrow lane, which wound its way down the hillside and towards the sea. Here, it was very dark and deserted. Anthony drove carefully around the sharp bends in the road as they made their descent. Occasionally, the headlights would pick out a night creature, scurrying around to get out of their way. Throughout the journey Rebecca said very little, just touching his knee and turning towards him every so often, and smiling.

The road ended at the beach. As they pulled into the small deserted car park, just off a short track, Anthony switched off the engine. The lights of the car had been quite comforting and now there was only darkness. All one could hear were the breakers as they rolled endlessly upon the shore.

He looked across at Rebecca, leaning his head against the back of his seat. He noticed that she was gazing up at the heavens.

'Just look at those stars up there. Aren't they beautiful?'

'I think you've been reading too many romantic novels, Becky.'

'Oh! Don't spoil it for me.'

'I know. I'm sorry.'

He leaned over and kissed her tenderly on the lips. It was a long, lingering kiss too. In the darkness, her eyes shone wide and bright. Then, taking his hand gently in hers, she smiled at him.

'If I'm not careful, I could find myself falling in love with you, Tony.'

'Me too.'

'What? In love with yourself?'

'No. I mean, feeling the same way towards you.'

She laughed.

'Don't worry. I knew exactly what you meant.'

'I'm sure you did. You know, Becky, that's another thing I like about you.'

'What's that?'

'Your sharp wit.'

'Well, perhaps you bring the best out in me.'

She leaned back in the seat and looked up at the stars again.

'I've really enjoyed this evening.'

'So have I. I just can't believe I'm sitting here with you. It's like a dream. You could attract any man you wanted. Why me?'

'Don't put yourself down.'

'But there are dozens of handsome young men out there and you'd only have to click your fingers to have them falling over themselves to take you out. I lost count of the lads who came over to you at the nightclub to chat you up, when you were talking to your friend.'

'Maybe so, but I prefer to be with you. It really doesn't matter that you're much older than I am. It really doesn't.'

Anthony smiled. She was so appealing. He adored that captivating smile, the one that had enchanted him right from the first time he had set eyes upon her.

'Why don't we stroll along the beach?'

'Yes. I'd like that.'

Getting out of the car, they walked over to the beach. The tide was in, leaving a small strip to walk along between the water's edge and the thick vegetation, which carpeted the land all the way to the top of the cliff. Becky took off her shoes and held them in her hand, whilst holding onto Anthony's arm with the other. She persuaded Anthony to do the same. As she walked along in silence, she could feel the soft sand between her toes.

When they reached the headland, they could go no further. In the darkness, Anthony turned to kiss her. She then placed her arms around his waist and hugged him. A large wave came in, washing over their feet. As it receded, she could feel the sand gently sliding away from under her soles and heels.

He put his arms around her and felt her shiver in the chilly night air.

'I think we should go back, don't you?'

She nodded.

'Tell you what. We'll leave the top down, but I'll turn up the car heater to keep you warm on the way home.'

'That's very considerate of you, Mr Lewis.'

They slowly ambled back to the car. In the glow of the door light, they put on their shoes again, and Rebecca straightened her seat into a more upright position.'

All the way back to her home, she held his hand. Anthony found it quite difficult to drive with only one hand on the steering wheel and two hands on the gear lever, when it came to changing gear. It was only a small problem though and not one that was going to spoil this wonderful romantic night.

Whilst he did not have the nerve to actually tell her, he knew that he was falling in love with this beautiful young lady who had made him feel so young again. He had no idea where this relationship was going or whether it could work out between them. The woman was, after all, less than half his age. All he knew for the moment was that he was happier now than he had been for many years.

Outside her house, Rebecca asked him if he would mind if she didn't invite him in. She excused herself on the grounds that she hadn't slept very well the night before, thinking about him. That much was true. In fact, her restlessness had awoken Jon, who asked her if she was unwell. In reply, she had convinced him that it was the sweltering heat of the summer night that had seriously disturbed her sleep.

Unfortunately, as this night was much cooler, she would need to think of a different excuse to tell him if it happened again. However, after seeing him so drunk earlier, he would probably be out like a light until late morning and there would be no need for one.

'Hey, I've just realised. It's my day off today. I don't work on Tuesdays, because I have to go in on Saturdays.'

'Are you going to have a lie in?'

'No! That's not like me.'

'Well! Why don't we go shopping in Plymouth, then? Shouldn't take us too long to get there.'

'Sounds good to me, but don't pick me up too early though.'

'What, and spoil all those romantic dreams of yours?'

She looked at him and smiled.

'You're asking for a clout.'

Anthony laughed.

'I'll pick you up around eleven-thirty.'

'Great! See you then.'

He watched as Rebecca walked up the path and opened her front door. As she went inside, she turned and blew him a kiss. He waited until she had closed the door behind her, and then drove back to his daughter's house. The roads were completely deserted. He glanced down at the illuminated clock on the car's fascia. It had gone three in the morning. He had never been out this late since his wife died. Back in those days, they would often visit friends and not return until the early hours of the morning.

He parked the car at the bottom of the drive and quietly closed and locked the doors, so as not to disturb the neighbours. He also put the top up for security reasons. Quietly opening the front door, he crept up the stairs to the guestroom. Feeling his way up the stairs without putting on the lights was a problem, but once inside the room, the moonlight streamed in through the windows, enabling him to find the bedroom light switch. As he went over to the window to pull the curtains, he looked up at the stars and smiled. They were of course the same stars that Rebecca had found so romantic earlier. Yes, he even found her silly dreamy ideals appealing too.

As he lay back in bed, his mind wandered onto beautiful thoughts of Rebecca. This holiday was becoming way beyond his wildest dreams, and he was so happy.

'I can't imagine anything that could spoil it for me now,' he mused. 'I must be the luckiest man in the entire world.'

Chapter Sixteen

Next morning, Anthony awoke. He looked around the room until his eyes fixed upon the tray of tea and toast beside the bed.

'Oh dear,' he thought to himself, 'if that's for me, I do hope Suzanne hasn't made it.'

He sat up in bed and stretched across to the cabinet. Picking up the tray with one hand, he balanced it upon his lap. As he was not entirely awake yet, he tilted the tray and some of the tea slopped over the side of the cup. Nevertheless, he was pleased to find that the tea was hot and the toast wasn't burnt. It was now obvious that Suzanne hadn't made it for him, so assumed that Julia must have been in a few minutes earlier and put it there.

'Hi Dad.'

Julia put her head around the door.

'Can I come in?'

'Yes, of course, love.'

She entered the room, holding a shirt of his that she had ironed earlier that morning. She opened the wardrobe door and placed it upon one of the wire hangers on the rail inside. In order to keep her evenings as free as possible, she frequently got up early to do the ironing, and where time permitted often included a bit of cleaning as well.

'So who was out on the town last night, presumably living it up with his female friend?'

'Oh, yes,' said Anthony, rather sheepishly. 'I am really sorry, Julia, about getting in late. I know I was suppose to look after Suzanne and....."

Julia cut in on him.

'I remember my dad used to go berserk when I came home in the early hours of the morning.'

'Yes, I know. I'm sorry, but I didn't realise the time. It had just flown by.'

Anthony was still grovelling.

'Do you know, that's exactly what I used to say, but it didn't cut any ice with you either.'

He then noticed that Julia was grinning.

'You're having me on, aren't you?'

'Yes, of course I am.'

She laughed.

'I've a good mind not to let you out for the rest of the week as a punishment.'

'Oh, OK, You've had your bit of fun.'

'Well! What do you expect?'

'Seriously though, Julia, I am really sorry about Suzanne. I know I should have been looking after her but she can be very persuasive when she wants her own way. She was determined to spend the evening next door.'

'Well! I think I've heard some excuses in my time, but that's one of the best. You're telling me, that a nine-year-old forced you to take her next door so you could go out with your girlfriend. Oh, really Dad!'

'I can't win, can I?'

'No, you can't. Creeping in at three in the morning - and at your age too.'

Julia came over and sat on the side of the bed.

'Where did you take her then?'

'For a meal. At least, for the first part of the evening.'

'And then?'

'And then, we went to a nightclub.'

'A nightclub! Good heavens!'

'I felt a bit out of place there though.'

'I expect the deafening music must have been a novel experience for you?'

'Yes, and the bar prices.'

Julia steadied the tray for him.

'The main thing is, did you enjoy yourself?'

'Julia. It was one of the best times I have had for years.'

'Then, I'm really happy for you, Dad.'

'And Suzanne?'

'Oh! She thoroughly enjoyed herself. Caroline lets her do all the things I won't let her do. Still, it won't hurt now and again.'

Anthony continued to eat his toast.

'I suppose I have you to thank for this?'

'Yes. Suzanne was going to do it for you when she gets back, but I thought you might prefer me to make it.'

'Too true!'

Suddenly a thought struck him.

'Oh, by the way! I almost forgot to ask. How is Gina?'

'They're not quite sure what is wrong with her, so they are keeping her in hospital for another day or two for some tests.'

'Is she all right, though?'

'She seems all right. Nothing to get too worried about at the moment.'

'I may go into Plymouth this afternoon, so perhaps I'll pop in and see her at the hospital in Truro on the way back. Take her some grapes or something.'

'Well, if you do, then make sure they're seedless or you'll never hear the last of it.'

As he finished the last slice of toast, Julia took the tray from him, leaving him holding his cup of tea.

'Is that Mike I can hear, tapping away on his computer like a demented gerbil?'

'Yes. He's rushing to get a number of e-mails sent off before going to work'

'That reminds me! What is the time? I'm supposed to take Caroline into school with her son's case.'

'Don't worry. It's only a quarter to eight. She's got to bring Suzanne back first, as soon as she's up. In fact, I'm surprised you're awake so early after such a late night. I only brought the toast in on the off chance that you might be.'

'Well! I've always been an early bird, haven't I? It'll probably catch up with me later in the day though. Then I shall probably keel over when someone is talking to me.'

'Well. Don't overdo it today, Dad.'

Anthony took another sip of his tea.

'Oh dear! I've just remembered. I forgot to leave a message last night, to tell you that Suzanne was next door.'

'It's all right. Caroline wrote a note and pushed it through the letter box, so you're in the clear.'

'It's so annoying. I'm getting so absent minded lately.'

'Yes, you certainly are doing things out of character, Dad. You're not in love with this girl, are you?'

Anthony was stuck for words. He had never lied to his daughter in all the years he had brought her up and now she was asking a direct question that he didn't wish to answer. She looked into his face and smiled.

'I think you've given me the answer to that.'

Holding the cup in both hands, he looked away.

'Yes, I suppose I am.'

'Oh, Dad. Do be careful. I don't want to see you hurt. I'd like to think it would work but....'

'But she's only twenty-four and I'm fifty-two. Is that what you're trying to say?'

Julia nodded.

'I know I have to be realistic, Julia. She is young and very attractive and I know that I'm old and past it.'

'No, you're not past it.'

'All right, but I expect there are going to be hundreds of young men out there, waiting to sweep her off her feet. I'm just, well; perhaps a father figure to her.'

'Look, Dad, enjoy each other's company. All I am trying to say is that you mustn't presume there'll be any future in the relationship. Just play it one day at a time. I am really pleased to see you so happy and I'm sure she's a very nice girl.'

'Thanks, Julia.'

She took his hand and gave it a squeeze. His mind reflected upon the times when her mother would do just the same. It was a sort of reassuring family gesture.

'Perhaps you'd like to ask Rebecca home for tea one evening? I'm sure we'd all get on well together.'

'Yes. I'd like that.'

'Mind you, we'd have to stop Mike fawning all over her.'

Anthony laughed. Mike had always fancied himself as a lady's man, but it was all in his mind. He never went any further than commenting on his fantasies. Truth of the matter was that he was absolutely devoted to his wife and daughter, and it would be unthinkable for him ever to go off the rails.

The tapping on the computer keyboard in the upstairs study stopped and they heard Mike go downstairs. The back door then opened, followed by the sound of voices and a lot of shuffling around.

'That'll be Suzanne back home. I'll just go down and get her ready for school. I'll let Caroline know you'll be round to pick her up in about half an hour.'

'OK, thanks.'

As Julia went downstairs, Anthony felt that this was his cue to get himself out of bed and ready for what the morning had in store for him. The next half an hour seemed to fly by. By the time he had finished his breakfast, Mike had already left with Julia and Suzanne. Now ready to go, he left by the front door. As he closed it behind him, he noticed that Caroline was standing by his car with a large case. He gave the door a couple of shakes to ensure that he had closed it securely and then walked down the drive to meet her.

'Good heavens, Caroline! How long is your lad going for?'

'I know it's big but it's the only case I've got.'

Anthony took it from her and opened the car boot. Fortunately, it fitted in but only just, as he had so much other clutter there that he had brought with him, mainly for the boat. Caroline then got into the passenger seat and they were on their way.

'Would you mind dropping me off at work after we've taken the case to school? I'm on morning shifts all this week.'

'No! Of course I wouldn't. After all, I've got all the time in the world.'

Well, if Caroline was off to work at the supermarket, she was certainly dressed to kill. Sitting low down in a sports car, her tight short skirt had risen so high that it almost met the plunging neckline of the blouse coming down the other way. In all, it left very little to the imagination. He noticed that her legs were long and very shapely. No wonder she had little trouble in attracting men, even though she tended to brush aside much of the attention she received.

Averting his gaze from her legs, Anthony fixed his eyes back onto the road ahead. He began to wonder how her husband could possibly have walked out on such a very beautiful woman. Besides, not only was she gorgeous to look at, but she had a fantastic personality as well.

'Thanks for helping me out with my problem last night, Caroline.'

'Oh, I don't mind a bit of childminding. If you ever get stuck again, just let me know.'

'That's very kind of you. Do you often help out with Suzanne then?'

'Now and again.'

'I'm sure Mike and Julia appreciate it.'

'Well. I suppose I don't go out all that much, whereas the two of them go to a lot of dinner parties. I must come in quite handy being only next door.'

'Yes. You're going to have to start charging them for the service.'

'What! Get money out of old Mike? You must be joking.'

'Well! You can certainly come round and baby-sit for me anytime. Even when Suzanne isn't there, if you like?'

She shook her head from side to side and grinned.

'I think I'm getting used to your saucy comments by now. Anyway, if I did, don't think that I wouldn't have you in bed by seven-thirty though.'

Anthony raised his eyebrow and smirked. It was then that Caroline realised the implications of what she had said. She slapped him on the arm.

'Just behave yourself! You know exactly what I meant.'

'Mrs McBride, I do believe you're blushing.'

'It's you! You're dreadful!'

Anthony couldn't stop laughing at Caroline's embarrassment. Her face had a gone a bright shade of pink.

'I've never had this trouble with any other man. What am I going to do with you?'

'Well. You bring the worst out in me.'

'That's right! Blame it on me! Still, I suppose you're harmless enough.'

'Oh! Don't go and spoil it, Caroline. I've got a macho reputation to keep.'

She leaned across and grasped his knee.

'Don't worry. Your secret is safe with me. You really are incorrigible!'

On arrival at the school, they managed to find a parking space that wasn't too far from the entrance. The coach had already taken the prime position outside, and the driver had left its engine ticking over. They got out of the car and Caroline waited whilst Anthony removed the case from the car boot and handed it her. She then went over to the awaiting coach.

Her son Mark was standing around talking to a group of other boys. She went up to him and hugged and kissed him, which must have been really embarrassing for the poor kid in front of his mates. Milling around the coach were many other parents saying "goodbye" to their children.

Within a short while, the luggage was stowed away and the children found their seats. As the coach pulled away from the school entrance, Anthony could see from the expression on their faces, that not all the children were happy to be parted from their parents for a few days. Needless to say that some of the youngsters and indeed some of their mothers too were in tears.

Mark was sitting at a window seat and waved shyly to his mum. He also noticed that Caroline continued to wave until the coach turned the corner at the end of the road. She then exchanged a brief word with some of the other parents and returned to the car.

As she settled in, she gave Anthony directions to the supermarket where she worked. It wasn't that far from the school, so Caroline knew that she would get there in plenty of time for the morning shift. As they drove along, she continued her conversation with Anthony.

'What are you going to do with yourself today, then?'

'Well, Becky doesn't work on Tuesdays, so we are off to Plymouth to do some shopping.'

'Is that where you're heading after you drop me off?'

'Oh, no. I promised her that I wouldn't pick her up until late morning.'

'I see. Actually, I'm surprised you managed to get up so early after last night. Julia told me what time you got in.'

'Does she tell you everything I get up to?'

'Pretty much everything. We women like to exchange all the juicy bits of gossip, you know.'

Anthony pulled up outside the supermarket and Caroline took off her seat belt, and opened the door ready to get out. She swung her legs around onto the pavement and then paused for a moment to look back at him.

'Where did you eventually go last night? You told me that you were only going for a meal.'

'Yes, we did, but then we went on to a nightclub.'

'What! Till three in the morning!'

'Actually, it was a bit earlier than that. We then went down to the beach to look at the stars.'

Caroline gave him one of those knowing looks.

'Oh, yes! You didn't? Well, you know. Get up to anything, did you?

Anthony was most indignant.

'Caroline McBride! Really! What a thing to ask me! No, we didn't!'

She stepped out of the car and shut the door. She had an impish grin on her face.

'Just checking. That's all. Just checking.'

She leaned over to pick up her purse that was on the seat.

'Are you sure there isn't something you're not telling me?'

'No.! There isn't?'

'You've gone very red in the face, though.'

'Just go to work, Caroline.'

She turned and went in through the doors, chuckling away to herself. She was delighted that she had got her own back on him for a change.

Chapter Seventeen

'Must you go out with this old fool, today?'

'Look! This is going to be the last opportunity I have to ask him for his boat.'

'Well! It seems to me like you're making such a meal of it. I would have thought you'd have sorted it out by now.'

'It takes time, Jon. I've got to find the right moment to ask him.'

Jon was feeling grumpy. He still had a hangover from the night before, although fortunately for Rebecca he couldn't remember very much as to what had taken place at the nightclub. She knew that she could also count on Kyle not to give the game away and telling him what had happened there either.

'If you haven't got that boat from him by tomorrow night, we're sunk.'

'Don't you think I don't know that?'

'Well, you don't seem to be taking it that seriously.'

'All right! But stop going on about it. Anyway, what's this package we're picking up?'

'Something pretty valuable.'

'So you keep telling me. I'm beginning to think that you have no idea what it is.'

Jon was annoyed at being questioned about the matter. He hadn't a clue as to what he was being asked to collect but he didn't wish to appear ignorant of the fact.

'And another thing. Who set this up? You don't know any master criminals.'

'Just get off my back, Becky.'

'No! Come on! Who's masterminding this? Don't you think I have a right to know?'

'No, I don't.'

He was now furious. Since they had got out of bed that morning, he had tried to establish what had gone on between Becky and Anthony the night before and she had been extremely evasive. So as to detract from his line of questioning, she was now cross-examining him about the job they had planned.

'I want to know what you and that old boy got up to last night.'

'I know you do but I'm not going to tell you. After all, you're keeping me in the dark over the scam.'

'Oh! Stop being so childish, Becky.'

'Who's the one being childish? I went out for a meal with this guy, went off to a nightclub and danced with him, and then came home again. That was all for the purpose of my getting to borrow his boat, so we can pick up some dodgey goods, which you're not going to tell me about.'

Jon had had enough. This was one argument that was going nowhere.

'I'm going out!'

'That's it! Typical! Run away, when you're losing an argument!'

Jon leapt across the room and grabbed her by the shoulders. Rebecca was not sure what was coming next but she could see his eyes were inflamed.

'I ought to punch your face in. I don't let anyone talk to me like that.'

Rebecca felt it best not to reply. Jon was so angry, that had she made one more inappropriate comment, he would have probably carried out his threat. He loosened the grip on her arms and left the room. A short while later, she heard the front door slam behind him.

Her arms really hurt where he had dug his fingers into her flesh. She examined the bruises. They were obvious for all to see, so she knew she had to wear something long-sleeved to hide them. She didn't want Anthony to be aware of their confrontation, as his natural reaction would be to take Jon to task over the incident. Everything would then come to light.

She had an hour or so to spare before Anthony came to pick her up, so she decided to go for a walk. It was possible that Jon would not return until after she had left, but she didn't want to take that chance. She couldn't face another quarrel. Slipping on something appropriate, she left the house, intending to come back again just before Anthony arrived.

After dropping Caroline off at work, Anthony returned to his daughter's home. The hot weather had made him thirsty so he went into the kitchen and poured himself a drink. Looking at his watch, he found that he had plenty of time to spare before going over to Rebecca's house. As it was a pleasant morning, he decided to sit outside in the garden.

He lay back on the sunbed and placed his drink on the lawn beside him. He could feel the warmth of the sunshine against his face as he shielded his eyes to squint at the few clouds, slowly drifting across the sky. Closing his eyes, he listened to the humming of the bees as they busily flew from flower to flower, and he only opened them again to observe the occasional noisy seagull that flew overhead. As it was all so relaxing after coming home very late that morning, he eventually fell asleep.

It was some considerable time later; when he was awakened by the light touch of a fly that had landed on his face. Brushing it aside with the back of his hand, he opened his eyes to look up at the clouds. He noticed that there were far more of them in the sky now, which signified to him that he must have been asleep for ages.

'Wow! I must have been tired.'

Casually, he looked around him and then lifted his wrist to look at his watch.

'Good heavens! It's eleven-twenty. I'm supposed to pick Becky up in ten minutes.'

Leaping up from the lounger, he rushed indoors to get ready. He had very little time to spare, except to close the windows and lock the back door. Picking up his car keys and wallet, he dashed through to the lounge. The clock on the mantelpiece only served to make the situation worse.

'Oh dear! I've only got seven minutes left now.'

He dashed out to the car, got in, and drove away at speed. Naturally, when one is in a hurry, there is inevitably far more traffic than normal and, unlike you, it always seems as if those other road users have all the time in the world. In his haste, he took a wrong turning and ended up taking a longer route to Rebecca's house. He eventually reached her turning fifteen minutes late. As he pulled up outside her home, she was sitting on the wall by her front gate.

'I thought you finance men were suppose to be very precise about time?'

'Sorry, Becky. I fell asleep on the lounger in the garden.'

'Can't hack the late nights, then?'

'Oh! Don't rub it in.'

She got into the car and they kissed.

'I've really missed you, Tony.'

'Well, it was only earlier this morning that I dropped you off at this very spot.'

'My goodness! As short as that, was it?'

They travelled across town and through the small villages until they hit the A30. Rebecca's conversation was all about her job and the amusing things that had happened at the shop, during the past few weeks. Anthony listened attentively, without comment, whilst he drove. She then got onto the subject of her past and in particular her education. She told Anthony that she hadn't been the brightest of pupils at school, although she had managed to pass the odd GCSE. When she left, she started work at the shop in the High Street, and that was where she had stayed ever since.

Throughout the conversation, she constantly referred to her poor school performance. She seemed to suffer from a lack of self-esteem in this area of her life, but Anthony reassured her that there was much more to a person than their standard of education. She appeared to judge herself as inferior in comparison to most of her friends, all of whom had good careers, overlooking the fact that her sharp wit, charm, and effervescent personality, more than made up for any lack of intellectual skills.

A short way along the dual carriageway, she changed the subject.

'Can I drive us to Plymouth?'

'I expect so.'

Anthony pulled into a lay-by at the side of the road, and they swapped places. Rebecca adjusted the driver's seat and the mirror and put the car into gear.

'Now just take it easy, will you?'

'I always do.'

He noticed that she had an impish look upon her face.

'Now careful with the accelerator, Becky. It can pull away quite fast.'

'What? Like this?'

Rebecca pulled away with such acceleration, that Anthony was thrown back against the headrest on the passenger seat. Within a matter of seconds, she was touching ninety miles an hour, and the needle on the speedometer was still rising. Anthony tried to regain his normal sitting position.

'Bloody hell, Becky! I'm not in that much of a hurry to reach the shops.'

He was trying desperately to shout above the wind noise, as it whistled over their heads.

'What did you say? You want to go faster?'

The mischievous young woman put her foot down harder and

the dial went on beyond a hundred miles per hour. Anthony had never driven the car at this speed before, but gained some comfort from the fact that it did seem to cling to the road quite well. He was finding the whole experience rather hair raising.

Remaining in the outside lane, she passed one vehicle after another until, mercifully for Anthony, she spotted a police car up ahead. Sensibly she reduced her speed to a respectable seventy.

'Hey! That was exhilarating! This car can really go some, can't it? How was it for you?'

'Out of this world, Becky! In fact, if you had driven just that little bit faster, we may both have been out of this world.'

Turning off the main arterial road, Anthony was pleased to see that Rebecca maintained a sensible speed along the single carriageway all the way to the Saltash Bridge. Upon reaching Plymouth, they parked down by the bus station. As he hoisted himself out of the passenger seat, still a little shaken, she dashed around the car to kiss him.

'Oh, you are a lovely man. Thanks for letting me drive your car.'

'It was a pleasure, Becky. I'll have to make sure we don't do it again.'

Anthony was considerably relieved that he had reached Plymouth safely. As he shut the passenger door, she handed him the keys to lock the car, after first putting the top back up. Linking her arm through his, she then looked up at him.

'I really do love you, Tony.'

Without verbally responding to the comment, Anthony leaned forward and kissed her upon the lips.

As they walked through the shopping precinct, Rebecca frequently stopped to look in the shop windows, to pass comments on the things that were on display. Each time she came across a place that sold women's clothes, she would take him inside to search through the racks for something that was suitable. Anthony then stood by and watched her try on various tops, skirts, jeans, and trousers. On each occasion, she would emerge from the cubicle to ask his opinion on how they suited her.

'Well, Tony! What do you think?'

Rebecca had such a beautiful figure that everything she tried on naturally looked great on her.

'Yes. They look really good on you. I especially like the trousers.'

'Tell me. Is there anything that doesn't suit me?'

Anthony smiled.

'In every shop we've been to, you've told me that everything I've tried on so far, looks good on me.'

'Well, of course it does. You're absolutely gorgeous.'

'Tony! I think we'd better take off those rose coloured glasses or I'll never get a sensible answer from you.'

'But you've had my honest opinion.'

'What? The same one each time?'

'Well. Yes.'

Rebecca looked into his eyes and shook her head.

'I get the feeling you must be in love with me or something.'

'Whatever gave you that idea?'

She returned to the cubicle to change back into the clothes she wore when she came in. Emerging from the changing room with her arms full of clothes that she had tried on, she replaced them onto the displays. She then took hold of his hand and the two of them headed for the exit.

'That's the fourth shop we've been into, Becky, where you've tried things on. Aren't you ever going to buy any of them?'

'Maybe one day, when I have enough money, I will.'

The remark brought home to Anthony, the simple truth about Rebecca's finances. A shop assistant's wages did not amount to a great deal of money. Admittedly, she paid no rent or mortgage whilst living in her dad's house, but such little income had to cover all the household bills and still provide some sort of social life for her.

'You'd like to have lots of clothes, wouldn't you?'

'Yes, and shoes too, if I could afford them.'

'Why don't you use a credit card?'

'I do, but I have to be very careful that I don't overspend and run up enormous interest charges.'

'I suppose it's nice to see a young person these days who doesn't want to be heavily in debt.'

'Well, if I did, I'd have to take to crime in order to pay it off.'

'Oh! Becky! I couldn't imagine for one minute that you would ever do anything like that.'

Rebecca paused for a moment to reflect upon her remark. This naïve man couldn't possibly conceive of her doing anything wrong. He thought far too much of her for that. He really had no idea what was going on in the background of their relationship either. Just for that instant, the reality of the situation hit her again. She still had to find the opportune moment to ask him to lend her his boat, and she also knew that the time in which to put forward that suggestion was getting nearer and nearer. Nevertheless, she committed the thought to the back of her mind and continued with the conversation.

'I do buy new things from time to time, but most of what I have in my wardrobe has been around for a few years now.'

'Well, anything you've worn since I met you, looks fantastic on you.'

'Romantic idiot!'

Putting his arm around her, they strolled along the streets and through the centre of the city. Anthony made a couple of small purchases for himself but nothing really worthy of note. Although he did enjoy wandering around the shops, there was nothing special that he wished to buy.

By way of a break from this shopping spree, they went into a coffee shop for something to drink. Sitting down at a table, Rebecca talked endlessly about her father, her friends, and her past. Anthony was so pleased to see her happy, that he just sat and listened patiently to what she had to say. She was such endearing company that he was mesmerised by her intriguing stories.

When they later emerged, Rebecca went across to a jewellers that she wanted to look in. Standing in the entrance, she viewed the items on display in the windows.

'I've always wanted a gold bracelet like that one.'

She pointed to a rather expensive item, which occupied its own separate position on the shelf among the trays. The two of them took a closer look.

'Just look at the price of it though, Tony.'

'That's understandable. There's a lot of gold in a 22-carat gold bracelet. Especially one like that.'

She laughed.

'I'll forget that idea, then.'

'Yes. I expect you'll have to.'

'One day, when I have enough money, I'll buy those beautiful earrings though.'

'Which ones are you looking at?'

Rebecca pointed to a pair of earrings on the shelf above the bracelet. They were really beautiful and sparkled in the bright lights of the jeweller's window. Anthony gazed upon them, whilst his young friend ran her eyes over the items on the other trays. There didn't appear to be anything else in the window that caught her fancy, at least, nothing that she specifically drew his attention to.

'Come on, let's go inside and see what those earrings look like on you. It'll make a change from trying on clothes.'

'Do you think we should? You know I can't afford them.'

'Yes! Go on!'

He guided her in through the door and over to the counter where a shop assistant was tidying a display cabinet. After a brief word, the assistant went over to the window, and Rebecca pointed out the items she wanted to try on. He later returned with the tray and placed it on the counter. Picking up the earrings, he handed them to her and she held them up to her ears.

'What d'you think?'

'I think they really suit you, Becky.'

'Now, there's a surprise!'

'No! I mean it! They really do look good on you.'

Rebecca grinned.

'Tell you what! Why not try on the bracelet too?'

'Oh, I couldn't do that.'

'Why not? You seem to have tried on everything else that the shops in Plymouth have to offer?'

'All right, then.'

Rebecca asked the assistant to fetch the gold bracelet.

'I know I can't afford it,' she whispered discreetly into Anthony's ear, 'but it'll be great just to see what it looks like on me.'

Anthony agreed.

Once more, the assistant went to the display cabinet, this time returning with the gold bracelet. She took the item from the counter and the shop assistant helped her to fasten the clasp.

'I feel like a million dollars with these on.'

'Yes. You certainly look like it.'

Anthony turned to the shop assistant.

'What do you think?'

'Yes. He's right madam. They really do look good on you.'

Rebecca continued to admire the jewellery, posing to look in a mirror on the wall nearby.

'Would you like me to buy you the earrings, Becky?'

'Well. I do like them but they're a lot of money.'

'That's not what I asked you, was it?'

'Honestly! I can't let you spend all that money on me. Mind you, they really are beautiful.'

Anthony turned to the shop assistant.

'That's settled then. The lady will take the earrings.'

'You mean, you really are going to buy them for me?'

'That's what I said.'

The assistant placed the earrings into the box.

'Can I take the bracelet back, madam?'

'Yes. Of course.'

She held out her wrist to enable him to unclasp it.

'It's really lovely but so expensive. Way out of our league, isn't it, Tony?'

The assistant took Anthony's credit card and the two of them went over to the till. Whilst she was waiting, Rebecca went outside to gaze once more at the trays in the shop window. Within a short while, Anthony joined her. He handed her the small bag with the purchase inside.

'Thank you so much for the earrings.'

'That's OK.'

'Do you realise that no one has ever bought me anything that expensive before. You really are a lovely man.'

She kissed him on the cheek.

'Come on. I want us to visit a relative in hospital now. I've seen enough shops for one afternoon.'

They walked briskly along the streets to return to the car park. On the way back, she told him how much she had enjoyed her shopping spree, even though she hadn't parted with any money. She had been quite contented to look at the things in the shops and try them on. Then one day, yes, that illusive day when she had enough money, she would know precisely what to buy. Upon reaching the car, she headed for the driver's side.

'Would you like me to drive us to the hospital?'

'No thanks. I think my nerves have been shattered sufficiently already today with your driving.'

They got into the car, and Anthony readjusted the seat and the mirror.

'I'm going to put on my new earrings before we drive off.'

'Why not? After all, they are yours.'

She delved into the bag and brought out, not one but two small packets. She opened one of them and took out the two pretty earrings. She admired them and then placed them onto one side.

'What's in this other packet?'

'You'll never know until you open it, will you?'

Rebecca was intrigued.

'What have you done now?'

She removed the wrapping from around the other package. As she did so, her eyes lit up in disbelief.

'Oh, Tony! You've brought me the bracelet too!'

She held it delicately in her hand.

'You must have spent a fortune on me in there. I honestly don't deserve this.'

Her eyes began to fill with tears and she placed her arms around his neck and sobbed.

'Becky! You should be happy. They're both what you wanted.'

'But I am happy.'

She brushed the tears from her eyes with the back of her hand.

'You really are kind to me, and I really don't deserve it.'

Anthony put his arms around her and held her closely to him.

'Let me be the judge of that. Nothing's too good for you.'

She looked down at the bracelet, which she now held in her hand. Each tear that rolled down her cheek slowly dripped onto the gold band. Anthony took his handkerchief from his pocket and handed it to her.

'Here. Take this. It is clean.'

She took the handkerchief and wiped her eyes.

'I really don't deserve all this. I can't believe how much you've just spent on me.'

Anthony leaned over to her and picked up the bracelet.

'Look. I'll help you put it on.'

She put it around her wrist and Anthony helped her fix the clasp, which was a little awkward for her to attempt with one hand, especially as it was new and rather inflexible. She then put on the earrings and turned to face him.

'I love you, Tony. I really do love you.'

'And I love you too.'

'If ever I hurt you, please remember, that I really do love you.'

'Oh, I can't imagine your ever hurting me.'

'Yes. But if I ever did, you must remember that I will always love you.'

Anthony didn't understand the significance of this remark. Ever since he had met Rebecca, she often appeared to talk in riddles. Problem was that he was so happy to be with her, that he let all these unexplained comments go straight over his head without questioning their meaning.

He started the engine and they drove out of the car park and onto the road out of the city. It was virtually the same way that they had come.

'Which hospital are we going to?'

'Truro.'

'Who are we going to see then?'

'It's my daughter's mother-in-law. Hope you don't mind?'

'No, of course not.'

Rebecca had now composed herself. It was time to pop the question that she had been dreading to ask of him for the past few days. As they drove along, the words she was about to say rolled over and over in her mind. She hated herself for the lie she was about to deliver but she knew that she had to follow through. How could she be so deceitful? She loved this man so much, yet everything that had happened between them had been based upon a lie. His incredible generosity towards her had only made matters worse. She looked across at him.

'Tony.'

'Yes, love.'

She struggled to force the words from her mouth. Her stomach churned within her. This wasn't right and she knew it. She was caught between two forces. Should she go through with the plan and risk losing Anthony, or should she go back to Jon and say she just couldn't do it? Right now, she wanted Anthony to take her away from it all, perhaps back to his home in London, where she could forget the past and start afresh. But then there was Jon. He would probably get great pleasure in telling Anthony the truth, especially if she failed do what he asked her to. Where would that leave her then?

'Would you let me borrow your boat tomorrow evening?'

'Well, yes, of course. Providing you drive it with a little more respect than you did my car.'

'Aren't you going to ask me what I want it for?'

'Becky, if you want it, you can have it. I don't have to know what for.'

Anthony wasn't making this easy for Rebecca. He loved her so much and was so trusting, that he would part with his beloved boat to her without even asking why she wanted it.

'OK. If it makes you feel any better, what do you want it for?'

'Well, you remember my friend, Lynn? She was the girl you met in the club.'

'Yes. That's the one whose boyfriend had two-timed her.'

'Yes. That's right. Well, I told her that you had a boat and she suggested that I ask you if you would lend it to us one evening so we could go out together.'

'Fine! That's good enough for me. You two go and enjoy yourselves. You say you want it for tomorrow?'

'If that's all right?'

'Yes. Mike and Julia are going out this evening, and I'm looking after Suzanne. If you come over to the house, I'll give you the keys. You can return them to me on Thursday.'

Rebecca was relieved she had got that over with. It didn't make her feel any better about herself though. She had still lied to a man who she was in love with - and it hurt, really hurt. Damn Jon. Damn his stupid scam.

It didn't take them long to get to the hospital. Although it wasn't official visiting hours, Anthony explained to the nursing staff his relationship to Gina and they were ushered into her ward. Before sitting by the side of her bed, he placed some seedless grapes that he had bought for her, into the bowl on the top of the cabinet. Throughout this time, Gina had been dozing and had not noticed them arrive. However, she opened her eyes when he leaned across to hold her hand.

'Oh. It's you Tony. How long have you been here?'

'We've only just arrived, Gina. How are you feeling now?'

Gina answered in a gentle, almost inaudible, voice.

'A little better. They said they would let me go home again in a couple of days. They muttered something about taking some more tests. I have no idea what they're up to.'

Averting her eyes from Anthony, she looked across to the other side of the bed and saw Rebecca.

'And who are you?'

'I'm Becky, Gina. I've come with Anthony to see you.'

She stared profoundly at Rebecca. From the expression upon her face, you could see her desperately trying to ascertain who she was.

'I thought you were Julia, Tony's daughter. You look very much like her.'

'No, Gina. Becky is a friend of mine.'

She continued to gaze upon the young woman, still trying to identify her.

'Come and sit here where I can see you more clearly.'

She beckoned to Rebecca to sit on the edge of the bed and then reached out to take hold of her hand. Anthony observed, as she held it tenderly in her own frail hand and spoke to her in a soft gentle voice.

She began telling her all about her daughter-in-law, Julia, and how her father had brought her up, after her mother had died. She said what a wonderful wife and mother she had now become, and how lucky her son had been to find such a loving woman to marry.

Anthony listened in mild astonishment. He couldn't believe this change of heart on Gina's part. Throughout the conversation, she hardly mentioned Mike, upon whom she normally bestowed such accolade. Rebecca showed genuine interest in everything Gina was saying and interrupted from time to time to ask her questions about the family. Surprisingly, she answered them too and in full. Perhaps this sudden illness and the ensuing time in hospital, away from home, had give her time to reflect upon the things that mattered to her most. Maybe she had now come to see her family in a different light and appreciated their concern for her.

Gina adjusted herself into a more comfortable position, as Anthony and Rebecca were ready to leave.

'Will you come and see me again?'

'Yes, of course. I'll ask Anthony to bring me along on another occasion.'

'It's been lovely talking to you. I still think you look very much like Julia, though.'

'Well, Gina, I will take that as a compliment.'

As the two of them left the ward, they turned to wave. Gina managed to lift her frail hand in an attempt to wave back and then settled her head onto her pillow again and shut her eyes. She appeared very tired.

The time during the brief visiting period had gone quickly, although they appreciated the fact that the staff had allowed them in at such short notice. On the way down the stairs and out into the car park, Rebecca compared the relationship that she had enjoyed with her father, to that of Julia and Anthony. There were so many similarities between them that she felt she almost knew Julia, even though she had never met her.

'I'd love to meet your daughter sometime,' said Rebecca, getting into the car.

'I'm sure you will do one of these days. Not tonight though, as they are going out and I am looking after Suzanne.'

'Oh, yes. I remember you saying earlier.'

Anthony got into the car and they drove out of the hospital grounds. He was pleased with his visit to Gina, having now seen her in a much better state of mind than she had been for some time.

'Look, Becky. Why don't you come round later and spend the evening with the two of us? OK, so it won't be that exciting as we'll only be watching children's videos or something equally as dull. Besides, as I said earlier, you can also pick up the boat keys whilst you're there.'

'Yes! Great! I'll come around later.'

'You don't mind?'

'Of course not! I love spending my time with you.'

Anthony drove them back to Rebecca's house and she wrote down his daughter's address before getting out of the car. She didn't need directions, as she was quite familiar with the area. She then waved him goodbye and watched him drive off down the road. As his car disappeared from view, she turned to walk down the path to the house.

Once inside, she went up to her bedroom and removed the earrings and the bracelet and hid them under some clothes in one of her dressing table drawers. She thought it extremely unlikely that Jon would go delving amongst her clothes and find them. Once again, she was very upset, not least of all for the fact that she couldn't openly wear the beautiful presents that Anthony had bought for her. She felt sad in the knowledge that they would probably never be worn unless she was out with him, even though she wanted to show the whole world what this lovely, kind man, who treated her with so much respect, had given her.

'Well. I shall have to smuggle them out of the house this evening in order to wear them just for him,' she muttered quietly to herself.

She knew that it would be easy to persuade Jon that she had to go over to see Anthony that evening, as she now had a genuine reason to meet him. Jon would be delighted to hear that she was picking up the boat keys at long last. However, she would have to think up some plausible excuse as to why she would need to spend the entire evening there.

Sadly, the situation in which she found herself had called for her to tell one lie after another, to both Anthony and Jon, and she found this very distressing. Whilst there are some people who have no qualms about deceiving others, telling the truth had been the one quality that her father had impressed upon her, since she was a child.

'What happens after tomorrow?' she thought.

She knew that come tomorrow, she would be unable to give Jon any more reasons as to why she would want to see Anthony. If she told him the truth, that she had fallen in love with this older man, Jon would search out Tony and tell him the entire story. What would Anthony's reaction be to finding out that she had lied to him, right from the beginning? It certainly didn't bode well. Right now, she wished she could wave a magic wand and it would all come right, but that was just fantasy. As she mulled the problem over in her confused mind, she decided that she had no choice but to see what would happen when Thursday came around.

Chapter Eighteen

Mike called out to his wife from the bedroom.

'Where's that new shirt of mine?'

Anthony had been sitting on the bed in the guestroom, keeping out of the way, whilst his daughter and son-in-law were getting ready to go out for the evening. They had been invited to a dinner party held by a senior partner in the firm of solicitors where Mike worked. Julia was in the bathroom at the time having a shower, and she obviously hadn't heard him. Mike repeated the question.

'Julia, where's that shirt I bought last week?'

This time she must have heard him call to her, above the noise of the running water. The shower was promptly turned off and Julia crossed the landing with a bath towel securely wrapped around her.

'It's downstairs, hanging on the cupboard door, Mike. It's a good job I'm one step ahead of you otherwise it would still be in its box with all the creases in it. Fortunately for you, I've just ironed it.'

'Thanks Julia. I don't know what I would do without you,' he said, kissing her on the cheek.

Mike scurried off downstairs and returned with the shirt. He unbuttoned the cuffs, the collar and the front and put it on. This evening was to be a shirt and tie affair, so he needed to look his best. Unfortunately, it was also bound to be extremely uncomfortable for the guests, having to put up with their collars secured on such a hot evening.

He was always the first dressed whenever they were due to go out and was then subjected to a long impatient wait for his wife to catch up. Ultimately, it was well worth the delay. Julia would dress in some very smart eveningwear on these occasions, in which she would look every bit, the successful solicitor's wife.

Mike emerged from the bedroom and went downstairs again to the lounge. He was now dressed and ready to go. Meanwhile, Anthony crossed the landing to the open bedroom door, where he could see Julia sitting in front of the dressing table mirror.

'All right if I stick my head in?'

'Yes, that's fine, Dad. I'm quite decent.'

He entered the room and sat on the corner of the large double bed. Julia was dressed except for the evening gown, which she had left until last to avoid it getting creased. He watched her making up her face with great care.

'I see Mike's ready.'

'Yes. It never does take him long.'

'He's been quite liberal with the after shave, as usual.'

'I know. He certainly does tend to splash a lot on, doesn't he?'

Anthony looked around the room. It had been tastefully redecorated since his last visit, and the dressing table and the built in wardrobes were new.

'Incidentally, is that a new suit Mike's wearing? I noticed it as he went downstairs.'

'Yes. New suit, a new shirt and a new tie. Do you like them?'

'Well, I wasn't aware that major department stores had a Pimp Collection.'

'Good Heavens, Dad! Don't say that to him. That's an Armani suit he's wearing. It cost him a fortune.'

Anthony laughed.

'I'm only kidding. It's very smart and modern. It suits him

too. I expect he'll be able to procure lots of clients in that.'

'You are dreadful!'

'Well, it is a bit...Well, you know what I mean.'

Julia looked up at her father's reflection in the dressing table mirror.

'I don't know why the two of you are always finding excuses to take pot shots at each other.'

'Yes. I'm sorry about that. He is actually a nice bloke and I couldn't wish to have a more honest and trustworthy husband for my daughter.'

'So what's the problem then?'

'I suppose it's just that he always seems so full of himself. Doesn't that drive you mad?'

'Sometimes it does. I think you'll find he's basically insecure and all that boasting and exaggeration is just a front.'

'So why does he always have a go at me?'

Julia put down her makeup and picked up her dress.

'Here. Help me on with this.'

Julia stepped into her evening gown and pulled it up over her shoulders. She then turned around for her father to zip it up.

'I think you'll find, Dad, that the constant digs he gives you are all due to insecurity as well.'

'What on earth has Mike got to be insecure about?'

'I think it's because he knows that you were able to look after me all those years, and he now insists on taking over that role. When you turn up, he feels threatened.'

'Oh, how daft! He's your husband - and a good father too. I don't play any serious role in your life anymore.'

'Yes, I know. But you try convincing him of that.'

Mike then entered the room and their conversation ceased. He had come to check up on his wife's progress.

'Come on, Julia, or we'll be late.'

'I am going as fast as I can, Mike. What's Suzanne up to at the moment?'

'She's watching the television and drawing in her sketchpad.'

Julia turned to her father.

'You won't mind looking after Suzanne tonight, will you Dad?'

'No, of course not.'

'You won't wander off this time?'

'No.'

Anthony smiled.

'Becky says she might come round later though. I hope that's all right with you.'

'Yes, fine. Anyway, you know where the coffee is, if you want to make her one.'

'Yes. Thanks.'

'And please don't let Suzanne stay up too late.'

'No. I'll see she's in bed at a respectable time.'

'Right! I'm ready then, Mike.'

'At last! Hallelujah!'

The three of them left the bedroom and went downstairs. In the lounge, Suzanne was doodling on her sketchpad. The television news had just finished.

'Would you do me a favour please Dad?'

'Sure, Mike.'

'The last match of the season is on the TV later and I wondered if you would video it for me. It isn't often that my team gets into the final.'

'No problem. I'll set it up after Suzanne has gone to bed.'

Having heard her name mentioned the youngster looked up from her pad.

'I know what the score is, Dad.'

'Well, I don't want to know.'

'But it was on the news.'

'Suzanne! I don't want to know what the score is before I watch the match. It'll spoil the suspense.'

The youngster shrugged her shoulders.

'Suit yourself then, but you won't see any goals.'

Mike's mouth dropped in disappointment. Standing right behind him, his wife and father-in-law couldn't contain their laughter. His young daughter however returned to her sketchpad, totally oblivious of the effect that her remark had had on her father's expectation of the game.

'Right, we're off now, Suzanne. Come and give us a kiss.'

Suzanne got up to kiss her mum and dad and then went over to the television to put on a video. Much to Mike's annoyance, Julia fussed around for a few more things that she had left behind in the bedroom before being finally escorted to the front door by her impatient husband. Anthony opened the door for them and Julia kissed him as she passed.

'I like the suit, Mike. It looks very smart.'

'Oh, really! Thanks.'

Mike was quite startled by his father-in-law's kind observation. However, Julia turned as she opened the passenger door of the car and waggled her finger at her father, who was now standing on the doorstep. Anthony silently threw his hands up in a gesture as if to say, "what am I supposed to have done now," knowing very well that she was referring to the sarcastic compliment about the suit. He watched them drive off and then went back inside the house.

Anthony returned to the lounge, where Suzanne was lying on the carpet with her head cupped in her hands. She was watching the film with her face only a few feet from the television screen.

'Come and sit back, Suzanne. You're sitting far too close and it won't do your eyes any good.'

'But I always sit like this.'

'I am sure you do; and I bet your mum tells you to move away just as I have done.'

Suzanne turned her head in his direction and frowned.

Anthony sat down on the sofa and Suzanne got up from the floor and came across to him to climb up onto his lap.

'What's this we're watching then?'

'It's called "The Lion King".'

'Oh! That's nice.'

'Honest, Granddad. You're beginning to sound like Grandma now.'

Anthony chuckled at the youngster's remark. He shifted her round so they were both facing the television and they watched the rest of the video together. Like most nine-year-olds, Suzanne had watched the film over and over again, and could tell him exactly what was coming up before each scene. When it had ended, Anthony suggested that they had something to drink and went off into the kitchen to fetch it. He returned with two glasses of lemonade and a packet of biscuits that he had found in the fridge.

'They're Dad's chocolate biscuits, you know.'

'Really!'

'Yes, and he knows exactly how many of them are left in the packet.'

'You mean, he doesn't share them with anyone?'

'Well, not very often.'

'Oh, never mind. If it worries him that much, I'll go up to the shop first thing tomorrow morning and get another packet. It isn't the end of the world, is it?'

Suzanne agreed. She took the packet and began to munch her way through them, dropping lots of crumbs onto the floor in the process. Anthony returned to the kitchen to fetch her a plate, and to collect the dustpan and brush in order to clean up the mess on the thick piled carpet.

It was then that the doorbell rang. Suzanne dashed across the room and out into the hall to open the front door. She then returned to usher Rebecca into the lounge. Anthony put down the dustpan and went over to her and they hugged each other.

'Wow!' said Suzanne, 'Granddad was right. You really are beautiful.'

'Well, that's nice of you to say so. I take it that you're Suzanne?'

'Absolutely correct.'

Suzanne held up her thumb in agreement.

'Would you like a cup of tea, Becky?'

'Yes please, Suzanne. I'd love one. That's very kind of you.'

Rebecca sat down beside Anthony on the sofa.

'I wouldn't thank her just yet, Becky, until you've had a chance to taste the tea.'

Thinking that Suzanne had scurried off into the kitchen to make the tea, Anthony leaned across to kiss Rebecca on the cheek. Suddenly up from behind the sofa the little head wedged itself in between the two of them.

'You weren't thinking of doing anything naughty whilst I'm in the kitchen, were you?'

Rebecca doubled up with laughter at the youngster's remark, which was made all the more amusing by the impish look on her face. She turned her head from one side and then to the other, first grinning at Rebecca and then at her granddad.

'Oh dear! I reckon you're going to have a sense of humour just like your granddad when you grow up.'

Suzanne paused for a moment to think of a suitable reply.

'Well, heaven help the rest of the family then!'

This brought even more hysterical laughter from their guest.

'Yes, I know, Becky. Nine-year-olds are so forward these days.'

The youngster disappeared into the kitchen. Rebecca looked over the back of the sofa to see that she had pulled the door to behind her. With Suzanne out of the way, she pushed Anthony back across the seats and climbed on top of him. She leaned forward to whisper into his ear and then to kiss him.

'Is this what Suzanne means by "being naughty"?'

Before Anthony could reply, the kitchen door opened again and Suzanne put her head around it.

'Would you like some toast, Becky?'

Rebecca raised her head to look over the back of the sofa to reply.

'No, thank you.'

'Are you sure you won't have some?'

'No. I had my tea before I came out.'

'I really don't mind making some for you. Honest.'

'All right, Suzanne. I'll have some toast.'

The little head disappeared back behind the kitchen door once again. Rebecca leaned forward in a second attempt to kiss him.

'That should keep her busy for a bit longer.'

'What! Don't you kid yourself, Becky, she'll be back again in a minute.'

Sure enough, within a few seconds, Suzanne returned to ask even more questions. Having frustrated her plans for a romantic evening, Rebecca decided to sit up. The two of them swung their legs around and sat side by side facing the television.

'Sorry about that.'

'Never mind, Tony. We'll be able to continue where we left off when she's gone to bed.'

'Doing what?' enquired the youngster, not wishing to miss out on something important.

'Never you mind, young lady,' Rebecca added. 'Anyway, what are you going to put on for us to watch?'

Suzanne hunted through her small collection of videocassettes for something suitable. Eventually, her hand rested on one of the boxes and she turned to address Rebecca.

'I thought we'd have "Winnie the Pooh". Is that all right with you?'

'Great! I always liked "Winnie the Pooh" when I was your age.'

She took the box down from the shelf and slipped out the cassette.

'Is that all right with you too, Granddad?'

'Yes, that's fine by me.'

She placed the film into the video recorder and then went off into the kitchen again as she could hear the kettle boiling. Within a couple of minutes, she returned with a tray. On it, were two pieces of toast and a wobbly mug of tea, some of the contents of which had spilt over the side of the mug. She placed the tray onto the floor and handed Rebecca the tea. She took one sip of it and winced. Not wishing to appear impolite, she took another mouthful.

'I hope it's all right. I couldn't reach the box of tea bags, as someone had put them away in the top cupboard. Still, I did find one in a cup in the sink and so I used that.'

Rebecca spat the tea back into the mug and hurriedly returned it to the tray.

'Not going to drink it then?' Anthony asked, mischievously.

'No. It's a little too hot at the moment and I want to try some of this lovely toast that Suzanne has made for me, before it goes cold.'

Rebecca began to eat the toast. It wasn't actually that bad. It was reasonably hot and had not been allowed to stay in the toaster long enough to be cremated. When she finished the last slice, she put the plate back onto the tray and then placed the tray onto the lounge table beside her purse and keys that she had put there earlier.

'Oh! That reminds me, seeing those keys of yours, Becky.'

Anthony got up from the sofa and went upstairs to the bedroom. A short while later, he returned holding a bunch of keys in his hand.

'Take these! I can never remember which one opens which lock, but the big one will definitely start the engine.'

He bent down and handed them to her.

'Oh, of course. I forgot all about the boat keys. That's the reason I came over this evening, isn't it?'

'I would hope that your prime reason for coming over here was to be with me.'

'Yes, of course it was.'

Rebecca placed the keys inside her purse. Surprisingly, she had actually said what she really felt, in her initial reaction to being handed them. She really didn't care a damn about the boat trip the next day, and in her excitement to be with the man she loved that evening, she had genuinely forgotten about collecting the keys.

She settled back into Anthony's arms and Suzanne got up onto the sofa and laid her head in Rebecca's lap. She felt so relaxed in this "family" atmosphere that she wished the evening would go on forever. She was dreading tomorrow evening. Not only would she be away from Anthony, but out with Jon and Kyle on some illegal escapade. Then there was Thursday. That could turn out to be even worse once Jon had considered that Anthony had fulfilled his useful purpose. It was all getting too much to think about.

'I know. Just lie back and enjoy tonight with people who love you, Rebecca,' she thought to herself.

Chapter Nineteen

Wednesday morning, Rebecca was up bright and early and ready to go to work. She had arrived home rather late the night before and assumed that Jon had already gone to bed. Creeping along the hallway and into the lounge, she was surprised to see him sprawled across the sofa, half asleep, and with the light turned off. He had decided to wait up for her. Although at first he grumbled at her for staying over at Anthony's place all evening, he was nevertheless relieved to hear that she had returned with the keys to the speedboat. As it was late, there was no further lengthy discussion on the matter before they retired to bed.

Without stopping to have breakfast, she left the house and made her way along the street towards the bus stop. She never took the car to work with her, as the bus proved to be such an easy journey, without the problem of finding somewhere to park the car when she arrived there. Jon of course was still in bed. He probably wouldn't rouse himself until ten-thirty and then waste the rest of the day, knocking around with his unemployed friends.

As she strolled along, her mind was on the previous evening that she had spent with Anthony and Suzanne. It had been such a long time since she had experienced that family atmosphere and she had enjoyed it immensely. In fact, she was so wrapped up in her thoughts that she failed to notice the car that drew alongside her.

There were two occupants inside the vehicle. One of them, a young man in his twenties, was behind the wheel. His passenger, a smartly dressed older man was sitting in the back seat. As they pulled into the kerb, this older man leaned across the seats and lowered the car window.

'Rebecca!'

She turned to see who was calling to her and noticed the large black car with the two men inside. By this time, the passenger had opened the door and was beckoning to her to get in.

She went over to the vehicle and stooped to look inside. Having satisfied herself as to the occupants, she ducked her head and slid across the seats. Closing the door behind her, she turned to face the older man, who welcomed her with a smile. Before settling down to speak with her, he instructed the driver to move off.

'Well, Rebecca. It's been a while since we last got together.'

'Yes. Must be a couple of months or so now. I've only ever managed to get to speak to your colleagues in recent weeks. How are you?'

'Fine!'

'I hope you won't mind me saying this, but I haven't got a lot of time to spare. I don't wish to be rude, but I've got to be at work in half an hour and I don't want to be late.'

'That's OK. I'll drop you around the corner from where you work, after we have had some time to chat about things.'

'Thanks. You realise that I shouldn't be seen talking to you.'

'I know. Relax!'

The car sped off and took the main road out of town. They experienced very little congestion in the direction in which they were heading, although the commuter traffic coming the other way was quite heavy and there were some long queues. Reaching the outskirts, the driver turned onto a much quieter road and headed along the coast. Throughout the drive, the two passengers conversed.

'Anyway Rebecca, how's your dad?'

'He rang me the week before last. He's keeping well.'

'Good. I got a letter from him about a month ago. That small business of his seems to be expanding. I hear he's got six men working for him now.'

'Yes. It's good news, isn't it?'

The stranger nodded in approval.

'He's invited me to go out there next summer. I'll be taking my wife along too. It'll be good to renew our friendship.'

'Well. The two of you do go back a long way.'

'That's true!'

Rebecca sat back and stretched her legs. She placed her shoulder bag on the floor between them and settled back into the seat. She then looked across at her companion again.

'I hear you're not doing so bad yourself, Jack. I understand you're in line for superintendent.'

'So rumour has it. It'll mean transferring to the Met though.'

'Will that bother you?'

'No. But my wife isn't too keen to move to London. She's got lots of friends in the West Country.'

'I hope you get the promotion though. You deserve it. Still, you haven't picked me up just to talk about my father, have you?'

'No, I haven't. How are things between you and Jon?'

Rebecca answered him with a sigh.

'Slowly getting worse.'

'How you managed to get yourself into this mess in the first place beats me. Your father would have a fit if he knew.'

'Jon was charming and attentive when I first met him and I was happy. Most women find him handsome too, so I considered myself very fortunate. I wasn't to know that he was a petty criminal when I invited him to move in with me.'

'I guess we all make mistakes.'

'Yes, and I'm beginning to regret mine.'

Rebecca observed that the driver had driven full circle and was now coming back into town again. This time he was making slower progress as he joined the rush hour congestion.

'You know, Becky, we nearly caught the three of them on the estate the other night. We had to leave the job to uniform as my officers were dealing with another urgent matter at the time. We caught one of them, but he was little better than useless under interrogation.'

'Yes. I noticed that Jon had come home looking rather unkempt. From the state of his clothes, he seemed as though he had been crawling along the ground on his stomach.'

'Not surprised. The two of them were being chased for some distance. They managed to give the officers the slip by taking to the back gardens.'

'I see.'

'There's just one thing that don't add up though, Becky. You told us that Jon was meeting this "Mr Big" that night.'

'That's right. That's what he told me just before he left.'

'Well, my officers know most of the trash on our patch, but all the ringleaders head up groups of petty criminals. We are at a loss to know who would mastermind a major crime of this sort, like the one you're taking on this evening.'

'I'm sorry, Jack, I can only pass on to you what he told me.'

In Jon's effort to appear someone of considerable importance in the criminal world, he had elevated Darren Baxter to that of master criminal in order to impress his girlfriend. Then, to ensure that such gross exaggeration remained undetected, he had conveniently dodged the questions that she had asked of him in her effort to establish the name of this seemingly important felon.

'So I take it that the pickup tonight is still on, is it?'

'Yes.'

'What about the guy who's supplying the boat?'

'Oh! He knows absolutely nothing about it. He thinks he's lending me the boat so I can take out a female friend of mine this evening for a trip along the coast.'

'Is he likely to get wise as to the real reason for the trip?'

'No. He's very trusting.'

'OK, then. I do hope you know what you're doing.'

'So do I, Jack!'

'I've alerted Customs and they're going to keep a watch out for the boat making the drop. They won't make a move unless the exchange takes place, otherwise there's no evidence.'

By now, the car had made its way down the back roads towards the High Street. The streets were crowded with commuters going to their workplaces. Just around the corner from where Rebecca worked, the driver pulled into the kerb. The senior police officer turned to her to give her one more piece of advice.

'Look, Becky. Be careful tonight. If you should change your mind about going through with this, then let me know as soon as possible.'

'I will do, Jack.'

Picking up her shoulder bag, Rebecca got out of the car and then watched it pull away. It soon disappeared into the traffic in the High Street. She then crossed the road and turned the corner, arriving at work just five minutes late.

Chapter Twenty

The next day, Anthony decided to relax in the garden and catch up on his reading. He fancied a rest from driving, and from sitting in the traffic jams that were all too frequent in this part of the country now that the tourist season had arrived. The weather report that morning had forecast warm sunshine throughout the day, turning to heavy showers later in the evening. With this in mind, he hoped that this would not spoil Rebecca's boat trip with her friend.

Much to Mike's disappointment, she had gone home the previous evening long before Mike and Julia had returned. Nevertheless, their daughter gave them chapter and verse as to what she was like and what they did together. She told them how much fun it had been for all of them that evening.

It was obvious to her parents that Suzanne liked her from the great praise that she lavished upon her, culminating in the fact that she really didn't want her to go home. Rebecca seemed to feel the same way too, and was happy to have the youngster around for the rest of the evening. It had gone midnight before Rebecca left and Suzanne had gone to bed, a fact which mercifully for Anthony, she had left out of the conversation with her mother. Julia would have been extremely annoyed that she had been put to bed so late, especially with a school day coming up the next morning.

Everyone looked a bit bleary eyed over breakfast, and getting ready for school and work had been quite a struggle for all three of them. Anthony however was in the enviable position of being able to go back to bed again after having breakfast with them. He didn't lie there for long though, as that would have been a waste of such a beautiful day. Hence his decision to soak up the sun in a deckchair in the back garden.

He thought it best to do something useful by mowing the grass, before settling down to read the novel that he had brought with him. It looked as if it needed a cut, and he felt that he should do it now lest the weather change for the worse.

It was a very neat garden, and one which Julia had given so much of her time and devotion to. Her mother had been a great one for gardens too, and always had a selected plot in which to grow fresh vegetables. She would often tell her husband that they tasted so much better when she had grown them herself. Julia, on the other hand, wasn't one to grow vegetables but instead her garden was a blaze of beautiful flowers.

When he had finished cutting the grass, and had returned the mower to the shed, Anthony sat back in the deckchair to read his book. He wasn't one to do a lot of reading, and this novel had already taken him several weeks just to get through the first few chapters.

As he lay there reading, his mind started to wander, and he found that after only a few paragraphs he was thinking about Rebecca again. Shutting his eyes, he could visualise her beaming smile and almost hear her endearing chatter. What an attractive girl! Surely a girl like that must have had a string of boyfriends over the years. The more he thought about it, the more perplexed he became. Her past was a complete mystery to him. She had never mentioned a single previous relationship, even though one could not imagine that such a good-looking girl could possibly have gone through her late teens and early twenties without at least one romantic affair to talk about.

Placing his book down on the lawn beside his chair, he began to relax. It would be at least another three or four hours before school was out, and Julia and Suzanne were home. The family had planned to take him as far as the local that evening, so they could sit outside in the pub garden and enjoy a drink. It was an ideal place for them to chat and unwind.

They were due to take Suzanne with them too. This would not have presented them with a problem as the pub catered for families with youngsters. However, before setting out for school that morning, Julia had received a telephone call from the mother of Suzanne's best friend, to ask if she could stay over at their place for the night. Naturally, Suzanne considered that an evening with her best friend was infinitely more desirable than one with her mum and dad.

Julia was happy with the situation too. It appeared that on the last occasion they took Suzanne to the pub, it had been most embarrassing for them. As they took their nine-year-old through the bar and into the garden, the landlord had asked them what they would like to drink. "Mine's a vodka and lime", Suzanne had yelled. Her father told her to be quiet, but she protested in a very loud voice that she'd always enjoyed a vodka and lime at home.

Although some of the drinkers in the bar had realised that the youngster was just being mischievous, many of the elder residents of the local community took her literally. They were shocked at the thought of a child being plied with drink by her parents at such a young age. It looked even worse when Mike placed his hand over Suzanne's mouth to shut her up and dragged her into the pub garden to give her a good reprimand. His daughter of course thought it was very funny to embarrass her parents in front of their neighbours. Maybe it was just as well that she was going elsewhere for the evening!

Meanwhile across town, two other characters were rather busily at work inside their small lock-up on the housing estate.

Darren Baxter and Nick Henderson were rummaging through their stolen property, which had yet to be fenced. The place was like an Aladdin's cave. There were stereos, hubcaps, and spare wheels taken from an assortment of vehicles, alongside cardboard boxes containing DVD players and discs, video recorders, and computer games. The latter items had all come from a warehouse job they had done a few days before.

'Just pile that lot up in the corner, Nick. We haven't got room to move in here.'

'When are we going to shift this lot?'

'When Dave comes back from his holiday. He's already got a buyer for most of it.'

Nick continued to stack the sealed boxes containing the stolen electrical equipment, on top of each other. They reached almost to the ceiling, leaving behind a convenient space in which to manoeuvre. When he had finished, he then began sorting through the DVDs, which were lying in a heap on the floor. In the meantime, Darren sat on a crate in the corner to watch him. It was obvious that something was troubling him by the expression on his face.

'You OK, Darren?'

'I'm just a bit peeved. That Jon really gets up my nose.'

'D'you think he did tell the law about us the other night?'

'He must have done. Who else would have known we were meeting up? I'll tell you, Nick, we are going to teach Jon a lesson. One that he won't forget.'

'Sound's good, Darren. Shall I go and get my baseball bat?'

'No, you pillock! We're not going to kneecap him.'

'So, we ain't gonna hurt him then, Darren?'

'No. I've a much better plan than that, my intellectually challenged friend.'

'Yes! Right! I like it. Intellect and challenge, eh Darren? Like in Mission Impossible?'

Nick held up the DVD for Mission Impossible II, to demonstrate his point.

'No, you buffoon! We're going to plant some of this gear on him. We'll put some of those DVD players over there in his garden shed.'

'Yes, but that's some of our most profitable stuff.'

'I know it is, but it's also got his fingerprints all over them. Remember when we got back from the job, he took his gloves off to take the players out of their boxes to examine them.'

'That's right. You told him he was an idiot for doing so.'

'Yep, and those are the items over there.'

Darren went over to a small stack of boxes. He removed six of them and carefully placed them into two sturdy black sacks, with the minimum amount of handling. After all, he didn't wish to add his fingerprints to those already there.

'Now! Whilst Jon is out on his spree this evening, I want you to store these in his garden shed. Make sure you hide them away under something suitable if you can, so they're not found straightaway. It's unlikely that Jon ever goes to the shed. He's too darn lazy to do gardening.'

'But isn't that his girlfriend's place?'

'Yes, but it won't make any difference to the forensic lads. He'll still be caught with his dabs all over the stolen gear.'

Nick looked puzzled. Most of Darren's plans had to be spelt out to him in very simple terms.

'How are the police going to know that they're there?'

'Because, my dense pal, I am going to tip them off. Then we'll see how Jon likes to be grassed on.'

'Right! I've got it now.'

'That's great, Nick.'

Darren drew breath. It was always a struggle, but he usually got through to Nick in the end.

'What happens next then, Darren?'

'Well. The law will find the stolen gear and link it straight to him. It's unlikely they'll need a warrant to go snooping around an unlocked shed. So there's no problem there. I've already got a good alibi for the night we nicked the stuff, just in case he blabs. Then, with that and his previous record, he's bound to go down for a fair stretch and be out of my way for a good while. I owe him that one for the other night.'

Nick paused for thought.

'So what is it you want me to do then, Darren?'

Darren put his head in his hands and groaned.

Whilst this conversation took place, Jon was standing outside Kyle's workplace, waiting impatiently for him to join him in the lunch break. As the expression goes, one could imagine that his ears were burning. He had thought it strange though, that Darren had not considered meeting him for a further update on the evening's plan. Nevertheless, he didn't wish to appear ignorant, and therefore intended to proceed on the basis of the information he had already been given.

Kyle came out dead on one 'o' clock and the two of them strolled across the road and down to the quay. As they sat on the wall, he got out his lunch box and began to eat his sandwiches.

'I've done really well at work today. The boss called me in and gave me a pay rise. He said I'd turned out a lot better than he thought I would have, when he hired me.'

'That's great, Kyle! Now! Let's get down to business.'

'He also says they're going to train me to do more complicated work, and that'll mean promotion.'

Jon was becoming frustrated with the interruption.

'I'm very pleased for you. Now, about this job this evening.'

Kyle was very disheartened by the fact that Jon was taking very little interest in his good news. It had been the first time he had ever been employed, and after such a long period on the dole, he felt very optimistic for once. The boss of the company liked the lad and found that he was willing to work, so he had encouraged his new employee to learn a variety of skills.

'You don't sound very interested, Jon.'

His friend was rather surprised by the remark.

'But I am, Kyle, although there are more important matters to talk about at the moment'

Kyle wasn't going to let the matter rest.

'Becky helped me to get this job and she believes in me.'

'Yes. I know she does.'

'Then there's my boss. He encourages me all the time.'

Jon showed signs of impatience, which were detected by his friend.

'I've been giving it a lot of thought lately, Jon. It seems to me, that all you're interested in is you.'

Jon's jaw dropped. He had never known Kyle to stick up for himself before. He had always managed to run roughshod over his feelings in the past. In fact, he was rather annoyed that other people were having such a great influence over his pal's attitude. He knew that if he allowed this to continue, he would lose control over him altogether. Although he felt aggrieved, his voice took on a more conciliatory tone.

'Come on, Kyle. We've been mates for a long time. It's great to hear that you're doing so well at work, but you've got to understand that we've still got another job to do. I hope you're not going to let me down this evening.'

'No. I promised I would go with you, and I will. But that'll be the last time. No more bent deals, no more scams, I'm going straight from then on.'

Kyle had a determined look on his face.

'Suit yourself! You're going to miss out on all the fun though.'

'What! Behind bars.'

'Rubbish! They've got to catch me first.'

'But your luck's going to run out one day.'

Although Jon bluffed his way through the rest of his discussion with Kyle, the earlier remarks had taken the wind out of his sails. As he explained about the job that evening, his friend showed less than his usual enthusiasm. By the time they parted company, he was feeling a little despondent.

To lift his spirits, he joined his other time-wasting friends at a pub in town for most of the afternoon. When he eventually arrived home, Rebecca too had a go at him for leaving a heap of washing up in the sink. It was clearly not his day.

Julia, Suzanne and her friend were the first to arrive home. They found Anthony on his hands and knees weeding the flowerbeds in the back garden.

'You didn't have to do that, Dad.'

'I know, but it kept me amused for an hour or so. I've just about finished now, which is good timing.'

Whilst her father put the gardening tools away, Julia took Suzanne and her friend across the road to her friend's house, where she intended to stay the night. By the time she had returned, Anthony had smartened himself up. He had also made a pot of tea for the two of them, and they chatted together as they waited for Mike to come home.

The time seemed to pass quickly, during which Julia prepared a salad for tea. Shortly after six, they heard Mike's car drive up. Anthony went out to meet him.

'So it's just the three of us up at the pub tonight then, Mike?'

'Yes. Suzanne wanted to go to her friend's house this evening instead.'

'I know. Julia told me.'

'It's worked out a lot better this way. We would have needed to return home much earlier if she had been with us; you know, what with school and all that tomorrow.'

'Mustn't have too many late nights then?'

Anthony felt rather guilty, as he had contributed to Suzanne's being very tired that morning, by allowing her to stay up so late the previous evening. Fortunately, she didn't tell on him.

'No. We don't mind her going over to Rachel's place. Her mum always sees that they get to bed at a reasonable time and also takes them both to school the following morning. We do the same for Rachel when she stays at our house.'

Julia then appeared at the front door.

'The food is ready when you are.'

Mike locked his car and they went inside.

Julia had decided upon a salad for the three of them, as a cooked dinner would have been too much on such a warm day. Throughout the meal, they had to endure Mike's recollection of his conversations with the partners of his solicitors firm, from the dinner party the evening before, which was about as riveting as watching paint dry.

Suitably fed, Anthony and Mike cleared the table and washed up, while Julia got herself ready. As she was dressing casually, the makeover on this occasion took very little time. She was in fact downstairs again long before her husband had found a spare moment to change out of his suit. However, once the three of them were ready, they strolled along to the local pub.

It was only a short walk of no more than a few minutes. As they arrived, it started to cloud over and looked very much as though they were in for some rain. Most of the drinkers must have been of the same opinion, as the pub garden was almost deserted. In view of this, they decided it was best not to drink outside. Mike went across and held the door open for them and once inside, they met many of Mike and Julia's friends and neighbours.

Anthony went up to the bar and bought a round of drinks for the family. He then carried them back to where the others had found a table that was free. For a short while, Mike continued with the less than scintillating conversation that had taken place at home during the meal. However, much to Anthony's relief, they were soon joined by a few of Mike's friends from his golf club, together with the neighbours who lived across the road from their house.

As the circle around them got bigger, they acquired another of the adjacent tables and some of the spare chairs. Being in the company of his golfing friends, Mike felt that he had to keep the discussion at a sufficiently intellectual level, which involved prattling on about the Government's shortcomings and the problems with the European Commission. Occasionally, his friends would interrupt him to add their own views on the subject, as Anthony and Julia sat silently and listened.

After an hour or so, the debate became rather tedious as many of the topics under discussion were often repeated. Even their neighbours looked as though they were about to nod off with boredom. Mike's views were to the right of the political scene. He had no great love for the current Government and could find no merits in any of its policies. Admittedly, he had a great knowledge of the subject upon which he was talking, but it was nevertheless a rather dull subject for a social evening out. Having ignored his father-in-law all this time, he decided to bring him into the conversation.

"What's your impression of the Prime Minister, Dad?"

Anthony just couldn't resist this one.

'Well, actually, I don't do political impressions Mike, although I can attempt one of Bruce Forsyth, if you like?'

Mike stared at him in utter disbelief. The remark had taken him by surprise and what was then to follow was to make him feel extremely embarrassed in front of his rather middle class friends.

Anthony got up from his seat to bend his head forward with his fist against his temple and taking up the well-known presenter's customary stance.

'How's this sound, Mike? Nice to see you, to see you, nice.'

It sounded quite authentic and brought a cheer from the neighbours, who now sat up and began paying attention.

'Keep going then,' said Richard, one of Mike's golfing friends. Even he seemed to be relieved that the subject had changed to one with a more light-hearted theme.

'All right, my love?' said Anthony, replying to him with another of the entertainer's expressions.

Just then the well-endowed barmaid came over to collect some of the glasses.

'We don't get anything for a pair!'

'Not in this game!' the others exclaimed. Even the barmaid joined in the merriment.

Mike was mortified. It was rather wicked to have ruined Mike's lecture, especially as everyone around the table was by now joining in the fun. Even his golfing friends had started to tell humorous stories, which brought peals of laughter from their audience.

When one of the group sits poker-faced whilst the other revellers are in stitches, he is inevitably going to be the butt of some of the jokes. Mike was no exception to this rule. They pulled his leg dreadfully. Sadly, he didn't see the funny side of it and sat there totally bemused by it all. The worst culprits were in fact his friends from the golf club. It almost seemed as though they had been waiting for an opportunity like this to take the rise out of him. Eventually, however, they decided that they had exhausted this particular topic.

'All right, all right, calm down! We've had our bit of fun at poor old Mike's expense,' said Richard. 'Let's change the subject.'

Mike looked relieved. Julia felt that she should apologise to her husband for joining in the fun at his expense, even though she still couldn't stop laughing whilst she was making the apology. Having now loosened up the party, several other drinkers joined them and the conversation became more diverse. Even Mike, after drinking a few more shandies, began to loosen up and join in the entertainment. For the next couple of hours, it was great fun. Anthony was really shocked at some of the things that Julia came out with, as they were quite outrageous. He had always thought of his daughter as being quite straight-laced and innocent.

Someone in the crowd then got onto the subject of fishing.

Unfortunately, it happened to be one of Mike's neighbour's favourite pastimes and one that his wife detested.

'There's nothing more relaxing than sitting on the jetty with your baited line in the sea and waiting for the fish to bite.'

'Oh, come on,' said his wife, 'you sit there for hours and hours. I'm sure you only do it to get out of the jobs that need to be done at home.'

'Good Heavens, woman! You've never experienced it, so how would you know of the pleasure it gives me?'

Julia decided to join his wife in the assault upon his hobby.

'How can anyone find pleasure in just sitting on a chair all day, holding a fishing rod, and looking out to sea?'

'People sit on the beach and do nothing for hours on end, just for pleasure, don't they.'

The man felt he had scored a point over the women with this remark.

'Of course! But it isn't quite the same, is it?'

'I think Julia's got a point there,' added his wife. 'At least on the beach you can read a book or watch the kids play.'

Julia was on a roll.

'Yes, and when they do eventually catch something, what do they do with it? They take it off the hook and throw the damn thing back in again.'

The man protested that it wasn't always like that. There were occasions when you did catch fish to take home to eat. Nevertheless, with two determined women hammering away at him, he was going nowhere with this argument. Finally, in order to bring the subject to a swift conclusion, he decided to concede the issue.

Near to closing time, the crowded bar began to clear. It was then that Anthony noticed Caroline, sitting on a barstool beside a guy, possibly in his early forties. He appeared to be trying to take her arm, as if to get her to leave, but she was having none of it and continually pushed him away. As he observed them, a rather heated argument then broke out between the two of them. Only those in the immediate vicinity would have been near enough to have heard the quarrel and establish what was taking place. He watched as the irate guy eventually got up from his stool and stormed out of the pub in a fit of temper, leaving her still sitting at the bar nursing her empty glass. Julia had noticed the confrontation too.

'I think I'll just pop over and see if she's OK, Dad.'

His daughter was naturally as concerned as he was.

'Yes. I think that's probably wise.'

Julia went over and sat on the stool beside Caroline. She then turned to engage her in conversation. Caroline continued to look across the bar with an almost blank expression on her face, and holding her empty glass in her hand. From time to time, Julia would lean forwards and listen attentively to what she was saying. From where he was sitting, Anthony assessed that the single mum must now have had a few too many drinks by the way she clung onto his daughter's arm whenever she spoke to her, presumably in order to maintain her balance on the stool.

To encourage the customers to drink up and go home, the pub lights were flicked on and off a couple of times. The bar staff then began to collect the empty glasses from the tables and take them out the back. Having indicated that closing time was near, people got up to leave and the conversation around the two tables came to an end. Soon, Mike and Anthony were left sitting there by themselves.

'I think we'd better go and rescue Julia,' said Mike.

'That actually wouldn't be a bad idea.'

The two men got up from their chairs and went across to the bar. By this time, Caroline was sitting the other way round and she could see them coming.

'Ah! Here comes the cavalry to take you home, Julia.'

She was really slurring her words.

'Can I buy you boys a drink?'

'No thanks Caroline. Besides, I think you'll find the bar is closed now.'

'But I've only just got here.'

If Caroline had only just got there, as she claimed, she must have been knocking back the alcohol rather fast. She was so drunk that she could barely hold herself up and continued to hold onto Julia for support.

'I think we'd better see you home,' said Julia.

Caroline nodded her head in approval. Julia took her by the arm and helped her up from the barstool. She wavered a bit in a desperate attempt to stand up straight, before the two of them were able to head for the exit.

As she walked towards the door, Caroline became very unsteady on her feet again, and Mike rushed over to her and put his arms around her to hold her up. Whether she would have actually collapsed upon the floor was questionable.

'Are you trying to get fresh with me, Michael? 'Cause if you are, I shall tell your wife.'

Mike had not anticipated her making a remark like that. He stood there in mild embarrassment, as Caroline locked her arms around his neck to maintain her balance. She kept blinking her eyes and swaying from side to side.

'Ooh! Your after-shave is rather potent. I bet it attracts lots of women.'

Mike didn't know quite what to say. Her head was practically resting on his shoulder. Out of the corner of his eye he could see his wife observing his actions and he perceived that all was not well. He was now beginning to wish that he had not been so gallant. To make matters worse, Caroline had started to slip down in the space between his arms. He then had to lower them in order to hold her tightly around the waist to prevent her falling onto the floor.

'Really, Mr Stevens! You're a very naughty solicitor. I noticed you had your hands on my bottom the other night at your party.'

Mike was horrified. He looked across to his wife.

'Julia, I didn't do anything. Honest I didn't. I have no idea what she's talking about. I only danced with her.'

From the expression on her face, Julia was not amused. Although it was hilarious to watch Mike's attempt to squirm his way out of an embarrassing situation, Anthony could see that this drunken dialogue could get a little out of hand. He therefore decided to intervene.

'Let's get her outside and into the fresh air. That should bring her up with a jolt.'

With one on either side of her, they gently eased her towards the door and out into the street. Anthony was right. The cool damp air did revive her to a large extent, at least enough to enable her to walk home with them, very slowly and unaided.

The pavement was very wet and evidence of the fact that it must have been raining earlier that evening. The downpour could well have been quite extensive too from the continuous flow of water along the gutter.

As they strolled along the road towards home, Caroline was yelling abusive remarks about her companion with whom she had argued earlier at the bar. Mike, who was walking alongside her, was doing his best to encourage her to keep her voice down as it was late and all the neighbours would hear her.

Arriving home, Julia suggested to her father that he should take Caroline inside her house and make sure that she found somewhere comfortable to crash out until morning. Mike was eager to help too, but Julia assured him that it only needed one of them to assist her, and that certainly wasn't going to be him. They said goodbye to Caroline and went inside, leaving Anthony to prop her up against her front door. His first problem was to get it open.

'Where's your front door key then, Caroline?'

She stared at him with bleary eyes, without speaking.

'Your door key, Caroline. Where is it?'

Again she swayed gently from side to side, without reply, so Anthony endeavoured to release her grip upon her purse and then searched through it for the key himself.

'Do you normally make a habit of riffling... fifulling... rifooling... going through a lady's handbag? I thought you were a gentleman.'

She was obviously attempting the word "rifling" but she was unable to pronounce it in her present condition.

'Caroline, if I don't find the bloody key, we'll be here all night and I shall then forget that I am a gentleman.'

'You don't have to shout at me. I'm perfectly capable of finding it myself. Anyone would think I was drunk or something.'

Anthony waited patiently whilst she fumbled through the pockets of her trousers. She managed to get hold of the key, and then got her fist stuck trying to extract it. It would have been quite comical to watch had it not started to rain again. She made several more attempts but her closed fist around the key kept pulling against the pocket's lining. Eventually, Anthony's patience ran out and he assisted in yanking her hand from her pocket, whereupon she let go and the key fell to the ground. Kneeling down, he hunted through the garden shrubs to retrieve it.

'What on earth are you doing down there?'

'What's it look like I'm doing?'

'Shall I get down there with you?'

'No, Caroline. Please, just stay where you are.'

Caroline knelt down to assist him. She was little better than useless in trying to find the missing key.

'Is this a game?' she whispered.

'No, it's not a game, Caroline. I'm trying to find it quickly so we can get in out of the rain.'

'I am trying to help.'

'Yes, but I could well do without it at the moment. It's got to be here somewhere.'

Anthony held the bushes apart and used the glow from his

daughter's security light next door to enable him to see. Suddenly, it shone upon a metal object. Picking it up, he was relieved to find that it was the missing front door key.

'What a clever man! You've found it.'

'Just move to one side, Caroline. It's going to pour down in a minute.'

Inserting it in the lock, he opened the door and guided her inside. He gently propped her up against the hall wall, whilst he closed the front door. Putting his arm around her waist to keep her steady, he searched for the light switch for the stairs.

'Right, young lady. Now to get you upstairs.'

'Upstairs, it is then, Mr Lewis?'

She raised her eyebrows and gave him one of those "knowing looks".

'Just behave yourself, Caroline.'

He guided her one step at a time to the top of the stairs. The first room he looked into had a small single bed. He deduced that this must belong to Mark, who was of course in Wales. Closing the door, he dragged her further along the landing until he found the main bedroom. She started to become very unsteady on her feet again and almost keeled over, so he picked her up in his arms.

'Ooh! You're very strong, Anthony. Did I ever tell you what lovely eyes you have?'

'No, but you can tell me in the morning.'

'Ah! So you're staying with your little friend Caroline then?' she said in a drunken little girl's voice.

Anthony didn't reply. He placed her across the bottom of the bed, and switched on the bedside light. He then pulled back the covers from the top as far as they would go. Flipping off her shoes, he rolled her inside. Her eyes were already closed. He turned her onto her side and rested her head squarely on the pillow, gently pulling the duvet up over her shoulders. Within seconds she was sound asleep.

'Sleep well, my friend,' he murmured.

He switched off the bedside and landing lights and went downstairs. It was quite simple to find his way to the front door again, even in the dark. Closing it behind him, he dashed across the drives so as not to get too wet. It was pelting down with rain again.

When he got inside, he noticed that all the lights in the house were out, signifying that Mike and Julia had already gone to bed. So as not to disturb them, he crept upstairs without putting on the light and quietly went to his room.

Chapter Twenty-one

Earlier that evening across the other side of the peninsular, Kyle, Jon and Rebecca were driving over to the marina to pick up Anthony's boat. It had been dry and sunny all day and unfortunately it had now turned cloudy. They were hoping that the predicted rain would hold off until after the job had been completed.

Jon seemed so excited at the thought of making several hundred pounds, merely by handling stolen goods from abroad and passing them on to a dealer, that he talked about nothing else all the way there. He told the others what he planned to do with his share of the money. In fact, just listening to him, you would be forgiven for thinking that he was about to come into a small fortune. Kyle however, who had reluctantly gone along with the scam, thought they were mugs for taking all the risks with no guarantee of any reward if they got caught.

After parking the car, Rebecca led them down to the marina to find the boat. Fortunately, it was moored in a fairly accessible position for taking out to sea. As they approached the pontoon, she pointed to the powerful craft.

'There she is. It's similar to the one my father had.'

Kyle was really interested. He had never been that close to a modern pleasure craft and he was greatly impressed.

'Cor! That's great, Becky. At least it's a reasonable size and really smart to look at too.'

He stood back and examined the vessel from bow to stern. It gleamed even though it was overcast.

'I imagined it was going to be like a little ferryboat with an outboard motor. Is it powerful?'

'Yes. She certainly is. She can plane through the water at up to 40 knots on a calm day.'

Kyle continued to feed his curiosity, like a schoolboy who had just experienced his first steam engine close up.

'Look, Jon, it's got cabins too.'

Becky laughed.

'Yep! Two of them, in fact. Come on, let's get on board.'

Jon had no desire to join in the discussion between Kyle and Rebecca. Anything associated with Anthony was of no interest to him at all. He even resented the fact that he had a boat, although it suited his purpose to borrow it for the evening.

Once on board, an argument broke out between Rebecca and her boyfriend as to who was entitled to take the wheel. Jon considered that he was in charge of the operation and therefore calling the shots. Rebecca, on the other hand, saw it from a different perspective.

'Be sensible, Jon! I'm responsible for this boat and you aren't.'

'So what are you saying? I'm incapable of driving the damn thing?'

Jon had begun to raise his voice, which was something he always did when he was trying to reinforce his point of view.

'Just calm down, will you? You've never been on a small boat in your life, let alone driven one. Be sensible!'

Jon was seldom rational when he was irate.

'Well, you're not in charge here.'

'For heaven's sake, Jon! The boat was loaned to me, so I've got to look after it.'

'And I won't, I suppose?'

'No. I didn't say that. I have lots of experience with a boat like this. You haven't.'

'Suit yourself then.'

Jon sat down on the deck and sulked. He looked away from his two companions, pulling his knees up to his chest and clasping his arms around them to hold them in place. She knew that when he was in one of these moods, he'd probably go the other way and not help out at all.

'Can I help, Becky?'

Kyle, in his usual inimitable way was endeavouring to keep the peace between them.

'No. That's OK, Kyle.'

Rebecca inserted the key and started the engine. The powerful craft burst into life. She went across to release the mooring ropes and then returned to the cockpit again. She glanced at Jon, whose face still bore a grumpy expression.

'Jon, why don't you show us where we're going?'

Jon didn't answer. He just wanted to be difficult.

'Don't be so objectionable, Jon. You've got to tell us where we are going.'

He looked across at her with a nonchalant expression on his face.

'Oh! So you want my help now, do you?'

'Don't talk stupid! You're the only one who knows where we're supposed to meet this other boat.'

'So!'

'So, how about some directions! Anthony keeps his maps in a locker over there.'

With one hand on the wheel, Rebecca pointed to the locker with the other.

'Well, good old Tony! Whatever would we do without him?' said Jon, sarcastically.

Ignoring her request, he sat back to watch Rebecca manoeuvre the boat across to the entrance of the marina and out to sea. She knew he was now going to be hard work, but she desperately needed to know whether to sail east or west.

'Right! I'll ask you again. Where are we going then, Jon? I need the map reference so I can get my bearings. Haven't you got those charts out of the locker, yet?'

Jon looked at her with a blank expression on his face. She may just as well have been speaking a foreign language.

'Jon, you do have the location, don't you?'

'Not exactly.'

'What do you mean by "not exactly"?'

Rebecca became concerned. Although he had so far withheld the details of this scam, the time had now come to impart a few of them.

'Well, the agreement was to meet a couple of miles out to sea off Lamorna Cove.'

'What! You've got to be kidding me! There's an entire ocean out there, you muppet. How are we going to meet this other boat in the dark with that sort of arrangement?'

'Well, I thought we'd just go out from the cove a couple of miles whilst it was still light.'

'And then what? You expect me to sail around in ever increasing circles until we bump into them?'

'No! Of course I don't. I expect us to wait for them.'

Rebecca was becoming very frustrated and couldn't understand his casual attitude to such an important part of the plan.

'I don't believe I'm hearing this.'

'Why? What's your problem?'

'You seriously suggest we anchor the boat offshore and wait for the coastguard to get suspicious?'

Rebecca shook her head in utter disbelief. If she said anymore to Jon right now, she would have blown her top. According to him, the meeting had been set for ten o' clock, when darkness would have fallen. How they were supposed to spot another vessel in the dark, give or take a mile or so, was anyone's guess.

Then there was the daunting prospect of other larger vessels running into them. What a moron! If she had a map reference, she could at least use the global positioning system to pinpoint where they were to meet. The thought of making some easy money was all that had concerned him. It was obvious that he had not made the slightest attempt to think this matter through.

The rest of the journey was made in silence. Jon sat up on deck, staring out to sea. He was now feeling petulant and had therefore decided to ignore his two companions. Kyle sat quietly in the cockpit seat alongside Rebecca, who was taking it easy.

A couple of miles out from the cove, she steered the boat around in a large circle before cutting the engine at the approximate position of the rendezvous, according to the rudimentary details that Jon had given her. Looking around her, there was nothing as far as the horizon in one direction and the coastline in the other. To add to the problem, darkness came much earlier than on previous nights, due to the black clouds which gathered overhead.

'This has got all the hallmarks of a king-sized cock up, you know, Jon,' said Kyle.

'Oh, don't you start on me too. Its enough having that rancorous reptile spitting venom at me.'

Rebecca gave him a blasé look.

'Yes, but she does have a point.'

'Oh! I'm glad it's only just the one. I'd have thought that by now she would have managed to dream up a whole list of complaints.'

'Be reasonable, Jon. Didn't it ever occur to you to ask for a map reference or for some landmark that was clearly identifiable? You know, - a rock, headland, bay - something like that?'

'No, it didn't. So we'll just have to sit and wait, won't we?'

For a few minutes they sat in silence. There was no sign of a boat on the horizon and it was now getting dark. Kyle was at a loss to know what to do, as his two friends were not talking to each other. He had always looked up to Jon as some sort of modern-day hero, but his faith in his best friend was now beginning to crack. With his new-style boldness, he began to question Jon's plans.

'Jon, I don't want to make a fuss, but where did you hear about this job?'

'I've told the two of you before, that's not for you to know.'

Rebecca had been standing silently at the wheel, listening in to the conversation. She was furious with her boyfriend and all this cloak and dagger stuff only served to make her even more angry. She was not sure how much more of it she could take before she packed up and went home again.

'Oh, come on, Jon. Just cut the crap and tell Kyle how you got us all into this mess in the first place.'

'Yes, Jon. I think we have a right to know.'

Angrily, he looked first at Kyle and then at Rebecca and could see from the expression on their faces that they were quite adamant. Although he was very reluctant to impart information to them, he could see that they were determined to question him until he did.

'Darren Baxter.'

'What?'

Rebecca's eyes lit up in amazement. The name was familiar to her. Jon looked at his two companions and noticed that they were awaiting his next remark.

'I met him at the nightclub.'

'What! Darren! I can't believe I'm hearing this,' said Rebecca. 'We are here because you listened to Darren Baxter?'

'Well, yes. He showed me some jewellery that had been smuggled in from the Continent. It was good quality stuff too. He told me how they get it into the country, and asked me if I wanted to make a few hundred quid, by smuggling it in for him. Of course, he wouldn't tell me exactly what was in the package we were going to pick up.'

Rebecca looked on in horror. She was so angry that she could hardly speak.

'Darren Baxter lives in fantasyland most of the time. That's why he hangs around with that idiot, Nick Henderson. He couldn't tell the truth if he tried.'

'But his mates backed up his story.'

'Of course they would, you clown. They're as brainless as he is. They were probably having you on.'

'How would you know? Darren was quite emphatic that this job was for real.'

'For goodness sake, Jon, Darren's only into nicking car stereos and the occasional shop theft. He's hardly some international jewel thief, is he? Besides, if there were a package, it would have more than likely contained drugs. Then we'd have been in deep trouble.'

For the first time since Darren had told him of the scam, Jon had begun to question its authenticity. It was still possible that there was to be a drop this evening, but at best he had entered into the arrangement ill prepared.

Fortunately, Kyle could see the funny side of their predicament and made light of Jon's stupidity. Rebecca, on the other hand, was not amused in the slightest. She had gone through several days of deceit, just to get him this boat.

'Have you any idea how many lies I have had to tell these last few days?'

Jon didn't answer.

'Well, have you?'

'Does it matter?'

'It does to me!'

'Well. It could still be true. There might be a boat out there. Anything's possible.'

Rebecca didn't answer him. As far as she was concerned, it was now irrelevant whether the drop was due to take place or not. She didn't want to be here this evening in any case. Over the past few days, she had found something more important to her, and the idea of handling stolen goods had become abhorrent.

Turning her back to the boys, she looked out across the sea. If only Jon had told her this at the beginning, she could have put him right and saved a lot of hassle for all of them. He should at least have found out from Darren exactly where they were due to meet this boat, and what was in the package. Then they could have weighed up the situation and decided whether it was for real or not.

She pondered further on the matter. Some good had come out of it. If it hadn't been for this stupid idea of Jon's, she would have never met Anthony. She had enjoyed those last few days with him but certainly not the deception.

She lowered her eyes to the wheel that she held in her hands and her anger turned to a smile. The last time she stood here, Anthony had put his arms around her waist and kissed her. That day had been so much fun and so had all the other times that they had shared since. To think that in just those few days, that man had become so enamoured with her that he was even willing to trust her with his boat.

She rubbed her arms as she was beginning to feel the cold. As her hand reached her wrist, she lovingly touched the area where her gold bracelet had been. Yes, to show his love for her the foolish man had even spent a fortune on her, buying not only the earrings but the bracelet too. As she left his daughter's house the night before, he had told her that he would be going out for a drink with his family this evening. Now she wished that she had gone with him.

Just then, she felt a few heavy drops of rain fall onto her shoulders. She tried to ignore them at first, but within seconds, the heavens opened, and it pelted down. A thunderstorm should have come as no great surprise after all those days of sweltering hot weather. Seeing that they were going to get wet, Jon headed for cover below deck, with Kyle closely following on behind.

'Hold on a minute! You're not going to leave me out here in the rain on my own? Come back and help me put up this canopy.'

Jon called out from his sheltered position in the cabin at the bottom of the steps.

'Well, you wanted to be in charge of the boat.'

'Yes. I know I did.'

'Well, now it's all yours.'

Rebecca realised that she couldn't leave the wheel to put up the canopy by herself. It would be too dangerous to allow the boat just to drift aimlessly in the dark. Heaven only knows where they would end up if she had allowed that to happen. As she quickly formulated a plan of action, the rain pelted down and in a matter of minutes she was absolutely soaked through. In view of this, she decided to abandon the idea of setting up the awning in favour of heading straight for home.

The rain swept incessantly across the deck and the visibility was really bad. The wind was blowing so strongly that she was having some difficulty in standing up. The boat was tossed from side to side in the choppy sea and she knew that she would now have to start the engine, and hurriedly make her move. It was hard to believe that the weather could change so dramatically in just a short period of time.

Rebecca fired up the powerful engines and turned the boat around. She was both upset and livid. It also made her angry to think that she was outside, fighting the elements, whilst her companions were below deck in one of the cabins keeping dry. She had only one thing on her mind now and that was to get back to shore.

'Right, you macho pigs, we're going back at full speed.'

She yelled her abuse to the two boys who probably would not have heard her above the noise of the wind and the rain.

The boat lunged forward as Rebecca pushed the throttle and accelerated her to the maximum speed. The sudden transfer of power raised the bow dangerously high in the water on such a choppy sea. John and Kyle, who were looking out through the door, fell backwards onto the cabin floor with tremendous force, as they weren't expecting to take off at such speed. They struggled desperately to haul themselves up again, clinging onto anything to hand. It wasn't easy at that velocity.

In the dark, she was driving mainly on instinct. It was risky, but she was really mad about the situation now. The rain that constantly rolled down her face only made her more and more determined to get back to the marina as quickly as possible.

The boat bounced perilously from side to side as it planed across the waves. In some places, it rose into the air only to belly flop down again upon another breaker. It was a credit to the boat designers that she didn't capsize, having been given such harsh treatment. She recalled how shocked Anthony had been at the way she had driven his car to Plymouth, but he would be having kittens now if he had experienced the way in which she was handling his boat at this precise moment.

Unlike Rebecca, John and Kyle were not used to the sea and the severe rolling was making them feel extremely queasy. Having given up on trying to steady himself into an upright position, Kyle was now lying flat out on his back on the cabin floor.

'I hope she gets back soon, Jon. The movement of this boat is making me feel sick.'

Jon was clinging desperately to the edge of the galley cupboard in order to maintain his balance. If he had let go, he would have fallen on top of his ailing friend.

'Well, if you do, don't throw up in my direction. When we put into shore, she's going to pay for this. You'll see.'

The boat continued to skim the waves. It would have been considered exhilarating had it not been for the adverse weather and the dangerous circumstances in which it was driven. Within a short while, Rebecca could see the lights of the town and the harbour. Although the wind had moderated, the incessant rain had not let up even for a moment's respite. Her hair was tangled and her clothes were now wringing wet, making her feel very uncomfortable.

Approaching the entrance to the marina, she decelerated so fast that it sent Jon flying back across the cabin to the opposite side. As he went down, Jon struck his head on something sharp.

'I'll kill that stupid bitch when I get out of here. Look, I'm bleeding.'

Kyle continued to lie on the cabin floor looking rather pale and disoriented.

'I feel sick, Jon. Help me up, will you?'

If the authorities had observed Rebecca's antics, there would have been all hell to pay. She was now anxious to get home as quickly as possible and away from all this stupidity that had made her so mad.

She carefully but speedily steered around the other boats that were gently rolling in the wind at their moorings. The bow of 'My Julia' thumped against the pontoon in her anxiety to quickly bring the craft to a halt. She switched off the engine and removed the keys. She then dashed across the deck, picking up the mooring rope as she leapt onto the platform. Hurriedly securing the boat, she marched off towards the exit and up the hill to where she had left the car. The two lads were still below in the cabin, sheltering from the downpour, with Jon nursing his cuts and bruises and Kyle holding onto his upset stomach.

'She's going for the car, Jon. I think we'll have to make a run for it.'

'It's still chucking it down outside though.'

'I know, but she'll drive home without us if we don't make a move.'

'She'd better not!'

Jon realised that Kyle did have a valid point. Rebecca was now in such a foul mood that it was quite likely that she would leave them behind.

They made a dash across the boat, and onto the pontoon. The suddenness of standing on something relatively firm again made Kyle giddy. Uncharacteristically, Jon waited for his friend whilst he threw up the contents of his stomach into the English Channel. It seemed to go on for ages, and Kyle still looked very pale and ill afterwards. Now, they too were soaked through in the torrential rain.

Rebecca reached the car after an exhausting walk up the steep hill. Fortunately, as she had been the one to drive there that evening, she still had the keys. She got inside and started the engine. Even though she was now in the dry, her wet clothes were so unpleasant as they clung to her body, that she could derive little comfort from it. The torrential rain had virtually ceased, now moderating to no more than drizzle. The temperature had dropped considerably and everywhere was cold and damp.

Whilst Rebecca had gone for the car, the boys had crossed the road from the marina and were now sheltering in a shop doorway on the corner. They expected Rebecca to come back down the hill again to go home, and therefore decided it was probably best to wait at the bottom. Besides, Kyle was doubled over in pain and was in no shape to attempt a steep incline.

Sure enough, within a short while, she drove down the hill at speed and round to where the boys were waiting. As they saw her coming, they left the doorway to stand by the kerb. Without showing the slightest intention of stopping, she swerved past them and through a giant puddle. The water sprayed like a gigantic wave over the two of them as she continued on around the corner towards home. The lads were drenched from head to foot.

Jon gasped as the cold, dirty water splashed his body.

'You cow! I'll have you for this when I catch up with you.'

He stood in the road, shaking his fist at the car as it disappeared into the distance. He turned to look at Kyle who was dripping with water and shivering.

'I don't feel very well, Jon. I want to go home.'

By the time Rebecca arrived home, the rain had stopped completely. She swiftly parked the car and went inside. She ran upstairs to the bedroom. Without switching on the light, she threw herself onto the bed, and promptly burst into tears. It had been a truly awful evening and she was so upset. With her head resting on the duvet, she once again ran her fingers around her wrist where the bracelet had been and sobbed her heart out.

Later on, having composed herself, she removed her damp clothes and dried herself with a bath towel. Wearily, she got into bed and soon fell asleep.

It was some hours later when Jon got in, having eventually persuaded a taxi driver to come and pick them up. As neither of the two friends had any money on them, he only agreed to take each of them home on the strict understanding that he would be paid when they arrived at the house. Upon arrival, Jon felt at liberty to raid Rebecca's purse for the fare, in view of the fact that she had gone home without him. Mercifully, by this time a lot of his anger had abated, and all he wanted to do now was to go to bed and sleep it off.

Chapter Twenty-two

Anthony had been at work all morning in his daughter's garden. He didn't mind a bit of weeding and cutting back some of the plants that had grown wild over the last few days. Besides, the sun had come out again after last night's thunderstorm and it was quite fresh and pleasant to be out in it.

It had been very kind of his daughter and son-in-law to let him stay with them, and their generosity extended to not accepting any money from him towards the food, even though he had offered it. Julia had also washed and ironed all his clothes during his short stay with them and so he felt the need to repay them for their kindness. Tidying up the garden seemed to be a way in which to thank them.

Just after midday, he went into the kitchen and made himself a drink and then sat in the garden to survey the work he had done so far. He had not been there long, when he heard the next door neighbour's patio door slide back. Looking through a gap between two bushes that he had just cut back, he observed Caroline McBride hanging up her washing on the rotary line.

He called out to her.

'So you managed to get up then?'

Without stopping to look at him, she continued to take washing from her basket and shake out the tangles, before pegging them up on the line.

'Yes. I've even been to work this morning as well.'

'I'm impressed.'

She briefly glanced in his direction.

'I don't let a little thing like a hangover stop me.'

She waited until she had finished pegging up the last of the contents of her basket before walking over to the fence to continue their conversation.

'So this is the casual life of a retired man, is it?'

'Well, I have done some clearing up and weeding so far this morning.'

'So I see. Julia will be pleased. She likes a neat garden.'

Anthony felt it was impolite to chat to her from the comfort of the deckchair and so he decided to get up and go across to the fence.

'You managed to make the morning shift then, you say?'

'Well, I was a bit late, but the manager seemed quite reasonable about it. I suppose it's you I have to thank for putting me to bed last night.'

Anthony nodded.

'I didn't disgrace myself in any way, did I? Only I have a habit of saying things I shouldn't when I have had too much to drink.'

'Oh, no. You were the perfect lady.'

'Well, I certainly can't believe that.'

Anthony grinned.

'Anyway, thanks for seeing me home, all the same.'

Caroline noticed that he had a drink in his hand.

'Would you like a sandwich or something to go with that? I'm going back indoors now to get some lunch for myself, so you're most welcome to join me.'

'Yes, thanks, Caroline. That'll be nice.'

'Tell you what. Come round and you can sit in my garden instead and then if you feel in the mood, you can weed that too.'

'OK! I'll put the tools away and I'll be with you in a few minutes.'

Anthony packed away the garden implements and folded up the deckchair. Having returned them to the shed, he then took his cup indoors and placed it in the sink. Picking up the house key, he went out through the front door and across the drives. As he approached Caroline's house, he could see that she had left the door ajar for him. Crossing the threshold, he went inside and called out to her.

'It's only me, Caroline. Where are you?'

'Come through to the kitchen, Anthony.'

He wandered along the passage and into the kitchen, where he found her standing at the table, slicing bread.

'This is very kind of you.'

'I wouldn't speak too soon. You haven't experienced my sandwiches yet.'

'Well, it's got to be better than Suzanne's toast making.'

'Oh! So you get the toast treatment too?'

'Why? Does she do it for everyone?'

'Oh yes! We all have to suffer Suzanne's toast, that's why I've been trying to teach her how to do something else, like baking her own little cakes and buns, when she comes over here for the evening.'

'I haven't had the pleasure of those yet.'

'You'd be surprised. They're really good. She's gradually getting the hang of it'

Caroline finished making some sandwiches and took them into the garden, together with two cold drinks.

'I take it you like fresh orange juice?'

'Yes. Fine.'

Her garden was about the same size as Julia's, but not so neat. She had done her best to keep the weeds down and to cut the borders around the lawn after mowing it, but it still could have done with a little more attention. Nevertheless, between the confines of her part time work and having only one pair of hands on the job, she had done remarkably well.

'I don't always get drunk when I go out, you know. It's only when I have a few problems.'

‘You don’t have to justify yourself to me, Caroline. We all have different ways of handling these things that are sent to try us.’

‘I’m sure you’re right.’

She placed the plate and drinks on the patio table. Then taking a dry cloth, she wiped the chair seats, where the previous night’s rain had made them dirty. Once they were seated, she offered him a sandwich, which he took and placed beside his glass.

‘I assumed you had something troubling you yesterday evening from the heated discussion you were having with your companion?’

‘You mean Ben?’

‘Well, he did seen rather annoyed, when he stormed out of the door.’

‘He’s just like all the men I’ve known. You see; I’m quite happy to go out with guys for an evening or two, maybe for a drink or a trip to the cinema, or perhaps bowling. It’s good fun and I enjoy it. Unfortunately, they’re not content to leave it at that. They always seem to want more than I am prepared to give them.’

‘And Ben got rather wound up about it, did he?’

Caroline took a sip from her drink and placed it upon the table.

‘Ben had been pestering me all day. He’s driving me mad. He rings me up at work and at home. Just because he has taken me out on a couple of occasions, he thinks he has the right to come over and stay with me, whilst Mark is in Wales.’

‘I see; but you’re not interested?’

‘Well, he’s a nice enough bloke, but he seems to think that just because he paid for the meal we had last Saturday, I should give him his money’s worth in kind. Life isn’t like that.’

‘Sadly though, Caroline. Life is all too much like that nowadays.’

‘But you wouldn’t act like that, would you?’

‘No! But then again, I am considered a bit old-fashioned.’

'Just as well really, seeing that it was you who put me to bed last night.'

Anthony smiled.

'I can't believe some of the things you said to me, Caroline.'

'Oh! I can. Dreadful, aren't I when I've had a little too much to drink?'

She leaned across the table and took his hand. Anthony placed his other hand on top of hers and held it tenderly.

'Caroline, why don't you find a nice man to go out with?'

'What? Like you, you mean?'

'No! I mean a younger man who is going to look after you and your son, and treat you with the respect you deserve.'

'Are there any such men? Just look at me! What smart solicitor in his BMW is going to want to take me to dinner parties and show me off to his middle class friends?'

Anthony shook his head.

'Well, perhaps if you dressed a little more - say, suitably?'

'My dear sweet man. You mean, I shouldn't dress so much like a tart?'

'Oh, Caroline! I didn't mean that for one minute.'

'Yes, you did! You don't have to apologise though. I know I shouldn't dress so flirtatiously, but it gives my deflated ego a boost, when men turn and look at me.'

'But you'd look gorgeous in whatever you decided to wear. You've got the figure to make any clothes look good on you, even those which are a little more subtle. Men couldn't help but notice you. Besides, you've got so much else to offer. Your great personality, for a start.'

Caroline smiled.

'You're right! Come to think about it, my figure hasn't changed a lot since I was in my last year at school. That's nearly twenty years ago.'

'I bet you filled a school uniform very nicely.'

'You know, you're a cheeky beggar. Actually, I think I've

still got it in the loft. I'll have to get it out for you one day.'

Anthony laughed.

She offered him another sandwich, which he took, and after taking a bite from it, placed it alongside his glass. He then sipped the fresh cool orange juice she had made. It was so refreshing to taste that he downed it all in one go.

'You obviously enjoyed that. Would you like another drink?'

'No. That's fine for me, thanks, Caroline.'

She left the table and went indoors, returning shortly with her own glass refilled. She sat down again and continued the conversation.

'Let's talk about you for a change. What's this I hear about you and that young girl you met, who came to look at your boat? I understand from Julia that the two of you have been inseparable ever since.'

'That's right! Rebecca is gorgeous.'

'Well, I gathered that; but not wishing to be rude, what's she up to?'

'You mean, what's a beautiful young girl like her doing with an old man like me?'

'No. I didn't mean it to sound quite like that.'

'Don't worry. It's a question that I keep on asking myself.'

Anthony picked up his sandwich and took another bite. Caroline leaned forward to look him straight in the eyes.

'Don't you consider it rather strange the way in which the two of you met? You're cleaning your boat as she just so happened to be passing by.'

'Yes, but there was a plausible explanation for that.'

'OK! But what about this sudden intense relationship which followed! It all sounds most peculiar to me.'

'Well. Certainly a lot has happened in a short period of time.'

'Yes, it has. But I'm sorry, Anthony. It becomes even stranger when you consider this girl is an absolute stunner and could have any male on the planet, by the sounds of her.'

Anthony paused for thought.

'You're right of course. I have gone over it in my mind at least a hundred times and I can't seem to work it out. I thought at first, it was because she looked upon me as a father figure, seeing as her own father brought her up on his own. Now I'm not so sure.'

'Look! Don't get me wrong Anthony, she could actually be madly in love with you. It does happen, irrespective of age.'

'Oh, I've no doubt about that. I'm convinced she really does love me. I'm not that blind.'

Caroline finished her drink. She didn't question Rebecca's love for Anthony. That appeared to come over loud and clear in Julia's discussions with her on the subject. After all, who else would be able to assess the situation better than his daughter would? It was some of the more practical things surrounding the relationship, which didn't quite add up and were therefore confusing her.

'You see, I'm more concerned about some of the normal things that couples do which are missing from this relationship of yours.'

'Such as?'

'Well, look at Ben, for example.'

'The frustrated boyfriend!'

'Exactly! He's desperate to come over here and stay the night, if only I'd let him.'

'But you don't want him to.'

'That's not the point! Here's a girl, madly in love with you and who, I understand from Julia, lives on her own. Yet, she has never considered inviting you into her house, even to wait whilst she gets changed. Then again, when you return home after the date, she still doesn't ask you in. Even my evening dates get a cup of coffee when they bring me home, irrespective of the fact that I throw them out afterwards. Don't you think that's very odd?'

'I suppose it is.'

'Have you ever suggested you'd like to see the inside of her home?'

'It's never occurred to me to ask. Whenever I have picked her up, she has always been looking out for me. So I haven't had to get out of the car.'

'What about when you take her home.'

'Well, it's usually been late and she's tired. If it's been earlier in the day, she's had to rush off to work, or to go shopping, or something. I must admit it does seem rather odd, but then I don't have a naturally suspicious mind.'

Anthony sat back in the seat and reflected upon their conversation. Caroline had only confirmed the unanswered questions that he had been mulling over in his mind, over the last few days. The problem must also have been worrying Julia too, as she was normally so confidential about family matters. It was obvious that she must have confided in Caroline on a number of occasions, telling her of her concerns for her dad and this mysterious young lady.

Caroline finished her drink and her sandwich before returning to the subject.

'There's another part of the puzzle as well, Anthony, that I don't quite understand. She may have told you something of the earlier part of her life, but what about those more recent events in the weeks before she met you. You surely didn't assume she spends her evenings sitting in front of the television knitting, did you?'

'Well, I did ask her what she did before I came on the scene, and she said that most evenings she would go out with her friends for a drink or to the nightclub.'

'All right. That's sound credible enough; but then she tells one of her pals that you have a boat. This pal then suggests to Rebecca that she asks you if they can borrow it to go out for the evening. Go out where? Surely, if you wanted to borrow a boat, you'd arrange for access to it on a sunny Saturday or

Sunday afternoon. Then you can go to a beach or for a trip along the coast.'

'Yes. I get your point. But every one of these mysteries could have a convincing explanation....'

'Come on, Anthony! Wake up! There are far too many mysteries for one young attractive girl to dream up in less than one week.'

Anthony reluctantly agreed.

'She also says some very strange things to me at times and I haven't a clue what she's on about. There's obviously something troubling her.'

'Why don't you ask her what it is?'

'I don't like to.'

'Why? Because you might find something out about her that you wished you hadn't.'

'No. I don't think it's that.'

It was good of Caroline to show such concern for him and to get him to at least query some of those unexplained areas of his relationship with Rebecca. She seemed to have given the matter a lot of thought, probably spurred on by his anxious daughter. Now that they had come to the same conclusion in that all was not exactly as it should be, the question was "what should now be done about it".

'Can I suggest something without offending you?'

'Yes. Fire away.'

'You obviously don't want to ruin a wonderful affair by making her aware of your suspicions, especially if they are subsequently unsubstantiated. As I said before, she might genuinely be in love with you, and there maybe some very good reasons that we haven't thought of that explain her rather bizarre actions.'

'Yes. I wouldn't want to upset her unnecessarily.'

'Well, then. Why not pay her a surprise visit when she gets home from work this evening. Take her some flowers. Say you bought them on the spur of the moment and they won't keep until the following day without putting them in water. She'll have to invite you in then, and who knows you may find that we've both been worrying needlessly.'

'Hmm! That sounds like a good idea to me. I'll try and get there around five-thirty. She would have just got in from work at that time. Hopefully, she won't mind my turning up unexpectedly. Thanks, Caroline.'

They got up from the table and went inside. He thanked her for lunch and for her advice. As he reached her front door, she wished him good luck and kissed him on the cheek. He in turn put his arms around her and gave her a hug. During this short visit to his daughter's family, he had made a good friend of their charismatic neighbour.

Chapter Twenty-three

For the rest of the afternoon, Anthony kept himself busy doing odd jobs around his daughter's home. He tried not to think about the unhappy possibilities that could arise from a visit to Rebecca's house, later that day. Instead, he decided to meditate positively. He knew that the love she had shown him was genuine, which was something he didn't doubt for a moment. As for his fears, brought on by some very odd unexplained situations in their relationship, he dismissed them as completely unfounded. He could not give credence to any convincing explanation as to why he should not think otherwise.

However, he needed to settle the matter once and for all. Caroline was right. Only by going over to Rebecca's home unannounced would he then know for sure. Although, he found the prospect rather daunting, he was nevertheless convinced that it was the only way forward.

It was crucial to get a present before the shops closed, so he popped out in the car to the nearest florist to buy a bouquet of flowers. He drew no pleasure from the assignment, as that awful nagging feeling inside him refused to go away. Feeling rather low, he couldn't bring himself to even write a message on the accompanying card.

When Julia and Suzanne arrived home from school, they found him still very active about the house. He had cleaned the wash basin and the sink and had vacuumed the carpets in all the rooms. As they entered the lounge, he had just completed the family's ironing and was about to put the ironing board away.

'You didn't have to do all that for me, Dad!'

He didn't answer her, but continued to fold up the board. He then returned the hot iron to the kitchen and sat it on its heel on the top of the work surface to cool down. She guessed that something was wrong.

'Julia, I've got to go out somewhere at five, so I'll probably have to skip tea. Is that OK?'

'Yes, of course, Dad.'

She knew better than to ask him where he was going. Her father was obviously distressed, which made any conversation between them very difficult during the remaining time before he left. Whilst Julia's lack of obvious questioning came as a relief to Anthony, it also signified that she knew that he had a problem and could probably deduce with a degree of accuracy what that problem was. Although Suzanne remarked upon the beautiful bunch of flowers on the hall table, Julia did not add to his embarrassment by commenting upon them further.

At five, he picked up the bouquet of flowers and went out to the car. He placed them on the passenger seat beside him and then readjusted the rear mirror that he had accidentally knocked askew as he leaned over. He sat for a while and stared out through the windscreen. He knew he was leaving far too early, but wanted to get out of the house before Mike came home. Whilst it was unlikely that his son-in-law would be home so soon after five, Anthony did not wish to take that chance. Mike didn't have his wife's diplomacy and would probably ask him point blank what exactly was going on.

At first, he drove down to the esplanade and parked overlooking the beach. He spent around twenty minutes or so, sitting in the car and watching the breakers roll onto the shoreline. He also observed that the previous night's thunderstorm had not dampened the expectations of the sunbathers, who were lying on the sands in the late afternoon sunshine.

As he drove across town and out to the suburbs, he sensed that this trip over to Rebecca's place was not going to bode well. It's strange how the mind subconsciously prepares you for that inevitable shock. It's almost as though one's brain adds up all the facts and comes to that inescapable conclusion that the heart just won't accept, until eventually confronted head-on with the dilemma.

About a quarter to six, Anthony reached the house. He parked outside, and taking the flowers from the seat beside him, got out of the car. He strolled down the path and up to her front door. He had never stood here before. His mind was racing, trying to cover all the possibilities as to what he would find behind it. He rang the bell and waited for what seemed like an eternity, even though it was probably no more than a few seconds. He knew Rebecca was home as her car was parked at the front of the house. Eventually, he heard a shuffling noise from the inside and the door opened.

He was not prepared for what he was about to encounter. To his complete amazement, the person who came to the door was Jon, the young man with whom he had become involved with in a dispute at the nightclub, a couple of days before. When Jon saw Anthony, his face broke into a wide smile.

'Hey, Becky! Come down here a minute. It's that stupid old geriatric again and it looks as though he's brought you some flowers. At least, I take it they're for you and not for me.'

Anthony stood on the doorstep, stunned into silence. Even in his worst nightmare he could not have anticipated being confronted by the hostile youth on Rebecca's own threshold. His heart sank and he began to feel rather faint.

Having heard Jon calling to her, Rebecca appeared at the top of the landing and slowly came down the stairs, only to stop halfway when she realised to whom he was referring. She gripped the banister rail and stared down at the figure in the doorway, not knowing what to say. It was obvious that she had just arrived home from work and was about to change into some casual clothes, due to her state of partial undress. Anticipating what was going through Anthony's mind, Jon spoke again.

'Yes, it's true. I live here with Becky. What's more, we both sleep together in the same room.'

Jon was enjoying this encounter and got some perverted pleasure out of adding the last unnecessary remark, merely to reinforce their relationship. It was cruel of him to do so, but the spiteful boyfriend was showing just how insensitive he could be.

Eventually, Rebecca mustered up the courage to speak, and did so in a quiet and almost pleading voice.

'Oh, Tony. I am so sorry. I'm so very, very sorry. I really didn't mean to hurt you. I didn't want you to find out like this.'

Her speech was very shaky and she was now visibly trembling. Meanwhile Anthony was doing his best to remain composed in the face of such an awful shock to his system.

'But you've humiliated me, Becky. Why?' he asked, in a gentle enquiring manner.

Her eyes were now filled with tears. She struggled anxiously to speak but the words just wouldn't come. Besides, what could she say? She wanted desperately to tell him that she did really love him but in the present circumstances, it would probably have sounded like hollow words.

'Well. What made you do it? Was it for a bet or a dare? What?'

Anthony's eyes moved across from Rebecca and back to Jon again. Her boyfriend could barely contain his excitement at the thought of giving this broken man a full explanation of what it had all been about.

'Yep! It's quite simple really. We needed to borrow a boat for a job we were going to do and you had just what we wanted. Becky was the bait and you fell for it. Isn't that just typical of men your age? Couldn't turn down the chance of going out with a gorgeous young woman, could you? Fancied your chances with her, I bet?'

Anthony felt like punching Jon in the face for that hurtful remark but considered that if he had done so, it would still not have made him feel any better about the situation. Although he had lost out to him on the girl that he thought was his, he wasn't prepared to compromise his dignity as well.

Rebecca was now sitting on the stairs, sobbing her heart out. Anthony wasn't angry with her. He still loved her very dearly and it affected him deeply to see her so upset. Even now, he wanted to run across to her and put his arms around her and to tell her not to cry. He longed to reassure her that everything was all right; and that this had all been a nasty dream that was about to fade away. Sadly, that was just a stupid romantic notion and the reality of the situation was facing him here and now.

Observing the manner in which Rebecca had reacted to Anthony, it more or less confirmed to Jon that there was more to their relationship than just plain friendship. Unfortunately, her outward demonstration of her feelings of love for this man, only served to make him more determined to be bitter towards him.

'Well, if there's nothing more you want to say to her, I think you should push off home.'

Anthony looked down and answered quietly.

'Yes. I suppose I should. There's really nothing else I can add.'

He hung his head as this huge feeling of rejection came over him. In the space of just a few minutes, his joy and happiness had been shattered as he realised that the girl he loved had never been his from the start.

Jon, on the other hand, was delighted with the effect his remarks were having on Anthony, and was determined to deal him yet another blow.

'Now, if you'd just like to get back to the old people's home where you came from, Becky and I have got some unfinished business to attend to, if you get what I mean?'

Without waiting to see if there was any reaction to his nasty remark, he started to close the door. When it was halfway shut, he stopped.

'Hang on a minute! I forgot something.'

Leaving the door ajar, he turned to take a ring of keys off the coat peg in the hallway.

'I believe these are yours.'

Instead of handing them to Anthony, he threw them out through the opening and then hurriedly closed the door.

Anthony put the bouquet of flowers down on the doorstep, whilst he fumbled on the ground to pick up the boat keys. His eyes began to water as he fought back the tears. He had never been so humiliated in his life and this final act concerning the keys had been the last straw.

After picking them up, he left the meaningless flowers behind on the step and walked back down the path to his car. He now wanted to get away quickly. Anywhere would do, just as long as it was away from this awful place where joy and happiness had been taken from him in such a cruel and insensitive manner. He got into the car and without looking back at the house, drove off.

He couldn't face the prospect of going straight back to his daughter's house. He needed some time to recollect his thoughts and to ponder upon his approach to telling the rest of the family what had transpired. Unfortunately, the rush hour traffic was bad, which only added to his frustration. He drove around the congested streets of the town until he could locate somewhere to park his car. Caroline had been right to get him to go and find the answers to the questions that had been puzzling him for some time, but now that he knew the whole story, it didn't make him feel any better. In fact, right this very moment, he felt a whole lot worse.

Eventually, he found a parking space. Locking his car, he wandered through the busy streets of the town. Many shops and businesses had already closed for the day as it was now almost six o' clock and their weary staff were making their way home.

The tourists, on the other hand, were looking in the gift shops which stayed open much later, with some beginning to fill the numerous cafes and restaurants for their evening meals.

From the cheerful look on their faces, it seemed as if the entire world was enjoying itself, apart from him. When he reached the promenade, he noticed that the sands were almost deserted. Walking further along, he found a relatively quiet spot in which to sit down, near to the beach cafeteria that had now closed.

Sitting on the wall overlooking the beach, his eyes began to well up again as the reality of the situation came to him. He was not known for his emotional outbursts, but the circumstances in which he found himself were too much for him to handle at this precise moment. He was upset at having been so foolish. How could he possibly have been so blind and not seen this coming? All the signs were there and he had stupidly chosen to ignore them. Losing Rebecca had been a painful enough experience, but Jon's sadistic attitude towards him had made it so much worse.

He sat there for some considerable time looking into the distance. Every so often, another tear would roll down his cheek as he reflected upon the wonderful times that the two of them had enjoyed in each other's company over the past few days. He had not experienced such happiness for such a long time, and now it had all dissipated in just a matter of minutes.

The more he thought about Rebecca's relationship with Jon, the less he understood the attraction between them. Surely she could not have been happy with him? She was after all a wonderful vibrant young lady and he was just an oaf and a moron. Maybe even after spending fifty years on this earth, he still failed to understand the complexities of human nature. He reached into his trouser pocket for his handkerchief. At this precise moment, he felt terribly alone and rejected, and it was difficult for him to contemplate his next move.

After a short while, he became aware of someone standing beside him.

'You know, from the expression on your face, it looks as though you could do with a jump start this time.'

He instantly recognised the voice. Without having to look up, he knew it was Natalie, in spite of the fact that he had only met her on one previous occasion in order to assist her with starting her car. She sat down on the wall beside him, and joined him in staring at the waves as they broke upon the shoreline.

'Thanks for getting my car started the other day.'

'It was a pleasure. Had any more trouble with it since?'

'No. My boyfriend purchased a new battery for it yesterday. Starts first time now.'

She could tell from the tone of his voice that Anthony was deeply distressed about something. For a short period of time, there was a lull in the conversation.

'You know. My father once told me that it was good to tell your troubles to a stranger.'

'He must be a very wise man, that dad of yours?'

'Yes, I suppose he is. He certainly has given me some good advice over the years.'

Anthony turned to face her. The breeze blew her long hair across her face and she constantly brushed it aside with her hand.

'And just what is your advice then?'

'Depends on the problem, although nothing in life is so bad it cannot be overcome eventually.'

'I expect you're right.'

Little by little, Anthony briefly related the events of the past few days to her. As he talked them through, it seemed to make him feel much better. She listened attentively, only interjecting a few words of comfort here and there when it appeared appropriate to do so. When he recalled the upset that he had experienced only an hour or so beforehand, even that didn't seem quite so bad now.

She was very sympathetic and in a gentle way, tried to reassure him that there was probably someone out there for him nearer to his age, who was infinitely better than Rebecca was. She meant well, although it was really the sort of thing that an older person says to a youngster, who has just lost his or her first love. Even so, it was enough to bring a smile to his face.

'Trouble is, Natalie, I now feel so foolish.'

'Don't worry about it. I suppose I shall do lots of foolish things too by the time I reach your age.'

'Yes. I expect you will. No one seems to be immune from making silly mistakes.'

'So I've got it all to look forward to, have I?'

Anthony grinned.

'What's that expression you older people use? Better to have lost than loved or something?'

'Better to have loved and lost than never to have loved at all. I think that's what you're trying to say.'

'Well. I was almost right.'

Anthony had cheered up quite a lot since Natalie joined him. She had obviously come at just the right time, before he had begun to wallow in self-pity.

'I expect I had better go and see what my boyfriend's been up to while I've been talking to you. I can see him standing over by the harbour wall.'

Anthony looked across in the direction she had indicated.

'You mean to say that you have left him waiting there all this time?'

'Oh no! When I saw you sitting on your own, he said he'd nip over to the garage whilst I came over to talk to you. He can't have been waiting more than twenty minutes.'

'Oh! Honestly, Natalie! You'd better not keep him hanging around any longer.'

'OK! But do take care, won't you?'

'Yes. I feel a lot better after talking to you. Got to go home now and face the family.'

'Catch up with you again sometime.'

'I expect so.'

He watched her walk along the promenade and over to where her boyfriend was waiting. They looked across to him and waved. Anthony in turn waved back and then watched the couple as they continued onwards in the direction of the town. Her comforting words had helped him to put his problem into perspective.

Anthony got up from the wall and made his way back to the car. Explaining all that had happened to his family was not going to be easy. However, he now felt in a better frame of mind to do so.

Chapter Twenty-four

Anthony took a slow drive back to his daughter's house. He had made up his mind that the situation wasn't going to get the better of him, and so he tried to think positive thoughts. When he arrived there, he let himself in and found Mike and Julia sitting in the lounge chatting. Julia could tell instantly that her father had been crying and got up out of her armchair and went across to him. She threw her arms around him and hugged him tightly.

'Come and sit down, Dad.'

He went over to the sofa to sit and his daughter came and sat beside him.

'Make Dad a cup of tea, please, Mike.'

'Yes. Sure.'

Mike got up and went into the kitchen to put on the kettle.

'Where's Suzanne then, Julia?'

'She just gone next door to Caroline's. I expect they're making cakes again.'

'Yes. She enjoys doing that, doesn't she?'

Julia waited patiently for her father to compose himself. He didn't feel like repeating the events of the last few hours but knew that she had a right to know what had happened. He started by relating the conversation between himself and Caroline, although it soon became quite obvious to him that she was already fully conversant with the details. Whilst he was out, the two women must have got together to talk, which probably also accounted for the diplomatic transfer of Suzanne over to Caroline's house to prevent her eaves dropping in on their present discussion.

Mike returned with a pot of tea and poured out three cups. He handed one of them to his father-in-law who took a few sips, before continuing with his story. He then settled back into his armchair to listen.

Anthony told them of his short visit to Rebecca's house and of the dreadful encounter that had taken place between them and her boyfriend, Jon. As he related the demeaning manner in which he had been treated, tears appeared in Julia's eyes. Her father was an honourable man and had always been well respected in both business and social life. It had been unpleasant enough to be made to look a fool, having been targeted by an unscrupulous group of individuals who were only after his boat. However, it had been even more distressing to hear how he had been subjected to such unnecessarily degrading treatment once he had found out about it.

He then spoke of his love for Rebecca and the many things that they had shared together.

'I was really happy with Becky.'

'Yes, I know you were Dad. It sounds to me as though she got herself too deeply into something that she just couldn't find a way out of it.'

'I'm sure you're right.'

'Well. It's so easy to say what she should have done with the benefit of hindsight.'

'But if she didn't want to go along with it, then why didn't she tell me?'

'Think about it though, Dad. Perhaps she did love you, but was frightened of telling you the truth. After all that had gone before, would you have still believed her.'

'I don't know. I'd like to think I would have understood.'

'Yes, I'm sure you would have. Remember! I've known you for many years, whereas she hasn't. I don't suppose she could afford to take that chance.'

Anthony placed his cup on the low table and sat back again.

'I think in all fairness to her, she did try to tell me time and time again that things weren't supposed to happen the way they did. Unfortunately, I didn't understand what she was on about.'

'Well, in a way that seems to bear out what I've just said.'

'Fine. But if you're right, Julia, it's such a pity it had to end this way.'

'Yes. I know what you mean.'

'Perhaps I shouldn't have gone over there and found out, and then maybe one day she would have plucked up enough courage to tell me.'

'Yes, perhaps you're right, but now we'll never know. I'm sorry it's over Dad, but do try to think of all the good times you had together. They were good, weren't they?'

'Yes, they were, Julia. It's years since I felt that good.'

Mike had been listening patiently, but sadly he wasn't prepared to be so forgiving.

'Really, Dad! Where was your common sense in all this?'

'Let it be, Mike. Dad feels bad enough about himself as it is, without your rubbing it in.'

'No, Julia. Let Mike have his say. I've let my heart rule my head. Common-sense should have told me that beautiful young women like Rebecca, don't go around picking up men more than twice their ages, without good reason.'

'Perhaps so, although it did lead to a loving relationship.'

Julia linked her arm through her father's and looked into his face. It had been a joy sharing in his happiness during the last few days and now it grieved her to see him so hurt. Mike continued.

'What about the boat?"

'In what way do you mean?'

Even Julia was puzzled as to what her husband was on about.

'Well, don't you think that Dad and I had better go over there and check it out right now. If that moron of a boyfriend of hers has damaged it, we may have to sue. In fact, I think we ought to let the authorities know, just in case they used it for something illegal.'

'Oh, Mike! Don't make such a drama out of it. You're not dealing with one of your matrimonial cases at work. I can now see how you solicitors make a breakdown in a relationship ten times more acrimonious than it was before you got involved.'

'But Dad's a fool to sit back and let them walk all over him. I bet she even got him to buy her presents too.'

'Well, I did buy her a couple of items.'

'There you are. What did I tell you?'

Mike was very annoyed and was ready to fight on his father-in-law's behalf.

'But Mike! She didn't force me to buy them for her. I did it because I was in love with her.'

'Then perhaps we ought to try and get them back. Were they expensive?'

Julia considered the matter was getting out of hand.

'For heaven's sake Mike, give it a rest. Dad's upset and you're not making things any easier.'

There was pause, whilst they waited for Anthony to comment.

'Look. I know you mean well, and it's nice to know you're really concerned about me, but let's forget it, shall we?'

'But you've got to act now, Dad.'

'Oh, come on, Mike. I'll go over to the marina tomorrow and check that the boat isn't damaged in any way. If it's OK, then that's the end of the matter.'

Mike persisted.

'But you can't let these people treat you in the way that they did, and then expect to get away with it.'

'I've said all I'm going to say on this subject for tonight.

Right! Let's see if there's a good programme on the television.'

Mike and Julia sat in silence whilst Anthony picked up the newspaper and looked through the programme page.

'There you are, "Neighbours from Hell". We'll watch that. Should be quite topical in the present circumstances.'

Anthony picked up the remote control and switched on the television. Julia looked across to her husband and gestured to him to drop the matter. Rather reluctantly, he acceded to her request. Although the three of them sat back and watched this immensely boring programme, it created a sufficiently lengthy interlude to enable the conversation to move onto a different topic once the fly-on-the-wall intrusion into other people's problems had ended.

Later, Julia went around to Caroline's house to pick up Suzanne and was gone for over an hour. She later returned with her daughter and got her ready for bed. After a bit of supper, they decided to turn in for the night.

In the quietness of his room, the full implications of what had transpired that afternoon came to him. His heart had been broken and he knew it would take some time to mend. Eventually, sleep came to him and gave him that much needed relief from his thoughts.

Chapter Twenty-five

After Anthony had left Rebecca's house, a row broke out between her and Jon. It had been brewing for some months now and his attitude towards Anthony had been the catalyst that eventually brought it to a head. Not only was she ashamed at the way she had deceived the poor man, but was utterly appalled at the callous manner in which her boyfriend had treated him as well. Jon, rather foolishly, tried to laugh the whole thing off as a big joke but Rebecca was very angry.

'That was sick what you just did to Tony.'

'Lighten up, Becky! The stupid old fool had it coming. We'd have had to tell him to push off eventually, especially as we don't need the boat anymore.'

'Yes. But you were so spiteful to him. You really are a nasty piece of work. You couldn't even be civil in handing him the boat keys.'

Jon did not like to be criticised.

'Don't you tell me what I can or cannot do.'

'Proud of yourself, are you then? Did you get some perverted pleasure out of humiliating him.'

'Yes, I quite enjoyed it, as a matter of fact. Anyway, what's it to you? Did you fancy him or something?'

'Yes, I did actually! He was a kind and loving man and I enjoyed being with him.'

'You do talk some romantic rubbish, Becky. He was far too old for you.'

She was extremely annoyed and was in no mood for his casual attitude towards the pain that he had inflicted upon the man she loved. She was determined to give vent to her anger on him.

'That guy was worth ten of you. It was shameful the way you treated him.'

'Oh! Come on! I bet he's forgotten about it already.'

'You're just scum, Jon. There's no other word to describe you.'

Jon laughed. There was very little she could say that would make him feel reprehensible for his earlier actions. In view of that, she felt it was pointless just to continue hurling abuse at him.

Rebecca went upstairs and was gone for ten or fifteen minutes. Meanwhile, Jon put on the television and began to relax on the sofa. When she returned to the lounge, she was carrying a huge pile of bed linen, which she dumped upon the carpet in front of him.

'What's your game then?'

'You're sleeping on the sofa tonight.'

'In your dreams!'

'No, Jon. This is serious. I've had enough of you, your scams, your laziness, and your arrogance.'

'But you can't do this!'

'Yes, I can. Perhaps you've forgotten. This is my father's house. You're just a guest here.'

Jon was taken aback by the suddenness of her change in attitude towards him. The smug look he had earlier quickly disappeared.

'How long d'you think you're gonna keep this up for. I guarantee you that it'll only last one night.'

'Just for once you're actually right.'

'There you are. I told you so.'

'Yes! Because I want you out of this house before I get home from work tomorrow evening.'

Jon's expression immediately changed. He leapt up from the sofa and came swiftly towards her with fire in his eyes. As he reached the door where Rebecca was now standing, he clenched his fists as if about to strike out at her.

'I don't take that sort of crap from anybody, especially a woman.'

Rebecca was angry too and stood her ground.

'I warn you, Jon. If you so much as hit me, even once, I shall call the police and have you out of here tonight.'

Jon stopped dead in his tracks. He could see the hatred in her eyes. She utterly despised him and he could tell that she meant every word of her threat. He already had one court appearance hanging over his head, and a bout of GBH on top of that would probably ensure that he went to prison for a long spell. Although he was reluctant to back down, common sense prevailed.

'I've had enough of this. I'm going out.'

'Fine by me! Don't forget to leave the door key on the side when you leave tomorrow, assuming of course that you're coming back to sleep here tonight.'

He didn't stop to argue. She heard the front door slam with such force that it shook some of the ornaments in the lounge. In the stillness that followed, she sat on the sofa with her head in her hands.

'Oh, Dad. I've really messed up big time. If only you were here.'

She muttered softly as she tried to see clearly through the state of confusion in which she now found herself. She longed to ring Anthony at his daughter's house and try to explain where she went wrong and to beg his forgiveness. She knew he was a kind gentle man and that it was just possible that he would understand.

She got up and went out into the hallway to where the telephone sat invitingly on a small low table. She picked up the receiver and quickly put it down again. Just suppose his daughter answered her call. She might not be so charitable and the whole conversation would then turn into a blazing argument. That's the last thing she needed at this particular moment. Besides, she'd probably blown it anyway. It would now be asking a lot of him to expect them to carry on their relationship where they had left off, as if nothing had happened.

She made a cup of tea and a sandwich and sat to watch the television for a while. There was nothing on that specifically interested her. In fact, she couldn't understand why she sat through 'Neighbours from Hell', as it was so boring. Eventually, she went up to bed and fell asleep.

The next morning, she was up at her usual time and ready to go to work. As she passed the lounge door she looked inside and could see Jon snoring away on the sofa. She had not heard him come in. From a distance, he looked and smelt as though he had drunk a lot of alcohol the night before. The covers she had left him were still in a heap on the carpet where she had originally dumped them. Closing the front door quietly behind her, she went off to work.

It was nearly eleven by the time Jon roused himself. He quickly washed and shaved with the intention of leaving the house in search of Darren Baxter. He had waited in all the previous day in the hope that he would contact him after the abortive pick-up the evening before that. He was anxious to ascertain what had gone wrong.

As he strolled along the quiet suburban road, he observed a large white Transit van come slowly past him. He would not normally have noticed something like that, had it not been for the fact that its side panel door was wide open. The vehicle then stopped on the corner, just a few yards ahead of him. He paid very little further attention to it and assumed that the three men who got out were workman engaged upon some local maintenance work.

As he drew alongside, he found himself being grabbed from the front and behind and bodily thrown inside the vehicle. Although he was extremely fit, the suddenness of the attack had given him no time in which to resist the assault. In a matter of a few seconds, the door was closed and the van sped away.

He looked up from his position on the floor of the vehicle and observed that it had no windows or access to the driver's compartment. The inside had been ply-lined throughout and the floor was completely clear of contents. Once he had sufficiently recollected his thoughts, he saw that there were four men looking down at him.

He tried to get up but one of the men punched him in the stomach. He lashed out at him in retaliation but another struck him in the face and a further blow hit him in the back of the neck and he fell forwards onto the van floor again. All Jon could then feel was a pain in his side as one after another they kicked him in the ribs. After a few seconds, the onslaught stopped. He attempted to turn over to look at his attackers but being very weak he fell onto his back.

'So! You're Jon Desner, eh?'

He stared up at the big man who spoke. Until now, this giant of a man had been standing to one side whilst his henchman had done all the damage to him. Although Jon was still feeling rather dizzy, he noticed that the van was now stationary. With great difficulty, he tried to answer him.

'You've got me at a disadvantage here. I don't know who you are or what you want. Are you sure you've got the right guy?'

'Oh, yes. We're certain of that. Does the name Darren Baxter mean anything to you?'

Jon was in such excruciating pain that it was very difficult for him to breathe properly, let alone talk. Nevertheless, he took a few short painful breaths before replying.

'Yes. Darren and I are good mates. We often go out on jobs together.'

'You didn't do very well the night before last though. You came back empty-handed.'

'I can explain that. It all went wrong.'

Seeing that Jon could barely move and therefore presented no threat to him, the big man crouched down beside him.

'Yes. It certainly did. That package was meant for me but it appears that the Customs were tipped off and seized the incoming boat. I've lost a lot of money. D'you know anything about that, Jon, my friend?'

'Oh! Come on! Surely you don't think I had anything to do with it? You ask Darren.'

'I'm sure we will. You see, Darren Baxter's my cousin and I gave him the job in the first instance.'

'What? He's only into small time stuff, like me.'

'So he is. His fence is a mate of mine.'

'Really! I always wondered where the gear from the lock-up went to.'

The boss looked up at his companions, smiled, and then looked back at Jon again.

'Perhaps you'd like to tell me where that is?'

'You're kidding! That's a place that only Darren, Nick and I know about. If you're Darren's cousin, then perhaps you should ask him yourself.'

The big man stood up again and looked over to his companions. One of the men who had previously kicked Jon spoke out.

'It looks as though your cousin was right after all, Lenny. Darren said he was the one who squealed.'

Jon was now becoming scared. This member of Darren's family was obviously no small time villain. He was possibly into drugs trafficking and the like. If Darren had told him that Jon was a grass, he might mysteriously disappear and never be seen again. Probably to the bottom of the English Channel with a large slab of concrete chained to his feet.

Jon manoeuvred himself into a kneeling position. He was bleeding from the punch to the face and was doubled up in pain where he had been repeatedly kicked. Taking a painful deep breath, he tried to put the record straight.

'I'm no police informer. You must have misheard what Darren said. We go back a long way, Darren and me.'

'Then perhaps you'd like to explain why he's now in police custody, along with his mate Nick?'

'What? I know nothing about that!'

'It appears that they found the stash of stolen goods and traced them to him. Now, seeing how only the three of you knew where it was, that just leaves you.'

Jon was lost for words. With Darren and Nick in the hands of the police, the finger of suspicion would point straight at him. He knew that he hadn't said anything. So who did?

The big man looked down at Jon again. There was a mean expression on his face. One of the men, who spoke to Lenny before, came forward and stood on the opposite side of him.

'What d'you want us to do with him, Lenny? I do hate a squealer!'

Lenny pulled back the panel door to leave. As he did so, he turned to his cohorts.

'Rough him up a little and then take him home. We'll let the police deal with him. We don't want to attract too much attention from the old Bill. It ain't worth it.'

The big man left the van and pulled the door shut behind him. The vehicle started up again and Jon tried to roll himself into a ball as the blows rained down up him. He almost passed out with the brutality of the assault.

The vehicle eventually stopped and the door was opened again. The three men threw him onto the pavement and then got back in and drove off at speed. Jon tried to stir himself. His vision wasn't very good where another unlucky blow had caught him just below the eye, leaving him with a cut that was bleeding. Nevertheless, he quickly established the fact that he was just around the corner from where he had been picked up, just a few hundred yards from Rebecca's home.

With difficulty, he rose to his feet and limped slowly along the road. The street was deserted. As he turned the corner, another surprise was waiting for him. Outside of Rebecca's house were two police cars. Unfortunately, he was so engrossed in the pain of his injuries that he failed to see them in time. As he turned to walk in the opposite direction, one of the officers spotted him.

The police came after him in the car, but Jon was in no fit state to run and they soon caught up with him. They put him in the vehicle and drove back to Rebecca's house again.

'Been in a fight then, Mr Dresner?'

The police officer could see that he had been on the rough end of a severe beating. Although battered and bruised, Jon was beginning to recover a little, although he still had difficulty in walking.

'I fell over the kerb.'

'From a great height, no doubt. I think we'd better get you some medical treatment when we take you down to the station.'

They took him across to the other police car, where they were loading numerous items of equipment into the boot.

'What's all this about then?'

'Well. It appears that you've got quite a lot of explaining to do.'

'I don't follow you.'

'Don't tell me that you don't recognise the gear. We found a lot of stolen items in your garden shed. Perhaps you'd like to tell us how they got there?'

'But I don't know anything about it.'

'So you'd be very surprised if our forensic boys found your fingerprints all over them?'

Jon now realised that he had been stitched up. It could only have been Darren or Nick who planted the stuff there, as they were the only two who knew where it was stored in the first place. Then again, they were now in police custody. So what made them do it?

Darren had told his cousin that Jon had informed on them to

the police and that's why they had been arrested, but they must have planted the gear in the shed before that happened. So did they think he grassed on them before that? Jon was now totally confused, as he could not establish how the suspicion arose in the first place. It never occurred to him that he had told Rebecca about many of his escapades, and even if he had, he would never have visualised her going to the police and informing on him.

'Aren't you going to let us come inside and have a look around, sir?'

'Not without a warrant, you aren't! Anyway, there's nothing in there that might be of interest to you.'

'We thought the same about the shed, Mr Dresner.'

Jon was in no fit state to conduct a conversation in the street. The police arrested him and took him to the police station for further questioning. It was there that a medical officer attended to his injuries. Fortunately, no bones had been broken, although he was severely bruised.

Chapter Twenty-six

That same day, Julia was doing some early morning ironing in the kitchen, when she heard a lot of activity coming from the guestroom. She went upstairs to investigate and tapped upon the bedroom door.

'Is it all right if I come in, Dad?'

'Yes, of course you can, Julia.'

She entered the room and found her father packing his suitcase. Most of the items from the dressing table drawers already filled the bottom section of the case, and he was now taking his shirts from the wardrobe and neatly folding them.

'You're not going home, are you, Dad?'

'Afraid so.'

'But why?'

Anthony placed the empty hangers back onto the rail.

'I've had enough excitement over the last few days to last me a year.'

'But you were going to stay with us for a second week.'

'I know, Julia, but I just can't face wandering around this area for another seven to ten days, dredging up all the old memories of Becky. I'd be far happier back at home.'

'Well, I wouldn't like you to rush off straightaway though Dad. Please stay at least until the end of the day. Mike's even taken time off work to keep you company.'

He stopped what he was doing and turned to face her. As her husband had specifically taken a day off to be with him, it would have been a personal affront to have then packed his case and left.

'Yes, all right, love. But I'm off home after tea.'

'And I can't get you to change your mind and stay for longer?'

'Oh, Julia. Please don't make me feel bad about it.'

'OK. I understand.'

She smiled. She understood exactly how he must have felt and staying on would have only prolonged the heartache.

'I'll go and get you some breakfast then. How do you fancy egg and bacon this morning?'

'Good heavens! You are doing an unhealthy fry up! This will be a treat. Are you sure it won't make you late for work?'

'I'm not actually going in today as I've arranged to have the day off too. I plan to go out later, but I'll be back long before you leave. Probably around lunchtime.'

'What about Suzanne?'

'Mike is just dropping her off at school for me at this very moment. He'll be back soon.'

She closed the bedroom door behind her and he heard her go downstairs. He accepted the fact that the two of them were trying to do their best for him. It didn't take too much to realise that both of them were so concerned that they were taking time off work to be with him during this upsetting period. For this reason alone, he was obliged to stay until the late afternoon. However, he felt that his decision to return home was the right one all the same, and nothing was going to change his mind.

Even Julia understood what it would be like for him to endure having to spend another week or so in familiar surroundings, prolonging those sad memories of Rebecca, her obnoxious boyfriend and him. Besides, many unanswered questions also came to mind. What if he bumped into her again? How would he feel? What would his reaction be if he saw her out with Jon? What if Jon was then rude to him again? This time he might not take it so lightly and whack him? How would that go down with

Rebecca? No, he knew he was making the right decision by returning home.

He continued to pack the case, until all the items were inside, apart from his shaver and flannel. He would put them in later after he had washed and shaved.

'Now for the piece de resistance,' he muttered to himself.

From a shopping bag by the bed he produced a dozen wooden hangers. He had bought them on his way to the florist the previous day, when he spotted them in a large barrel outside a shop nearby. He placed them onto the rail in the wardrobe and removed the metal ones. At first, he threw the old ones into the bin in the corner of the room and then thought better of it.

'Knowing what an old skinflint Mike is, they'll probably turn up in Suzanne's wardrobe next,' he mused.

He took the old hangers and placed them into his suitcase, with a view to throwing them into the wheelybin, when he got home. His next job was to get ready, although he had no idea what he would do for the rest of the day, before driving back.

After he had washed and shaved, he finished packing the suitcase. He zipped it up and stood it down by the door. The beautiful smell of bacon had now wafted up the stairs and made him anxious to get down to breakfast. When he reached the kitchen, Julia had set a place for him just as if he had been staying at a guesthouse. There was fruit juice, toast and jam and a large pot of tea.

'You're really spoiling me this morning, Julia.'

'Can't I give my dear old dad a treat, once in a while?'

'Oi! Not so much of the old.'

Breakfast was great. I don't suppose the Stevens' household had experienced a fry up for years, as that would have been considered too unhealthy. Whilst he was eating, Mike returned from taking Suzanne to school.

'Hey, Julia! That smells great! Any chance of some for me?'

'Don't worry. I wouldn't give a treat to one of my boys without the other, otherwise the two of you would be squabbling again.'

Julia took another plateful of food that she had kept warm under the grill and placed it upon the kitchen table for Mike. He tucked into it as though he had never had egg and bacon before in his life. Meanwhile, Julia was getting ready to leave.

'I've got to go out in a minute and should be back around lunchtime. I trust you will be OK if I leave the two of you together without me around to keep you from scratching each others eyes out?'

'Yes, we'll be all right, Julia. Oh, by the way, you'll want the key to the car.'

Mike fumbled in his pocket and took out the key and handed it to her.

'If we go out, I'm sure Dad won't mind taking us in his.'

'Yes. Sure, Mike.'

Julia got ready and then left, leaving the two of them to continue their meal. With plenty of time on their hands, Mike and his father-in-law chatted.

'Dad. I'm really sorry about last night. I didn't mean to be so insensitive. It's just that it all seemed so unfair on you.'

'That's OK, Mike. I know you meant well.'

Anthony was anxious not to dwell upon his break-up with Rebecca so he changed the subject.

'So what's all this about your having the day off? At the rates you solicitors charge, it must be costing you a fortune.'

'I only had one client originally booked in to see me this morning. My secretary rang me yesterday evening and told me that she has rescheduled that for next Monday, at his request. The rest of the work I can do over the weekend as I have all the necessary papers in my briefcase.'

'What about the garden gate?'

'Oh, blow that! Julia's been going on at me for weeks to get that fixed. I'll do it whilst I'm off work for a week in July.'

Anthony poured another cup of tea for the two of them. It had been many years since they had sat and talked together, without Julia present.

'When we've finished breakfast though, Mike, I would like to go over to the marina to make sure the boat has been locked up securely. I take it, you won't mind coming with me?'

'No. Of course not.'

After they had cleared away the breakfast things, Mike followed Anthony out to his car. They spent some time looking it over and his son-in-law seemed to take quite an interest in it. Time however was marching on.

'I don't mean to rush us, but I suppose we'd better get over to the marina soon.'

'Yes, I suppose we should, especially as you're leaving to go home later today.'

Mike went back to the house to lock up and then returned to the car.

'Would you let me drive us over there, Dad? I've never driven an open top car before.'

'Yes, sure you can, son.'

Anthony took the top down and got into the passenger seat. Mike sat in the driver's seat and adjusted the mirror.

It was quite a relatively sedate drive across town, compared with the last time Anthony allowed someone else to take over the driving. Although Mike was a careful driver, he certainly didn't hang around and really enjoyed the experience. Shortly, they arrived at the marina and Mike managed to find a parking space nearby. Wandering across the pontoon, they found the boat securely moored.

'Everything looks OK from a distance.'

'Yes. But let's get on board and see if there are any problems.'

The first thing they noticed was the open cabin door. It was a little worrying as anyone could have just walked in and stolen things. They looked around below deck and fortunately nothing obvious seemed to be missing. The place however was a tip, with items that had fallen from open cupboards, strewn all over the cabin floor.

'Good Heavens! It looks as though a bomb has hit it.'

Anthony viewed the mess. He had left everything so neat and tidy on the last occasion he had used the craft.

'I think they must have had a rocky ride back in that thunderstorm. Mind you, she seems to have survived it intact.'

'It appears so. At least nothing seems to be broken.'

They spent an hour, cleaning and tidying up after the escapade of the night before last. Anthony checked the engines over and the mechanics seemed fine. There was no visible harm to the hull either. Nevertheless, to be absolutely certain that there had been no damage, they decided to take her along the coastline for a couple of miles to check the performance.

By the time they returned to the moorings, they had satisfied themselves that everything was all right. As it was now just after one and Julia would be returning home for lunch, they decided to lock up and return to the house.

Chapter Twenty-seven

Although Rebecca had made it to work on time, she was very tired after having a restless night. Even the other staff in the shop had noticed that she was not her usual self. Normally, she was bubbly and full of life and always cheerful and helpful even with the most difficult customers. She had been known to brighten up the most downhearted staff on the busiest of days when everything seemed to be going wrong for them.

However, today her face displayed a more serious expression. Some of her colleagues thought that perhaps she was ill, and so she settled for that as a suitable explanation for her low vitality, thereby avoiding the need for in depth probing into her personal life.

The morning seemed to drag on very slowly and by ten 'o' clock she was desperately in need of a cup of coffee to perk her up. She left the cash desk in the hands of an assistant whilst she went across to the stockroom to make herself one and was surprised to bump into her father's friend, the high ranking police officer, on the way. She cheered up a little when she saw him. He had been loitering around the freestanding racks displaying the latest in summer skirts.

'Do you usually hang around women's clothes shops, Jack?' Rebecca's impish grin had returned to her face.

'Not unless my wife is with me. Actually, I came to see you.

Is there anywhere we can talk privately?'

'You can take me across the road and buy me a coffee if you like.'

'OK!'

'Right! I'll just square it with the manager. Fortunately, she's in today, which puts her in charge of the store instead of me. It's therefore not so essential for me to remain on the premises.'

Rebecca went out to the back of the shop to talk to her boss and later returned with her jacket and purse. The two of them strolled over to the coffee shop where Jack bought two cappuccinos. It was surprisingly empty for a Friday morning, so they were able to find a vacant table where they could talk without being overheard.

'So to what do I owe this pleasure. That's twice we've met in one week, Jack. If we carry on seeing each other in such a clandestine way, people will think we're having an affair.'

Jack laughed.

'You've always had your father's wit. In fact, I can see a lot of his character in you.'

'Must have come from the close proximity in which I grew up with him all those years. Anyway, is this a fatherly chat or strictly police work?'

'Neither, really. I've just got a few things to tell you that won't take too long. I've got an appointment at eleven back at the station, so I can't leave here too late.'

'So, I expect you're going to quiz me about our abortive boat trip on Wednesday evening?'

'No. Customs have already dealt with that problem. That's why you had a wasted journey.'

'I wish you'd told me earlier.'

'Didn't know myself until yesterday.'

'I see. So if it isn't anything to do with the boat trip, I'm intrigued.'

Jack picked up his cup and took a drink.

'I thought you ought to know that we've picked up Darren Baxter and Nick Henderson. We actually caught them at the lock up, checking out their stolen goods. They couldn't believe it was a police raid. This time we took sufficient officers to ensure that they didn't get away from us. I'm much obliged to you for letting us know the location.'

'Well. At least, two villains are now out of the way. I left the other one fast asleep on the couch this morning. He's a bit upset as I've told him I want him out of the house by the end of the day.'

'Well, he'll be even more upset when my officers pick him up. Darren tipped us off that your garden shed was full of bent gear.'

'What? There are no stolen goods in my garden shed. At least there weren't, when I last used the mower.'

'There are now, Becky. But don't worry about it. I expect Darren had his moronic friend plant them there earlier in the week.'

'But why would they do that?'

'Must be to implicate Jon in some way. I expect we'll find his fingerprints all over them.'

Rebecca sipped her hot coffee.

'Your mob won't think I had anything to do with it?'

'No. I wouldn't let that bother you. Still, there is one thing I should warn you about.'

'Oh!'

'Darren and his pal are under the impression that Jon had turned police informer.'

'But won't that take the heat off me?'

'In a way, it will.'

'You don't sound too convincing, Jack.'

The police officer leaned across the table to speak in a more subdued voice. Rebecca became more attentive.

'That package you were due to collect contained Class A drugs.'

Rebecca thumped the table with her fist.

'I knew it had to be something like that. I told that idiot of a boyfriend of mine not to get involved with anything big-time. He just wouldn't listen. I think he thinks he's Lex Luther or something.'

'Lex who?'

'You know, the master criminal in the Superman films.'

Jack shrugged his shoulders.

'Where does that leave us then? After all, Jon was contracted to go and collect it.'

Rebecca was visibly nervous. She was frightened that Jon had now brought her into contact with real criminals.

'Darren's cousin is a chap called Lenny. He's into the importation of illegal substances. Surrounds himself with a lot of muscle too. If he thinks Jon's a police informer, I'd hate to be in his shoes when they catch up with him.'

'And me?'

'I don't think anyone's going to suss out your involvement in it all. If Jon doesn't suspect you as the one who shopped them, then it's unlikely that anyone else will. Besides, we've also got enough evidence to put Darren, Nick, and Jon well out of your way for a good while.'

'But what about this chap Lenny? Isn't he dangerous?'

Rebecca sat patiently waiting for a reply whilst the police officer paused to finish the remainder of his coffee.

'Why don't you go and pay your father a visit in Australia? You've never been out there to see him and it'll be really good for both of you – and for your stepmother too. I'm sure even she will be pleased to renew your acquaintance after all this time.'

'Are you trying to frighten me, Jack?'

'No! Of course I'm not. All I am suggesting is that you lie low for a while until all this nasty business blows over. Besides, I hear they're short of the odd attractive 'Sheila' or two out there. You'll have a whale of a time.'

Rebecca thought for a moment. It was obvious that Jack was suggesting that she should keep well out of the way until the whole sordid affair had been resolved. It was likely that the three petty criminals would go to jail and that Darren's cousin would moved on to other criminal activities, and put this minor setback behind him.

The prospect of going to visit her father had been something that she had contemplated for some time. The outcome of recent events had only made her want to be with him even more. It wasn't that she was lonely here in England, but she did miss his comforting advice and fatherly protection.

She knew she could always leave his house in the hands of a local managing agent to rent out fully furnished, while she was away. That would guarantee some income and also ensure that the place was looked after and properly maintained. Should she decide not to return, her father could then give them the necessary authority to sell up. After all, the only reason he had not sold the house before was due to his daughter's desire to live in it.

'I think you're right, Jack. I'll have a word with Dad and then book a flight out there.'

'Good. Make it soon though, Becky.'

'OK!'

Jack looked at his watch. The previous half an hour had just flown by.

'My goodness, is that the time? I'd like to stay and chat some more, but I really must go.'

'I understand. Thanks for coming over, superintendent.'

Jack grinned.

'That's a little premature, I think.'

'Go on! You'll make Chief Constable one day.'

'I wish! Just you look after yourself, Becky. Tell your father we'll be over to see him in the near future.

'OK! You take care!'

Her father's friend left for his eleven 'o' clock appointment. He had given her some good sound advice and she felt that she should take it.

Instead of returning to work, she decided to go straight home. As her colleagues thought she was ill in any case, they would not have been all that surprised to hear that she had taken the rest of the day off. She intended to ring them when she got in to let them know.

She now had a thousand and one things to do if she was to make arrangements to go abroad in such a short period of time. She would have to wait until some time later to ring and discuss the matter with her father, due to the time difference between England and Australia. He and his wife would have probably already gone to bed by now. Nevertheless, there were lots of other arrangements to make and so she decided to start planning for the move right away.

Chapter Twenty-eight

Jon sat alone in the room, sad and dejected, and looking around him at the four stark walls. Apart from the table upon which he rested his elbows, and a couple of basic chairs, there was little other furniture worthy of mention. After the officers had arrested him, he had been brought here. He had been cautioned and then processed through the system like a common criminal with the vivacity knocked out of him. His feelings of depression were exacerbated by the claustrophobic nature of his environment, there being no windows in the room and therefore no natural light.

The medical officer had attended to his ailments. The blood on his face was fortunately only superficial and they soon patched up the small wound and stopped the bleeding. He also had a lot of bruising which still caused him considerable pain, but he was assured that all of it would heal in time. His ordeal could have been much worse had he not been so fit.

As he sat, deep in thought, the door to the room opened and a police officer entered.

'Your brief is here, Mr Dresner.'

He held the door open for the solicitor to enter. Jon was relieved to see a familiar face.

'Hi, Jon! How are you feeling now?'

'I'll survive, thanks, Mr Barrett.'

The door closed again and the solicitor sat down in the seat opposite him. So much had happened since their last meeting in his office, a couple of weeks ago.

'Well, you always wanted to play with the big boys, Jon. It seems as though you got your wish more quickly than you expected to.'

Jon hung his head and quietly nodded.

'Do you think I'll get bail.'

'Who knows! That'll be up to the magistrate to decide. You're technically of no fixed abode and the police are convinced that you'll abscond if they let you go.'

The solicitor opened his briefcase and took out a notepad. He then reached inside his jacket for a pen.

'The police will want to interview you shortly. Is there anything you want to tell me before they do so? I don't want any surprises.'

'No. Do you think they'll formally charge me today.'

'I think you'll find there's a lot involved in this one. They've got to check out your fingerprints on the stolen goods found in the garden shed and in the lock-up. I expect there'll be a number of witness statements to check out and then there's corroboration with whatever Darren Baxter and Nick Henderson has been telling them.'

Jon forced a smile.

'They won't get very far with Nick. He confuses even the most patient of questioners.'

'So I've heard. Still, the police can only hold you for thirty-six hours. It'll then be up to the magistrate to decide whether you remain at liberty, or held for another seven days.'

'Is there any chance of Becky coming to see me, Mr Barrett?'

'Well. I rang her before I came here, to see if you could still claim her place as your home. I'm afraid it appears that she's leaving shortly to go abroad. Australia, I think she said.'

'I expect she's going to see her dad. He lives out there with her stepmother. I can't blame her in wanting to get away so soon after all that's happened recently.'

'Yes. I understand she's having the locks changed on the doors too and letting the house out whilst she's away.'

'I see.'

'I'm sorry to say this Jon, but at this precise moment in your life nobody loves you, apart from God of course.'

Jon placed his head in his hands. He spoke in a very quiet and subdued voice. Gone were the customary pretentiousness and arrogance that had been such an inherent part of his character. His solicitor could not fail to notice the change in him and in some ways, felt almost sorry for the young man.

'I guess I've messed up big time, Mr Barrett.'

'I'm afraid so.'

During the pause that followed, the solicitor looked pitifully at the dejected young man before him. Although he told himself on that previous occasion that he would never wish to see the lad again, somehow his heart now went out to him.

'I'll do what I can for you, but I still think you're looking at a custodial sentence. We'll apply for bail but there may be some opposition from the police. If you do get turned down, I've got another seven days in which to come up with something. Anyway, right now you'll probably be safer on remand as you seem to have upset a number of very influential people in the criminal world. I wouldn't like to see anything else happen to you.'

Jon didn't reply. He sat with his hands in his lap, staring across at the older man. He never expected things to turn out the way they had. He could now imagine Darren and Nick blabbing to the police, making out that he was the ringleader and that it was all his idea. His solicitor was spot on. At this precise moment, he didn't have a friend in the world.

'I really hate to see a young man like you make such a mess of his life. It's never too late to go straight, you know.'

'Yes. I think you're right. All of this just isn't worth it.'

'Well. Take it a day at a time, Jon. For the moment, I think we should get through the interview and then discuss your defence.'

The young man and his solicitor proceeded to review the allegations made. Unfortunately, there was little mitigation that could be used to justify his actions. Jon was a broken man, and one could only hope that he would now follow his intention of avoiding crime in the future.

As their discussion was coming to and end, the door opened again and the police officer stepped into the room.

'Are you and your brief ready for the interview now, Mr Dresner?'

'Yes. Let's get it over with.'

Chapter Twenty-nine

Julia was out in the garden, when Anthony and Mike arrived home around half past one. She had already set out the place mats on the patio table in order for them to have lunch outside. After having cooked such a big breakfast, she decided to give them only a light meal.

'I've heard some good news about your mother when I rang the hospital, Mike. They tell me that the results of her tests are negative and she can go home tomorrow, providing there is someone to keep an eye on her.'

'That's great news. It's such a relief to know that it wasn't anything serious.'

Julia brought out the food and the three of them sat down to eat the meal.

'I hope you won't object, Mike, but as Dad has decided to go home this evening, I thought we'd bring her back here to stay. She can use the guestroom.'

'No, that's an excellent idea.'

Over lunch, the two men informed Julia about the state in which they had found her father's boat and how they had spent time clearing up the mess. The conversation came over quite light-hearted as no permanent damage had been done to the craft. When everyone had finished their meal, Julia poured them some tea and they relaxed in the deckchairs on the lawn. During a lull in their discussion, she felt it was a convenient moment to bring up a completely different matter.

'Dad. There's something I think I should tell you.'

Anthony placed his cup on the ground beside his seat and sat up to listen attentively to what his daughter was about to say. From the tone of her voice, she seemed as though she was about to discuss a rather serious subject.

'I went to see Rebecca this morning.'

'You did what?'

Anthony was dumbfounded.

'At first, I went over to the shop that you mentioned she worked at. I was told there that she had left earlier with a friend and then rang in later to say that she was taking the rest of the day off. The assistant suggested I try to reach her at home. Naturally, I didn't know where she lived, and it would have been improper to ask her for the address. Not that I expect she would have given it to me in any case.'

'So, how did you find out where she lives?'

'Well, from a rough description of where you said you collected her each time you went out together, I went over to the vicinity and asked a few neighbours. Eventually, I managed to track her down.'

Anthony was amazed at what he was hearing. He could never have imagined his daughter attempting such a thing. He looked across at his son-in-law.

'Did you know she was going over to see Becky, Mike?'

'Yes. We discussed it in bed last night. It was something that Julia wanted to do and I wholeheartedly supported her in her decision.'

He turned back to address his daughter. She was sitting there quite bemused by his reaction.

'I can't believe you did this.'

Mike interjected.

'Look, Dad! The whole episode had been left on a sour note

with lots of unanswered questions. I think she did the right thing in attempting to find out what it had all been about. I know it's none of our business really, but please don't blame her for trying.'

'Don't get me wrong, Mike. I'm not annoyed. I'm actually intrigued.'

He looked across again at Julia, eagerly awaiting what story she had to tell.

'Well, go on then, Julia. Don't keep me in suspense.'

Julia leaned forward in her seat.

'Now! Before I tell you what was said, I want to make it very clear that I didn't make a scene. Meeting her was all very civilised.'

'I bet it was a shock for her, when you told her who you were?'

'Strangely enough, she said it wasn't. She had been expecting me to come and see her and would have been more surprised if I hadn't.'

'Really!'

'Yes. She said she would have done exactly the same thing if it had been her father who had been hurt.'

'Was lover boy there?'

'No. It appears that after you left there was an almighty row between them and she kicked him out. She's since heard that the police have arrested him.'

'Good for Becky! She can do better than a guy like that.'

Anthony listened further as his daughter related the conversation between the two women.

'Fortunately, when Rebecca came to the door, she didn't hesitate to invite me in. She's got a really nice house.'

'Well. I've never been further than the doorstep.'

'Yes, I know. You wouldn't believe it, but it's spotlessly clean inside and all the curtains and the wallpaper in the lounge are colour co-ordinated. I adored the three-piece suite that she said her father bought, just before he went off to Australia. Do you know, she's also got one of those fireplaces that we looked at in Cheltenham, Mike.'

'What the one we saw when we went over to visit your old school friend?'

'Yes, that's right. If you remember, we were sheltering out of the rain under that shop awning when we saw it in the window of the department store across the street.'

'Oh yes, and Suzanne threw a tantrum because we wouldn't take her to the leisure centre.'

'That's right! But I recall that you gave in to her in the end and we all finished up in the pool for the rest of the afternoon.'

Anthony interrupted.

'Can the two of you find another time for a trip down memory lane? I just want to know what the hell she said to you.'

'Patience! Patience! Father dear. I'm telling the story. It's for you to listen.'

Anthony sat back in the deckchair and continued to drink his tea.

'I loved your flowers that you bought her. Rebecca had put them in such a beautiful vase.'

Anthony huffed.

'All right! All right! I'll continue. You never did have the patience to sit back and listen to what I had to say, even when I was a kid.'

Julia put her cup to her mouth and sipped her tea. She knew that her father always insisted on you getting straight to the point in any conversation. He wasn't one for social chat.

'Rebecca rang her father earlier this morning. She has decided to go and spend some time with him and her stepmother in Australia. They have even discussed selling the house if she wanted to stay out there and live with them. However, she told me that she wanted to see how things transpire first.'

'I see. There is one thing that does puzzle me though. How did she get mixed up with a bunch of crooks in the first place?'

'It's rather a long story, I'm afraid. Briefly, when she found out that Jon was a petty thief, she wanted to have nothing further to do with him. Then, a friend of the family who was a police officer got her involved in catching him and his friends with the stolen property. Sadly, it all went wrong and now she'd rather not be around. In case she doesn't return for some time she's leaving the house in the hands of a local managing agent.'

'When is she going?'

'As soon as she can buy a plane ticket, probably within the next day or two.'

'My goodness! That's not long.'

'No, she just wants to get away and be with her dad again as soon as possible. I don't suppose she even mentioned to you that she's got an aunt living in the next street and a cousin and his family living in Pendeen.'

Anthony shook his head.

'It never ceases to amaze me what you women find out from each other when you chat together. I don't suppose she's got a cat, by any chance?'

Julia laughed.

'Oh no! That was Jon spying on you both. She was furious with him, especially the way in which he treated you in the nightclub, and again when you collected the keys.'

'Well, the guy's an oaf.'

'I think she knows that too. He was always very jealous when any man looked at her, so he must have gone berserk when the two of you went out together.'

'But he must have known what was going on, surely? Chatting me up in order to borrow the boat was probably his idea in the first place.'

'Well, not exactly. She didn't tell him anything of what you did when you were out together, so I suppose he didn't really know what was going on between the two of you.'

'So, it was all one big lie then?'

Julia patted her father's knee.

'No, Dad. The important bits weren't. She really does love you, and I am convinced she means it. She was prepared to be realistic though, in understanding that your relationship would have had to come to an end one day as you're poles apart. I don't just mean in age either. Mind you, she said some really lovely things about you and I agreed with her.'

'What were they then?'

'I'm not going to tell you! That's private between the two of us. Just you take my word for it.'

Mike had been listening attentively to the conversation.

'What were these things that Dad had bought her?'

Only Mike could have asked such a tactless question. Anthony looked across to his daughter and began to show embarrassment.

'She showed me the earrings you bought her. They were really lovely. She was actually wearing them when I arrived. As for the gold bracelet she showed me, she said it was the most beautiful present she had ever been given. She's going to treasure that.'

Anthony's eyes began to well up.

'She's a lovely girl, isn't she, Julia?'

His daughter paused and then smiled.

'Yes, Dad. She's beautiful.'

Julia leaned down to pick up a bag that was on the grass beside her chair. She opened it and dipped her hand inside.

'Before I left, she asked me to give you this. She found it whilst she was packing away some of her things.'

Julia took from the bag a small model of a boat and handed it to her father. It was similar in style to the speedboat that he owned.

'I understand that her dad had a motor cruiser just like ours. A friend of the family had a replica made of it when she was a little girl. She has treasured it all these years and she now wants you to have it. Oh, yes, and she's given me a note for you too.'

His daughter passed him the letter. It was all too much for Anthony. Tears came to his eyes as he carefully examined the model of the boat, which he held in his hands. So that part of the story was also true. Not to add to his embarrassment, Julia and Mike got up and went indoors, leaving him to sit alone and ponder.

He opened the sealed envelope and took out the short note. It read:

> "My dearest Tony,
>
> Words cannot express how sorry I am for hurting you so much. It was never my intention that you should ever find out about me in the way that you did. I had always meant to tell you, but somehow I just couldn't find a way to do so.
>
> When I first saw you on your boat, I hid my true reasons for meeting up with you. Had I told you the truth, you would have sent me on my way, so I chose to be devious. At the time, I could never have anticipated falling in love with you. Then, when I did, I was so deep into that false façade that I had created that I just had to continue lying to you to avoid losing you. I know now that I should have come clean and taken a chance. I'm convinced you would have understood. With the benefit of hindsight, I realise that it was just a completely unnecessary deception.
>
> Tony, I can assure you that my love for you was real. I just hope in time that you will find it in your heart to forgive me.
>
> Your ever-loving, Becky."

He sat outside for some time, there in the garden alone with his thoughts. He was pleased that Julia had taken the initiative to visit Rebecca. At least, he now knew that she was all right and that she was well away from that troublesome boyfriend and his criminal activities. He also knew that the love she professed to have had for him was real too.

'Better to have loved and lost, than never to have loved at all. Isn't that what Natalie had tried to say?' He mused.

Anthony went inside and packed the model boat into his case, and then after saying "goodbye" to Mike and Julia, left for home. It was not until Christmas, that he returned to spend some time with the family again. The model took prime position in the glass cabinet on the wall of his lounge, and brought back many happy memories whenever he took it out to dust it.

By the following summer, he was back on his boat again. As usual, he grumbled about the state at which his son-in-law had left it in after a family trip out. Nothing had changed! He often chuckled to himself as he sailed across the calm waters and past the cove where he and Rebecca had sat on the warm sands on that peaceful Sunday afternoon.

On the last visit, he took the long way home just to drive down her road to pass her house. He had done this a couple of times before. However, on this last occasion, he noticed that it was up for sale and so presumed that she must have decided to stay in Australia with her father and her stepmother.

He never met Rebecca again, but the fond memories of her and those few wonderful days that he had spent with her that summer, remained with him forever.